THE SAHA DECLINATION

COLONIAL EXPLORER CORPS BOOK 3

JULIA HUNI

IPH MEDIA

The Saha Declination Copyright © 2021
by Julia Huni. All Rights Reserved.

All rights reserved. No part of this book may be reproduced in any form or by any electronic or mechanical means including information storage and retrieval systems, without permission in writing from the author. The only exception is by a reviewer, who may quote short excerpts in a review.

Editing by Paula Lester of
Polaris Writing and Editing

Cover Design © J. L. Wilson Designs
https://jlwilsondesigns.com

This book is a work of fiction. Names, characters, places, and incidents either are products of the author's imagination or are used fictitiously. Any resemblance to actual persons, living or dead, events, or locales is entirely coincidental.

Julia Huni
Visit my website at http://www.juliahuni.com

IPH Media

ISBN - 9798473524727

BOOKS BY JULIA HUNI

Colonial Explorer Corps Series:
The Earth Concurrence
The Grissom Contention
The Saha Declination

Recycled World Series:
Recycled World
Reduced World

Space Janitor Series:
The Vacuum of Space
The Dust of Kaku
The Trouble with Tinsel
Orbital Operations
Glitter in the Stars
Sweeping S'Ride
Triana Moore, Space Janitor (the complete series)

Tales of a Former Space Janitor
The Rings of Grissom

BOOKS BY JULIA HUNI

Planetary Spin Cycle

Krimson Empire (with Craig Martelle):
Krimson Run
Krimson Spark
Krimson Surge
Krimson Flare

If you enjoy this story, sign up for my newsletter, at juliahuni.com and you'll get free prequels and short stories, plus get notifications when the next book is ready.

CHAPTER ONE

The senior lounge at the Colonial Explorer Academy was a fixture on the potential cadet tour. The plush room—with comfortable seating, bar, vendo machines, Crud table, and virtual gaming corner—offered a glamorous counterpoint to the austere dorms and classrooms.

The tour guides liked to bring kids through when we were there and encouraged us to talk about our experiences at the Academy. We didn't mind strutting our stuff and spinning war stories—as seniors we ran the whole place. Or so we pretended.

This day was different. The entire senior class had crammed into the lounge at the behest of our commandant, Admiral Nathanier Kassis.

My dad.

We knew what was coming—we'd seen it twice before but always from the other side of the door. The seniors would enter in nervous silence and exit either elated or disappointed, depending on what had been announced. Today was Placement Day for the Senior Tour.

Aneh Jones, my roommate and best friend, perched on the extreme edge of our couch, her leg bouncing in quick time.

On her far side, Chymm Leonardi di Zorytevsky shut down whatever program he was tweaking on his holo-ring and put a hand on her knee.

"Stop. You're bouncing the whole sofa. Shaking the room apart isn't going to make this happen any faster."

Joss Torres leaned over the back of the couch and put his big hands on Aneh's shoulders, pulling her against the thick padding. "Chymm is right. Settle."

"Easy for you to say." Aneh craned her head around to look up at our big friend. "You're the pride of Earth. You're sure to get a good slot. I'm a nobody from Grissom."

"You've got the top grades from our class," I said. "They're going to send you to an amazing research opportunity. It would be a huge waste to do anything else."

Across the room, Felicity Myers and Derek Lee huddled in a corner, talking and glaring daggers at the rest of us. Since our plebe summer, they'd been virtual outcasts. Their own flight, Delta Black, liked them but mainly because they both had credits to spend. The rest of us ignored them whenever we could and tolerated them when required. None of us thought they'd last this long, but apparently their legacy stubbornness ran strong.

"I wonder where Peter is," Aneh said for what had to be the tenth time.

"He's with the commandant," Joss, Chymm, and I said together.

The door swung open. "Attention!" We all leaped to our feet.

Commandant Kassis strode to the front of the room, followed by the three squadron advisors and the cadet unit commander—Peter Russell.

"At ease," Dad said, and we relaxed a fraction. "Take your seats." Chair legs scraped the floor as we settled quietly—all of us sitting on the edge of our seats now.

"As you know, my team and I have been reviewing your records and assigning you for the Senior Tour. You will be assigned to an active stage 2 mission. Each mission will have multiple cadets and will last three weeks. Mission commanders have reviewed your records and agreed to accept you. Your performance and behavior will be constantly evaluated and reported back to us. Do not sully the Academy's reputation. When you return, if—and only if—your SenTo commander signs off, you'll be commissioned."

He turned to scan the room, seeming to take stock of each cadet.

"Assignments have been posted to the senior board and will be released when I leave the room. Do you have any questions?"

For a brief second, Dad's eyes met mine. I straightened my spine and nodded. I wouldn't let him down. The corner of his mouth twitched in the barest of smiles, and he looked away.

Dad and I hadn't always had a good relationship. Before I started at the Academy, I'd been…I believe my "uncle," Tam Origani, referred to me as "high maintenance." Coming from a CEC officer, that was the worst of insults. I hadn't realized that until I'd started here. My maintenance levels had decreased dramatically.

Dad pointed. "Cadet Myers?"

Felicity stood in her corner, back ramrod straight. "What if our mission commander doesn't like us?"

Snorts of laughter went around the room. No one liked Felicity, so that was a good question.

His lips thinned. "Active duty officers know better than to let their personal feelings endanger the mission. If your commander doesn't like you, that will have no bearing on their evaluation. These missions have been selected because we trust the judgment of the officers in charge."

Captain Fortescue took a step forward. "But it's a good idea to make yourself likeable."

We all snickered.

Felicity lifted her chin. "I am likeable."

Sounds of disbelief rippled through the crowd.

Dad held up a hand. "Then there won't be a problem. Any other questions?"

No one moved.

"You have the room." Dad turned smartly on his heel and marched to the door, the three captains following.

"Attention!" Peter bellowed.

We all popped to our feet, frozen for the interminable seconds required for four officers to walk through the door.

"At ease."

Every holo-ring in the room flicked to life as we searched for our names on the SenTo assignment list.

We'd read the stage 1 reports from all five planets currently under exploration. Brahe, a young planet with heavy volcanic action but mineral riches that demanded exploration. Goryu, a pastoral planet that would be an excellent agricultural colony if proven safe. Auzout and Harawi, both older, more stable worlds, were excellent locations to support high tech manufacturing, if they were colonized. And Qureshi, the least likely to be approved for colonization. Although the initial tests showed a stable environment that would respond well to terrraforming, it was low on valuable minerals and slightly below the optimum temperature range. Its proximity to Gagarin made it a likely military base.

Voices whooped around me as the lucky cadets found the most coveted assignments next to their names.

I scrolled down the board, past *Abdul, Argawal, Franklin, Jones*, not stopping to check my flight mates' assignments. There it was: *Kassis, Serenity*. Assigned to Qureshi.

Aneh yelped softly. "I'm going to Harawi! Part of the geographical assessment team." Aneh had developed an interest in geology and geography after our exercise on Sarvo Six. "The possibilities on Harawi are amazing. Did you know they've detected traces of both senidium and platinum? And the rock formations in the northern hemisphere—"

I tuned her out. She's my best friend, but when she starts yammering about rocks, I find it difficult to keep my eyes open.

Joss, still standing behind Aneh, caught my eye and snorted a laugh. "Siti, where are you going?"

I put on a bright smile. "Qureshi." I scrolled through my orders. "My team will be doing a broad analysis of the southeastern quadrant of the planet. They think it might be a good location for a military base. What about you?"

He grinned, stretched the file in his palm, and highlighted his name. "I'm going to Qureshi, too."

A wave of relief washed over me. The chances that at least one of my flight mates would be on the same mission was high—there were forty-eight seniors and only five planets. But since they assigned us based on our field of study, it wasn't random. "It says there'll be ten of us, but that doesn't mean we'll be working together. I think they spread the cadets out to—" I pushed my hands out.

"Limit the liability?" Chymm suggested.

I pointed at him. "That. Where are you going?"

"I'm with Aneh."

We all nodded. Sending Chymm to a world destined for manufacturing made the most sense. Once we graduated, he expected to spend most of his career in a lab, but we all had to do the SenTo on a stage 2 team. It was supposed to foster leadership skills, or make us well-rounded, or something like that. It was also the only time some officers would spend in the field.

"Attention!" Peter's voice echoed through our implants. We snapped to. "Command is releasing us for the rest of the day to prepare for our SenTo assignments. You can stay here longer or go about your business. Dismissed!"

As cadets filtered out the door, comparing assignments with their friends, Peter waded through the crush to our little island. "Where's everyone going?"

As the others shouted out their assignments, I watched Felicity and Lee cross the room. A little eddy of empty space surrounded them. Felicity noticed me watching and gave me her patented legacy glare. Lee murmured something, then arrowed away, making straight for me.

"I see we're going to Qureshi together, Kassis."

Perfect. My spirits dropped even further. Crappy planet and crappy company. It would be just my luck if Lee and I were assigned to the same location.

"Joss and I are going there, too." Peter winked at me. "Just like old times."

"Without the Hellions, I hope," Joss put in.

Lee ignored them. "I guess your dad thinks we'll be a good team."

"Or he trusts me to keep an eye on you."

"That works both ways."

"Does it?" I sized him up. "I don't think my dad would ask *you* to keep an eye on anyone."

"Yeah, watching Siti's back is *our* job." Joss punched Lee lightly on the arm. Lee staggered. The rest of my flight closed in around me, facing off against the Delta Black cadet. Lee muttered under his breath as he stalked away.

I smirked at Joss. "Cuts both ways, Earth boy. I've pulled you out of trouble more times than I can remember. Come on, Blue."

CHAPTER TWO

With a quiet thump, the shuttle touched down in the landing bay of the *CSS New Dawn*. My braids, which had been floating around my head during the flight, dropped to my shoulders as the ship's gravity wrapped around us. Liam, my sair-glider, thumped down with them, chittering in my ear. I stroked his silky blue and white fur.

Beside me, Joss grunted. "That transition always gets me."

"You'll get used to it. You've done a lot less travel than most of us."

Peter and Joss had both been born and raised on Earth. Their first interplanetary trip had been the flight to the Academy. Since our plebe summer, we'd all been back to Earth twice and had done cadet exercises on several other planets. But the boys were still relatively new to artificial gravity.

Around us, the other cadets chattered quietly. In addition to Peter, Joss, and Lee, our shuttle carried two cadets from Yellow and one each from Purple, Red, and Green. We knew them, of course, but not as well as we knew our flight mates. This mission would be our first without our usual, dependable team.

The captain's voice echoed through our implants and the body of the shuttle. "Landing check. Systems connections green. Passengers may release their restraints."

The cargo door rattled and clunked, then ratcheted slowly down to form a ramp to the ship's deck. We unfastened our five-point harnesses and waited for the crew chief to unbuckle the luggage pallet. Then, bags in hand, we filed out of the shuttle.

"Cadets, over here!" A short, barrel-shaped woman wearing a master sergeant's uniform waved as she called us through the audio. We crossed the landing bay and gathered around her. Liam scampered down my arm and into my pocket.

"I'm Master Sergeant Suisei, assistant load master for the *New Dawn*. As such, responsibility for billeting passengers falls to me. You'll be quartered with your explorer teams. Don't ask me to change your rooms—ain't gonna happen." She glared at each of us in turn. "Every year, a cadet wants to bunk with his friends. This isn't a pleasure cruise, kids."

Lee cleared his throat. "We are cadet officers. Not kids."

Suisei stared him down. "Y'all are *cay-dets*. Do you know what rank *cay-dets* hold? None. Someday, you might be ensigns, and I'll be happy to call you 'sir' *if* that happens." She didn't sound happy.

She swiped a link to our holo-rings. "This is the assignment board. It lists your billet and duties for the duration of this flight. There's links to everything you might need—team allocations, mess schedules, latrine assignments, maps in case you get lost."

Jirati, from Yellow flight, raised her hand, but Suisei ignored her. "Your supervisor is your primary point of contact for everything. Don't bother me or any of the crew unless your supervisor tells you to. This is a working ship, and we all have better things to do than babysit a bunch of kids." She glared at Lee.

Lee's chin came up. "I'm sure we have better things to do as well."

"Oh, yeah, you got things to do." She bared her teeth in an unpleasant grin. "I helped build the duty roster. Now get out of my cargo hold." She made a shooing motion, pushing us toward the door.

I flicked the link she'd sent and ran a search. "Here's the map." With a swipe, I sent a direct link to Joss and Peter. I poked my finger through my billet listing, and a location lit up on the map.

"Where'd you get those?" Lee asked as the boys and I moved toward the exit. "Send me a link."

"Find it yourself," Joss snapped back. "The sergeant gave us board access."

"Thanks for the help, Neanderthal." Lee dropped his bag in front of Joss's feet while he pulled up the assignment board.

Joss pulled back a foot as if to kick the bag, but I grabbed his arm. "Don't. We're being evaluated, remember? Professionalism."

Joss's eyes slid toward Lee, who smirked back.

"Not worth it, dude." Peter pushed Joss around the bag. "Eyes on the prize."

As we left, Lee sneered under his breath, *"Dude."*

Peter's map took him away from us at the first corridor.

"See ya, wouldn't want to be ya," Joss called after him.

"Not if I see you first." Peter threw the words over his shoulder. Four more cadets followed him down the corridor.

"I'm this way." I turned left at the next junction.

Joss followed me. "I think we're assigned to the same team." He held his map up beside mine. "We're both headed to the same place."

"I'm amazed my dad put the three of us together."

"You are? I think he stuck us in the least desirable assignment so no one would accuse him of playing favorites. Peter said—" He broke off.

"Peter said what? Did he give recommendations?" As the cadet commander, Peter had given input to the assignments. His position gave him duties and responsibilities—as well as privileges—the rest of us didn't have.

Joss shrugged. "I think it was more like they pumped him for information and let him see the list first when it was done. But he said we were divided between planets first, then slotted into missions based on our studies."

"So, where does that put us? You focused on security. I did project management. Not really the same thing."

"Maybe they need both?"

We stopped at a hatch labeled D-8. I waved my holo-ring, and the red light on the panel flipped to green. Joss pulled the handle in a downward arc, and the hatch swung inward.

We stepped into a lounge with drab, functional furniture. Individual curtains partially covered a grid of bunks along the bulkheads on either side. Lockers lined the far wall. A handful of people in CEC uniforms sprawled around the room, some reading, others sleeping, a couple playing cards at the table.

"Home sweet home," Joss whispered.

A woman with a single bar on her collar looked up from her cards. "The cadets have arrived. I'm Ensign Okazaki. Welcome to Team Foxtrot." She pointed at the wall of bunks, four stacks, each three high. "You got the top row. Lockers in the back—if it opens, it's yours. Don't bother unpacking, we're only on this bucket for five days. That's Rigel, Morse, Sterling, Leng-wei, Parthensky, and Ferris. The others are in the gym—you can meet 'em when they get back. Go ahead and get settled." She shuffled a pack of cards. "Then we can play a round."

"I'm not sure playing a round with the boss is a great idea," I muttered to Joss as we crossed the room.

He twitched the open curtain of a top-row bunk. "You want this one?"

"Go for it—they're all the same." I moved to the next stack. Liam crawled up my arm and leaped to the bunk. He made a circuit of the space, chittering at me as if he were critiquing our quarters.

"You got a glider?" An explorer—the one I thought was Sterling—wandered over to look at Liam. "Mine's here somewhere." She looked around the room, then pointed. "There she is. Squeaky." I followed the line of her arm. A bright green glider perched on the edge of a middle bunk.

"You got a friend over there, Liam." I held out my arm, and my glider jumped to my hand. I swung my arm and flung him across the room. He arced high and spread his limbs, using the membranes between his arms and legs to catch the air. "Are there any others on our team?"

Sterling shook her head. "Not many. Just Squeaky in here. Half a dozen others on the whole crew. The mission commander ain't a big fan."

"Is that likely to cause problems for us?"

She shook her head. "Not if you keep out of trouble."

I drew the curtains shut to claim the bunk. "Thanks."

She nodded. "You can get extra chow for her."

"He's pretty self-sufficient on the dirt, but he does like protein bars." I gave a dramatic shudder.

Sterling laughed. "Did you say 'he'? I thought all CEC gliders were female."

"I did, too, but Liam is male."

"And he's approved? They ain't worried about a ba-jillion little gliders?"

"He's been cleared. I've got his certificate on my holo-ring. Maybe gliders aren't as prolific as everyone assumes." I stuffed my bag into a locker. My handprint activated the locking mechanism.

"Which one's mine?" A familiar, hated voice brought me around. Derek Lee stood just inside the hatch.

Perfect.

Okazaki waved at the wall. "Whichever one they left you."

I pointed to the bunk beyond Joss. "That one."

Lee pulled the curtains shut and smirked at me as he passed to claim a locker. "See, told you the old man wanted me to keep watch on you." His eyes traveled over Joss, from feet to head and back. "Probably doesn't trust the Neanderthal around his little girl."

"Could you be any more offensive?" I growled. "I don't need a keeper."

Okazaki stood and stalked toward us. "I don't tolerate any -isms in my team. No genderism, racism, planetism, none of that crap. Let's get one thing straight. You're all cadets—which means you're all equally nothing on this team. You'll do what you're told by any member of my squad."

"We're supposed to follow orders from enlisted people?" Lee's eyes bugged out. "We're going to be ensigns in less than a month!"

"Maybe." Okazaki moved closer, until her nose was almost touching Lee's chest. Despite her tiny size, the force of her glare made me grateful I wasn't the target. "Maybe not. If you've got enough brains to make it through three years of the Academy, you should know to listen to the enlisted folks. That's why they send you on these missions—to show you how little you know and how completely you must rely on your enlisted team. These folks—" She waved at the people lounging around the room. Every eye was on us. "They are your superiors in every way. And when—if —you pin on a pair of gold bars, they will still be superior to you in experience."

Lee's eyes dropped. "Sorry, sir."

Joss and I exchanged an amazed look.

Okazaki swung around. "You two got that, too?"

"Yes, sir," Joss and I barked together.

She swaggered to the table and dropped into her chair. "Good, then let's play cards. You kids got any credits?"

Lee slammed his locker shut. With a little nod to himself, he crossed the room and dropped a ten-credit coin on the table. "I'm in."

"Ooh, big spender!"

Someone whistled.

"What about you two?" Okazaki eyed me. "Does the admiral's little girl have any coin?"

"If I did, I wouldn't bother betting, I'd just hand it over to you, sir. I'm crap at cards."

The whistler laughed. "Smart girl."

"Too bad you aren't as smart as she is, Ferris, or you would have saved yourself a lotta cash." A short blonde woman smacked Ferris on the back of his head as she passed the table and stopped in front of me. "I'm Parthensky. They call me Rocky."

I knocked knuckles with her. "I'm Kassis, this is Torres."

"Kassis?" Rocky swung around and pointed at me. "Hey, Ensign, we got the Hero's kid!"

"Yeah, I know who she is. So?" Okazaki dealt out cards to Ferris, Lee, and a pair of explorers who were Morse and Leng-wei, if I remembered correctly.

"That oughta be worth something."

"If it is, I don't know what." Okazaki slapped the deck onto the table and flipped the first card. "Ante up, boys. And leave the kid alone, Rocky. She's just a cadet like any other."

I shrugged at Rocky. "Sorry."

Rocky grunted and turned to look Joss over. "This one is right tasty."

"Hands off the cadets, Rocky." The words were sharp, even though Okazaki was still focused on her cards.

"Yeah, Ensign, I know. But I can look." She licked her lips.

Okazaki slammed her cards down on the table and erupted from her chair. "Did you completely miss my -isms speech, Parthensky? Stop treating the boy like a piece of meat, or I'll send you to sexual harassment training. Again."

Rocky winced. "Yes, sir. Sorry, sir."

Okazaki jabbed a finger at Rocky. "Last warning. If I hear the slightest whisper of an innuendo from you, I'm turfing you to ship's maintenance. I don't need any troublemakers on my team."

Rocky ducked her head. "Got it, sir."

"Good, now get out of my sight." Okazaki flicked her holo-ring and swiped.

"You're on latrine duty."

Rocky's lips pinched together, but she snapped a salute. "Aye, sir." She waited for Okazaki to return the gesture, then hurried away.

The ensign gave each of us a narrow-eyed stare, then returned to her card game.

"Sir?" I asked tentatively. "Do you mind if we take a walk around the ship—to familiarize ourselves with the layout?"

"Don't get in the way of the ship's crew. You've got kitchen duty at sixteen hundred."

CHAPTER THREE

"What did you make of that?" Joss asked as soon as the hatch shut behind us.

"Rocky? I dunno. You'd think a second term explorer would know better than to harass anyone."

"Exactly." He pulled up his map and started toward the stern of the ship. "I think it was a setup—like that kid on the shuttle when we landed at the Academy."

"You had a kid on your shuttle, too?" Joss and I had arrived on different shuttles almost three years ago. On mine, a kid had demanded answers and the commandant had reprimanded him. Later we were told he'd been expelled for insubordination. Later still, we learned the kid had been an actor hired to teach us not to question authority. But that commandant was gone, and this wasn't an Academy ship.

"Maybe Okazaki thought that was an effective way to train newcomers?" Joss stopped at an intersection, sticking out an arm to stop me, too. A team of explorers ran by in formation. After they passed, he dropped his arm. "Rocky didn't strike me as the sexual harasser type. And the whole thing was really awkward."

A full circuit of the ship would have taken more time than we had, so we identified the latrines closest to our bunks, checked out the gym, and visited the lounge. This room looked like a larger version of our quarters but without the bunks along the walls. More drab furniture, a couple of virtual reality booths, and a screen playing sports vids. Under the rev-ball tournament, a small bar stood empty. A sign on the counter read, "Open at sixteen hundred. One drink per customer."

"I'm betting we won't have the opportunity to test that." Joss tapped the sign before pulling up the map again. "We've got kitchen duty—in ten minutes."

We followed the map to the mess hall and presented ourselves at the kitchen door. Cadets Weng and al-Jhiri were waiting by the closed hatch.

"What's up?" Weng asked. Al-Jhiri simply nodded.

The hatch swung open, and a tall, thin man with a long face waved us in. Scuffed white cupboards were topped by gleaming steel countertops. Pots and pans hung from the overhead, and a huge stove took up the back wall. A bank of industrial-sized Autokich'ns took up another wall.

The man spoke over his shoulder as we followed him into the kitchen. "Most of the kitchen is automated, but they like to keep you kids busy on the flight, so they dump you on me. I'll have you doing prep work. Any of you worked in a kitchen before?" He stopped in the middle of the room and turned to survey us.

Weng raised his hand. "I've baked bread with my grandma."

Al-Jhiri snickered.

"You can laugh, girl, but that gives him a better job." The man pointed at Weng. "You come with me. The rest of you—time to peel potatoes." He opened a metal hatch in the wall, and a pile of brown vegetables poured out into a trough. "Scraps go in the recycler. Peelers and scrap bowls in that drawer. Grab a stool and get to work."

"I've peeled enough potatoes to last ten lifetimes." Joss pulled a stool close to the bin and wedged a bowl between his knees.

"You'll have to show me how to do it." I grabbed another stool.

Al-Jhiri picked up a peeler. "Me, too."

Joss tossed a potato at each of us. "Unbelievable."

THAT DAY SET the tone for the rest of the cruise. We spent three of the five days on kitchen duty and the other two on latrines. On those days, we were responsible for cleaning the bathrooms, despite the fact that bots usually did this job. As the cook had said, they wanted to keep us busy. By the time we reached Qureshi, my hands were rough and dry. In our spare time, Joss and I worked out with the other cadets, played games, and studied our mission briefs.

After dinner on the last evening, Lt Okazaki called us together. "We arrive in orbit at oh-four-hundred, ship's time. This ship is scheduled for a quick drop and depart—they have several moons to survey—so we will be on the shuttle and ready to launch by oh-three-forty-five. Pack up your gear and hit the rack now."

I pulled the few items I'd left in my bunk and stowed them in my duffle. As I shoved the bag into my locker, Lee sauntered up and fanned out a handful of credits.

"Shoulda played poker, Kassis. Easy way to pick up a few credits."

"For you, maybe. I know my skillset, and poker is not in it." I closed the locker and engaged the lock.

"I could teach you." He leered suggestively.

I rolled my eyes as hard as I could. "No, thanks."

He grabbed my arm as I started to move. "You think you're better than me just because my mom got taken down and your dad survived. It's only a matter of time."

"I think I'm better than you because I didn't try to hurt other cadets on our training missions. Because I don't have to profit from every human interaction. And my dad survived because he wasn't doing anything underhanded. Your mom was stealing from the Corps."

Lee snorted. "That's the way it's done. You don't make admiral if you play by the rules."

I pulled my arm out of his grasp. Liam launched himself from my bunk and landed on my shoulder. He stood up, balancing a hand against my ear, and chittered at Lee. I stroked his smooth flank, quieting his agitation. "My dad played by the rules, and he made admiral. Besides, there are things more important than credits or rank."

"I know. Love, friendship, and cuddly sair-gliders." Lee sneered. "The sooner you learn that nice guys finish last, the better off you'll be. But if you want to live in la la land, be my guest. Don't look to me for help."

I stroked Liam. "We obviously live in different universes, Lee. I'm happy in mine. Enjoy your miserable fight for power."

Too few hours later, the lights snapped on in my bunk. I kicked my blanket aside and pushed open the curtain. After a quick run to the latrine, I grabbed my bag, made sure Liam was safe in my pocket, and waited for the others.

Controlled chaos filled the compartment. Most of the team stood ready by their bunks while Rigel raged through the room, upending chairs looking for something. Morse grabbed clothing from his overfull locker and jammed it into his duffle, muttering under his breath. Sterling lay halfway in her bunk, apparently trying to coax Squeaky out of the corner.

Liam crawled up my arm, then launched toward Sterling. He landed on her rear end, and she squealed. An arm came around to swat him, but he jumped again and disappeared into the bunk. Seconds later, he and the green glider reappeared, clinging to the curtain. As Sterling extracted herself from the bunk, Liam scolded the other glider, then sailed back to me.

"How did you get him to do that?" Sterling scooped up the little green creature and pushed her into a tiny ventilated crate.

"I didn't. He just did it. I don't have to put Liam in one of those, do I?" I pointed at the crate.

"It's easier to carry her this way. Most of us use 'em." Her eyes narrowed as she stared at Liam, perched in his usual place on my shoulder. "I've never seen a glider like that one."

I ran a finger down Liam's silky back, and he arched against my hand. "I guess I got lucky."

"Enough fun pet times." Okazaki stalked past me. "If you can't stay on schedule, Sterling, you'll have to give up the glider."

"I've got five minutes, sir. I'll be ready." Sterling set the crate on her bunk and hurried to her locker.

Okazaki turned on her heel to look at me. "That's definitely a well-trained glider, Kassis. See that he continues to be an asset to the team."

"Yes, sir." I'd do my best, but Liam did what Liam wanted. Fortunately for me, that had usually been to my benefit.

At Okazaki's command, we grabbed our duffels and shuffled into the corridor. Sterling and Rigel staggered in behind the others, and Joss, Lee, and I brought up the rear. A voice barked, "On your left!" and we all jumped to the right side of the corridor. A quartet of ship's crew—identifiable by their beige coveralls—hurried past, intent on their duties.

We reached the shuttle deck a few minutes later and filed up a ramp and into our shuttle. Half of the forward-facing seats were already filled with sleepy explorers.

"Go forward as far as you can and take the first empty seats." Okazaki slapped my shoulder and pointed down the central aisle.

I dropped my duffel on the pallet, to be strapped down before launch, then followed Rigel between the seats into the shuttle. We reached a partially empty row and side-stepped in. Rigel plopped down next to a woman with first-term rank and started a low conversation.

I dropped into the next seat and pulled the straps over my shoulders. They buckled to the straps across my waist and linked to one between my legs.

"Seems like overkill." Beside me, Lee waved the end of one of his straps.

"Standard configuration for a shuttle without gravity." I snapped them into place and pulled them tight.

"Duh. I'm a pilot trainee. I'm just saying, when's the last time you needed 'em?" He wrenched his into place. "Those crappy commercial shuttles they used for PSW, yeah, they need all the safety gear, but CEC ships are way better."

"Feel free to leave yours off, if you want." I leaned forward, my head brushing the seat in front of me, to peer past him. "You good, Joss?"

Joss gave me a thumbs up.

"Sorry, shoulda let you sit next to your boyfriend." Lee leaned back in his seat and waved at the half-meter of space over his lap. "You two want a good morning kiss?"

I leaned back and closed my eyes. "Do you have to be so immature?"

"Drop teams, prepare for launch!" The voice echoed through the hold. "All aboard?"

"Alpha team, all aboard," another voice yelled from the front of the ship.

"Bravo team, all aboard!"

"Charlie team, all aboard!"

"Delta team, all aboard." I ducked as Okazaki's voice roared from directly behind me.

At "kilo," the calls stopped. The first voice took over. "Drop teams are prepared for launch. Close the hold doors!"

"Hold doors closing." This calm voice came through the audio link—the co-pilot, if they were following standard protocol.

The rattle of machinery, followed by a resounding boom, confirmed the closing of the ramp.

"All hands, we are clear for launch," the co-pilot said, her voice calm and smooth. "Thirty second count-down begins now. Double check your restraints—landings on Qureshi are known to be bumpy. Total flight time, approximately twenty-three minutes." The voice paused. Then, "Five. Four. Three. Two. One. Launch."

On her final word, we were shoved back in our seats. Someone whooped, and a sprinkling of laughter followed. The acceleration dropped, and we were weightless. Liam chittered in my ear, then pushed off my shoulder and sailed to the overhead. Around us, several other gliders took to the air, flipping and twirling between the seats and the bulkheads.

When the ship hit turbulence, the gliders returned to their owners. Liam crawled down my arm and curled up in my pocket. As my hand curved around him, I got the distinct impression he was there for my benefit, not his own.

The co-pilot had not been exaggerating. The drop to Qureshi included ten solid minutes of tooth-rattling turbulence and several sudden drops and bounces. I closed my eyes, cuddling Liam against my stomach, and tried to ignore the occasional sound of vomiting.

Lee swore under his breath, and my eyes popped open. He scrabbled in the pocket of the seat in front of him, barely getting the barf bag to his face in time. I bit back a smirk and tried to look sympathetic. That didn't last long. The smell got to me.

Rigel leaned past me and tapped Lee's arm. "Hold the bag closed, would you? You wanna make us all sick?"

"Sorry." Lee squeezed the top of the bag between his fingers.

I took a careful breath and nodded gratefully to Rigel. He rolled his eyes.

The shuttle dropped then rebounded. I squeezed my eyes shut and made deals with the Almighty.

Then it was over. We dropped for a few more minutes, then landed with a soft thump. Our audio implants pinged, and the co-pilot spoke. "Shuttle *Arco-Seven* to *New Dawn*, we have landed. All passengers, remain in your seats until you're cleared to exit the shuttle. Crew cross check." The feed went quiet.

Around me, metal clashed as my teammates unlatched their restraints. Once I'd unbuckled the shoulder belts, Liam climbed to his usual perch, holding lightly to my ear. I unfastened the other straps and waited.

Beside me, predictably, Lee stood.

"Sit down, Lee," Okazaki hissed. "Didn't you hear the pilot?"

Lee froze, then dropped into his seat. "What's the big deal? We're down."

"What if we had to launch again?" Joss asked. "This is an unexplored planet. Who knows what's going on out there? You wanna risk being slammed into the ceiling if we launch?"

"We've already got our straps off, Cave Man."

"Whatever," Joss muttered.

"You shouldn't have your restraints off," Okazaki's voice carried from behind us. "You're supposed to stay latched in until she gives the—"

"Cross check complete." The co-pilot cut her off. "Passengers may unbuckle their restraints. Rear hatch opening…now."

The rumbled and groan of the door was accompanied by a waft of cold air.

And a stench to rival Lee's barf bag.

Voices rose in the cargo hold. "What is that smell?"

"Pipe down!" Okazaki barked.

"Sorry for the perfume, folks." The co-pilot's voice was laced with laughter. "Qureshi has its own special welcome. Don't worry, you'll get used to it."

"I'm not sure I want to get used to that," Rigel complained as he stood.

I followed his example and turned to look out the back hatch. I'm taller than average, but all I could see was pale pink sky. As those in the rear shuffled off the shuttle, CEC modules came into view. Their white exteriors reflected bright sunlight into the vehicle, all but blinding us.

I flicked my holo-ring and adjusted the filter on my personal shield. The glare decreased but the stench remained. "How can that smell get through our shields?"

"Whoever discovers the answer to that will win the Sharavelli Prize," Okazaki replied. "The good news is they're supposed to protect us from anything a planet can throw at us. So, I guess the stench ain't dangerous." She side stepped toward the aisle. A few seconds later, we followed.

CHAPTER FOUR

Qureshi was beautiful—at least this corner of it was. Tall mountains with thick white snow, vast plains of green and blue, studded with pink, red, and yellow flowers. The sky was a pale blue—almost white. The glare off the snow caused our personal shields to darken more in response as we stepped off the shuttle.

Too bad the stink ruined the beauty.

We had landed in a rocky valley below the snow line. A stream, crystal clear and sparkling, trickled down the center of a wide riverbed. Five CEC modules stood well back from the water, and the usual meter-high pylons with their blue force shield surrounded the camp.

"Foxtrot, grab your bag and a landing pack, and follow me." Okazaki's voice blared through my audio. "We're in Module Three." She set off at a trot toward the farthest white cube.

The luggage pallets lay on the ground near the shuttle. Each was clearly labeled with the team's symbol, and our individual bags had our names emblazoned on the side in big, white letters. Beside the luggage, six more pallets held our landing packs. These contained the equipment each explorer would need on the planet and were labeled by size. Grav belts, parkas, gloves, helmets, emergency rations, communications equipment, all packaged in a regulation backpack. I grabbed one from the pallet labeled medium and hurried after Okazaki.

The module was set up the same as our module on Earth, except each team had their own room. By the time Joss and I arrived, the other team members had taken all the top hammock hangers. The lower level was easier to get into, but you were more likely to have something dropped on your head, so the top row usually went first.

Okazaki had a head-high partition around her hammock, separating her sleeping area from the rest of us. One of the perks of rank.

I picked a location away from the door and hung a hammock. Rocky strolled over and put a possessive hand on the bag above me. "Guess we're bunk buddies."

"I guess so. What does that mean?"

"Nothing." She glanced over her shoulder.

I followed her look—Okazaki was staring back. She raised an eyebrow at me—at least I think it was at me. I raised a hand. I wasn't sure what I was agreeing to, but I wasn't going to make any waves.

Liam crawled out of my pocket and conducted a thorough inspection of the hammock.

Rocky watched the glider, a bemused smile on her face. "He sounds like he's pointing out all the good and bad points."

I smirked. "Glider product reviews—very helpful."

"May I?" She reached a tentative hand toward Liam.

"That's up to him." I watched carefully—Liam had an uncanny ability to read character, and he had no problems protecting himself or me, as a couple of people had learned the hard way. Glider bites hurt like the devil and healed slowly.

Liam's bright eyes glittered at Rocky. He turned to me and chirped, then jumped to the other woman's hand.

"He's so soft!" She stroked the creature's blue and white fur, murmuring to him under her breath.

"Haven't you touched Squeaky?"

Rocky shrugged. "Squeaky don't like me much. She don't like anyone, except Sterling. In fact, most of the gliders I've seen don't like other folks."

I nodded. "I've noticed that. But Liam is friendly. He'll be even more friendly if you feed him. He'll eat anything."

She cuddled the little creature. "I'll save some of my lunch for him." She glanced around the room and noticed a couple of our teammates staring. "What's the matter? Ain't never seen a girl with a cute pet before?" She scowled, and the others turned away.

My audio pinged. Everyone else froze, as if they were also getting a message. Then an androgynous voice announced, "Mission briefing in ten minutes."

"Where do we go for that?" I asked.

"We'll meet in the cafeteria." Rocky give Liam a little toss and he flew to my shoulder. "Only place big enough. Wear your coat—you want to keep that with you on a planet like this."

"Thanks." I opened the backpack and pulled out the first item. The jacket was made of thin, high-tech fabric that could be set to different ratings. I pulled it on over my other layers—undershirt with built in support, long-sleeved shirt, and a thicker pullover. With the coat set to its lowest heat conservation level, it was almost too warm inside the module.

I shoved my backpack and personal bag into a locker, activated the handprint lock, and followed my teammates out the door, with Liam on my shoulder.

The cafeteria was an open patio in front of the kitchen module. Widely spaced beams of plastek stretched overhead, defining the space and providing a framework for an awning that could be retracted. Although the force shield would protect us from indigenous creatures and the sun, it didn't retain heat. And a torrential downpour could overwhelm the shield projector if it was low on power. Extending the awning allowed us to conserve juice.

And, as Dr Abdul-James had told me on our mission to Earth, a smart explorer uses the lowest necessary technology to do the job.

We gathered under the awning, taking seats on the benches at each table. Although it was cold outside, the number of bodies gathered and our excellent clothing kept us warm. I pulled a cap over my braided hair and tucked my hands into my pockets.

A wiry man with gray hair climbed onto a table near the kitchen. He held up his hands, and the space quieted. His voice carried easily through the thin air with help from the audio implants.

"Welcome to Team Qureshi Four. For our newcomers, I am Lieutenant Commander Lishan Jankovic. My deputy is Major Liz Bellincioni." He gestured, and a short, tough-looking woman with a blonde crew cut and a tattoo of the CEC emblem on her neck stepped onto the bench beside him. She raised her hand, then jumped backwards off the bench.

"As you know, our job is to explore this planet. The phase 1 team gave the sign-off to further exploration—despite the smell." He laughed, and we joined in. "They tell me you get used to it. We have additional landing teams around the planet. Team Four's responsibility is this continent. We're lucky—we got the temperate location."

Voices groaned and exclaimed.

"That's right—it's colder everywhere else. The bad news is the other teams will probably finish their evaluations faster—no point in wasting time on an uninhabitable location. For that reason, their teams are much smaller. Since we have the livable area, we'll do a full investigation. Complete biological and environmental workup. I leave those briefings up to your team leads. For now, welcome to the team. Anyone want to chicken out?"

We all leaped to our feet. A hundred voices bellowed, "Hell, no!"

Okazaki raised her hand, catching our attention. "Foxtrot, you have twenty minutes for chow, then meet at grid seven for mission briefing."

Joss and I grabbed meal pacs and ate quickly. Leftovers went into pockets and belt pouches—a smart explorer didn't waste potential snacks. Liam finished off my remaining stew, then leaped into the rafters to meet the other gliders. After a quick trip to the latrine in the back of the module, we met at grid seven.

The entire camp was broken into virtual squares ten meters on a side. Each square was designated by a number, and those coordinates were programmed into our holo-ring mapping systems. An explorer could look at the map to find a location or set their ring to direct them through haptics. Grid seven was a table on the edge of the patio.

"Our first mission is to explore sector forty-three." Okazaki set a projector on the table and threw a map of the area onto it. A wedge to the south was outlined in green. "We'll collect samples of any native flora and vid of any fauna we encounter. Teams of two, staying in contact at all times."

She looked around the small group, pointing at a couple of people. "Make sure your audio is set to this channel. Each team will pick up a radio as well. We've got comm microsats up, but this planet has weird atmospheric conditions that interfere on occasion. Pairings are listed here." She flicked her fingers and a list replaced the map. "Any questions?"

When no one replied, she bellowed out the familiar call to action, "Anyone want to chicken out?"

"No, sir!"

CHAPTER FIVE

Before I could find my name on the list, a deep voice spoke through my audio. "Kassis, you're with me." A tall, muscular man with thick dark hair glowered down at me. His nametag read Unida. "Let's get our supplies."

As I followed Unida across the gravel toward the supply module, Liam soared away from the rafters and landed on my shoulder.

"You can keep that thing under control, I assume." Unida glared at Liam.

I put a protective hand against Liam's side. "He's very well-behaved. And helpful."

"Really." His dry response did not invite me to explain. "Tether that crate to your grav belt and let's go."

"I—I didn't wear my belt." My face heated, and I looked away from Unida. "I didn't realize we'd need them so soon."

Unida folded his arms over his massive chest, his expression bland. He half-sat against our crate. "I'll wait."

I took two steps, then turned back. "Is there anything else I should bring? This is my first real mission."

"I thought you went to Earth?"

"I did, but that wasn't a regular mission, you know." I opened my mouth to explain, but he held up a huge hand.

"I've read the report. Inside your landing pack, there's a smaller survival bag. Bring that, plus your hat and gloves."

I did my best CEC salute.

Unida frowned. "Don't do that—I work for a living."

I hurried to my locker and returned a few minutes later with the equipment he had listed. I threw in an emergency ration pack for good measure. Unida showed me how to strap the gear to the crate and double checked my tether settings. Then we lifted off.

From the sky, the area was even more beautiful. Our camp sat in the middle of a wide bowl, with mountains on three sides. A narrow valley led away to the west and eventually—according to the map—the sea. We had been assigned a section on the far edge of Foxtrot's wedge.

"Set your belt speed at eighty percent and follow me." Unida swung his arm in a circle, then dropped it, pointing southwest, and zipped away.

I followed behind, the cold air stinging my cheeks and making my eyes water until I remembered to turn my personal shield up. Tears dried on my cheeks as the wind dropped to almost nothing.

Liam crouched on my shoulder and held onto my ear. He chittered a bit, then rubbed his fur against my face.

I shouldn't be able to feel that, should I? Unless he's inside my shield. Why hasn't anyone else ever noticed this? Liam had proven his ability to pass through CEC shields on Sarvo Six. Were other gliders able to do that? I'd never remembered to ask. When we filed our training report for Sarvo Six, we'd mentioned Liam's ability, but no one had followed up. Of course, the entire situation on Sarvo had been complicated. This detail might have been lost in the clutter. Or it was unimportant. I'd ask my dad when we returned to the Academy.

Ahead, Unida slowed, angling toward the edge of a forested area. I adjusted my direction and landed beside him.

The plants bore little resemblance to trees. Tall white stalks stuck up from the ground—ranging from seedling-sized to sixty meters high. Long, flat, serrated triangles projected horizontally as if the points had been driven into the stalks. The meter-long "leaves" were dark green with red edges and flexible. I reached out a gloved hand.

Unida grabbed my wrist and yanked my hand back. "The edges of those fronds are toxic. Didn't you read the reports?"

I jumped back. "I read them—it's not life-threatening. And shouldn't my force shield protect me?"

"Yes, but no point in tempting fate." He released my arm. "Explorers need to learn when it's smart to take risks and when it isn't. We know those trees are potentially dangerous, and we don't need to take samples. That's been done. No point in touching them. Save your daring for something that hasn't been seen yet." He pointed into the forest. "We'll go that way."

The bottoms of the taller stalks were bare, with horizontal scars as if the triangular leaves fell from the trees as they grew. But there were no discarded fronds on the ground—we walked on clean packed dirt with no detritus or undergrowth. The botanists would undoubtedly study that for years to come. But for now, it meant we could walk between the older trees without risking our lives. Unida led me deeper into the forest.

We stopped to launch a pair of drones—one flew ahead of us and the other trailed, recording our movements and discoveries—if there were any. The feed from their cams went through a program that compared what we saw to what had already been catalogued. If it found a new species of plant, we took a sample. If it identified a new creature, we launched another drone to observe it.

Liam watched everything from my shoulder, alert and vocal, but made no attempt to leave his perch.

After a few hours, all of our drones were up. Unida called a halt, and we settled on some flat rocks to take a break. Liam jumped down and scampered across the rocky outcropping, racing in circles.

"We'll recall these drones." He poked a protein bar at the vid in his palm. In it, a snail-like creature slowly oozed up one of the massive spikes. "We've marked the location and recorded the area. We can send a drone back in a few hours or a couple days to document any changes."

"Is this what you do all day, every day?" I snapped off a piece of my own protein bar and held it out for Liam. He ignored me, continuing to get out his pent-up energy. "Record stuff?"

"Most planets don't come with indigenous sapient life." The words came out dry, but a spark of humor lit his eyes.

"You mean like Earth?"

He nodded. "According to the reports, your first mission was much more exciting than anything I've done. It kinda set you up for disappointment. But the reality is much more—"

"Boring?"

"I was going to say routine." He lifted the cloth in his lap and wiped his hands, then folded it meticulously to contain the crumbs and returned it to a small pouch in the crate.

I followed his example, not wanting to contaminate an unexplored planet with an external source of food. Our travel rations were designed to break down quickly, but that was another risk we didn't need to take. Destroying the planet's ecosystem was left to the settlers.

We finished our survey and returned to our initial entry point. Unida recalled most of the drones, and I packed them back into the crate.

"Hey, look at that tree." I pointed to one of the stalks. "One of the fronds has fallen off." The red-edged triangle lay in the dirt at the foot of the stalk. I lifted off and flew toward the plant, Unida close behind.

"It's our snail friend." Unida stood beside the fallen leaf, his hand-held vid cam focused on the creature. Its shell was a rough blob rather than a smooth spiral, but the creature looked similar to an Earth snail, with a slimy body and four antennae sticking out of the head end. Or maybe those were spikes on a tail?

I looked at the stalk. Clear fluid dripped from a horizontal gouge where the frond must have been. I filmed some vid, then dropped to the ground to crouch beside Unida.

The snail crawled along the broken edge of the frond. "Is it eating that?" I asked.

"Or dissolving it. It's pretty fast." As we watched, the creature reached the edge of the frond and turned a hundred and eighty degrees to make another pass along the broken edge.

A flicker of movement caught my eye—another snail scooting across the dusty ground, directly toward us. "We might want to lift off." I set my belt to one-point-five meters, and my feet left the dirt.

Unida pointed as he rose. "Look, they're converging on this frond." Dozens of snails oozed toward us, moving faster than a creature with one foot has any right to move. Within minutes, the perimeter of the frond was covered in snails. They crept around the edge, each one shaving a little more off.

"They're working together." I lifted a little higher. Ravenous, slime-oozing snails gave me the heebie jeebies. *Coordinated*, ravenous, slime-oozing snails were terrifying.

"Don't be ridiculous." Unida smirked.

"They're going counterclockwise. All of them." The frond grew smaller by the minute, the snails rotating around the edge, shaving it down in increments.

Unida reprogrammed one of the returning drones, setting it to watch the frond. "We'll recall it when we get back to base. No point in us staying here."

I nodded. "That explains why the ground is clear of fallen debris. Natural garbage disposal."

"Maybe. There's no guarantee they eat anything but the fronds, but you're right, they seem to keep the forest floor clear. Let's grab a specimen." He pulled a pair of extendable tongs from his belt and reached toward the snails.

I pulled out a clean specimen jar and opened it. "Should I punch holes in this?"

He dropped the snail in. It stuck to the side. "Not necessary. Twist the lid to the first click. That allows air to circulate."

I twisted and it clicked. The snail oozed around the inside of the jar, a couple of centimeters above the bottom. The jar flexed in my hand. "Aren't these supposed to be rigid?" I lifted the jar to eye-level. "I think the snail is eating through the jar."

CHAPTER SIX

"It's eating through plastek? Impossible." Unida drifted closer, squinting at the thing in my hand.

I held the jar by its cap. The snail had made its way halfway around now, a gap in the clear material edged by a layer of pink goo left in its wake.

Unida flicked his holo-ring. "The biologists are gonna want to see this."

"How are we going to bring in a specimen if it can eat plastek?" I held the jar at arm's length. The bottom now hung at an angle, barely connected to the rest of the jar. As we watched, the snail oozed back to its starting point, and the bottom of the jar hit the dirt. The snail landed beside it and went to work on the remains.

"We need to get the crate off the ground." I arrowed back to our supplies, hitting the lift control on my belt. I flew around the crate, examining all sides for snails. "That is some scary crap."

"I'll call it in." He lifted higher, checking the bottoms of his boots as he spoke. "Ensign Okazaki? Unida. We have a code yellow. We found a snail that cuts through plastek like a spoon through pudding!"

While Unida gave a detailed report, my audio implant pinged. The automated voice came on. "Attention, Explorer Team Four. A code yellow hazard has been identified in sector forty-three. All teams are advised to stay airborne until further notice. Vid and stills posted on the team board. Check all equipment for infestation before returning to base. Details in the linked brief. Message repeats. Explorer Team—"

I hit the green check icon, and the voice cut out.

Liam chittered at me, then leaped from my shoulder, landing on the crate. The crate bobbled then steadied.

That shouldn't have happened. The grav lifter on the crate was more than capable of compensating for Liam's tiny mass without reacting. Liam perched on the edge of the crate, chittering at me. I swooped closer.

"Unida! We have a problem!" I grabbed Liam and sped to my partner's side.

He held up a finger, still talking at top speed. He listened for a minute, then responded to a series of questions. "Yes, sir. No. No, sir. Understood. Unida out. What's up, Kassis?"

"The snails got into our crate." My voice shook as I stared at the box floating a meter away. I'd forgotten to untether the thing, and it had followed me. The beginnings of panic curled up through my stomach, and my hands went cold. "Crap!" I scrabbled at my belt controls.

"Easy." Unida put a hand over mine, stilling my frantic fingers. "They can't get to you through the tether. We're safe." He released my hand. "Untether the crate, cadet."

The authority in his voice calmed my nerves, and the shaking of my fingers decreased to a nervous tremor. I swiped the belt screen and flicked the tether setting to off.

"Good. Now we're going to move." He flicked his own belt and backed away. Before I could reach for my controls, I started moving backwards. I peeked at the screen—he'd connected us. At least one of us was staying calm.

We stopped about five meters away.

"Should I put it down?" I asked.

He watched the crate, but nothing happened. "I don't suppose there's any reason to. We probably aren't getting that lifter back—it'll be nothing but wires and silicon connectors by the time those things are done. Unless they eat those, too." He swiped his holo-ring, and two of the drones lifted out of the crates. "Looks like the ones on top are still operational. I'm getting no response from the other two."

"I put them back into their boxes—they're powered down." I swallowed hard. "Should I have not done that?"

"No," he replied absently as he programmed the drones. "You followed protocol. I'm setting these to record from above. When the others return, we'll set two more to watch from below." He peered through the hologram at me. "You okay?"

"Yeah." It came out as a whimper, so I tried again. "Yes, I'm good. You're so calm. Have you seen this before?"

Unida waggled his head side-to-side. "I've seen reports from other teams of code yellows. And we get extensive simulator training to deal with this stuff. Didn't you do that at the Academy?"

"Kind of—not like this, but we had sims of dealing with reports like yours—basically Okazaki's role—managing the situation after it's been reported."

"Cadets become officers, not explorers, so that makes sense." He flicked another control as a third drone appeared on his holo. With his finger, he drew a flight path in the holographic display and set the cams to their target.

"We should be trained to deal with this end, too, though. I mean, Okizaki's out here with a partner, right? She could have been the one to find the snails."

He shrugged. "She is, but she doesn't have to be. A lot of the officers stay in camp to coordinate the team. That's harder to do from the field if something goes wrong."

"It seemed to work fine today." I told him about the alert.

"Yeah, I got it, too. And most of this stuff can be done remotely. But if she was in the middle of something tricky, it might have been different." He swiped away the drone program, then snapped his fingers in dismay and pulled it up again. "Let me walk you through what I did."

While he showed me the surveillance parameters he'd set, I kept one eye on the crate. He finished explaining and had me alter the flight path of the fourth drone.

"That wasn't too hard." I grinned as I watched my drone feed drop low, then circle the crate from ten centimeters above the ground, cam pointed up at the target.

"It isn't, once you learn the—" He held up a hand. "Did you hear that?"

"It sounded like—"

The bottom of the crate crashed to the ground.

"Did your drone catch that?"

I nodded. "Yes. Do you want me to watch the crate or the bottom?"

"Leave that one on its current course. I'll redeploy one of the others."

The audio pinged. "Code yellow team on approach. Please remain in place for debrief."

A rank of people swooped through the trees, led by Major Bellincioni. Dark uniformed explorers set up a perimeter around the crate.

"That isn't enough, sir." Unida saluted the major. "This whole forest should be quarantined. We spotted those snails at multiple locations." He swiped a file to her.

"I listened to your report, explorer. Well done." Her head turned toward me. "And you, cadet."

I saluted.

She returned the salute and turned back to Unida. "Send your drone controls to Watson. You two head back to base."

"We can stay and help—"

She cut me off. "That's not how this works. Unida, explain it to her—on the way back to camp. Full decon procedures are in place." She turned away before either of us could respond. She buzzed away to speak to a white-clad civilian scientist.

Unida swiped at his holo, then made a pushing motion at me.

With a jerk, I dragged my eyes away from the crate and pushed my drone controls to the icon labeled Watson.

Unida watched over my shoulder, then clapped me on the shoulder. "Let's go."

When we arrived at camp, a second set of force shield bollards were being deployed three meters outside the perimeter. Explorers with flame throwers burned the ground between the two, creating a blackened no man's land. A long, white temporary building had been erected extending from the outer bollards at the main gate, through the second set gate, and another twenty meters beyond.

We dropped to a black pad hovering a few centimeters above the ground at the entrance to the tent. The landing panel moved into the open end and paused between two metal bins hovering on a pair of similar panels. A wall dropped into place behind us, and a heat source turned on, bathing us in warmth.

A voice sounded in my audio. "Remove all gear and clothing."

Liam jumped from my shoulder to the edge of the bin. Unida turned away and began shucking his gear.

I faced opposite him and pulled off my grav belt and jacket. A quick glance over my shoulder confirmed my guess, so I loaded my gear into the bin. As we peeled off the layers, the temperature slowly rose. By the time we'd stripped, only my toes were still cold.

"This is pretty nice for decon," Unida said from behind me. "At Walther Training base, there's no heater."

"Isn't it pretty warm at Walther?" I asked, trying to sound nonchalant—as if standing back to back with a man I hardly knew, naked and on a moving panel was part of a normal day for me. Liam jumped from the bin to my shoulder and rubbed against my chin.

"Place the glider in the crate," a female voice said. "He can't go through decon with you."

Another hover panel swung in over the bin, holding an animal crate. I pointed at it. "Off you go, Liam."

The glider chittered in a disgusted tone, then scampered down my arm and jumped to the crate. He went inside, still scolding as I latched the door shut. The crate zipped away, and the bin holding my clothing followed.

"Stand still," the automated voice said. "Decontamination procedure initiated."

A blast of air hit me, blowing back the strands of hair that had worked free from my braid. The heater panel intensified, and my skin prickled. A wave of blue sparkled over me, like passing through a force shield turned to the lowest setting. This process repeated several times, leaving my skin red and prickly. A new panel swung up beside me, holding a set of clothes.

My body tingled as I pulled on the underlayer, the fabric scraping over sensitive skin. With each layer, my sense of helplessness diminished. Balancing on one foot, I yanked the sock and boot on, then switched to do the other.

"You can sit down, you know."

I half turned to see Unida perched on the edge of the panel, his legs dangling over the side. He lifted one to pull on his remaining boot.

I grinned sheepishly. "Sorry. I'm feeling…"

"Powerless? Violated? Terrified?"

"Yeah, all of that." I dropped beside him, sitting cross-legged. "What happens now?"

"I suspect they'll quarantine us for a few days, run way too many tests, and finally let us go."

"Oh, good. I was afraid they were going to lock us up and throw away the key."

"Same thing."

CHAPTER SEVEN

As the hover panel emerged from the tent, we passed through a faint blue shield, fritzing through our bodies. Cold air hit us, dampening the tingle.

"That's the force shield," Unida said. "The gate is set to the highest setting that allows people through. Everyone who returns to base will have to go through decon, but only those of us who came in direct contact with the specimen will require quarantine."

"But we didn't come in direct contact. You used the tongs. I held the outside of the jar."

"Doesn't matter. We were there and could have gotten pink snail slime on us. They'll watch and test us until they're sure we're clean."

"Does that mean our whole team will be with us? How many years is that going to take?"

Unida shrugged. As we talked, the panel took us to a new, smaller module that had been installed near the front gate. It had large windows in the front and an airlock at the door. Our conveyance stopped in front of the airlock, and we stepped onto a gray mat.

The door opened onto a short, empty hall. We entered, and the door shut behind us. The internal door popped open.

We walked into a small, gray room. Beds with med-pod equipment stood on either side of the room. A table with two chairs filled the space between the beds, and a door on the far side gave into a utilitarian bathroom. A small crate sat on one of the beds, and Liam chittered at me from inside.

As I hurried across the room, he reached through the grate and unlatched the door. He pushed it open and jumped from the bed to my arm. I winced as his tiny claws pricked my sensitive skin through the jacket. I stroked his soft fur. "That wasn't so bad, was it?"

Liam chattered loudly, as if he were criticizing not just the decontamination procedure, but the CEC as a whole. I giggled and murmured back at him.

"We have an audience," Unida said.

I swung around. I hadn't noticed the big window over the other cot—or maybe it had been opaque. But now, a rank of faces stared in at us from a room containing counters filled with equipment I recognized from my short stint in Li Abdul-James' lab on Earth.

My audio pinged. "I'm Dr. Samson." Behind the window, a plump man waved and grinned. "I'm head biologist on the mission. We thought this was turning out to be a big nothing for us, but you took care of that!"

A woman's voice replace Dr. Samson's. "I'm Dr. Florentine Vardel y Ortiz van Kranken, medical doctor. I'll be monitoring your health while you're in quarantine. I will run extensive tests while you're here. We'll do a health survey every morning, as well as daily exams. If you have any unusual symptoms—anything other than perfect health—you will notify me at once."

"I'm getting a headache from the yammering," Unida muttered.

I snickered.

Dr. Vardel wasn't amused. "Commander Jankovic promised us your complete cooperation. I don't want to have to report that you've been less than one hundred percent helpful."

I held up a hand. "We'll keep you completely up to date. However, we'd appreciate a bit of down time, if you don't mind. We've had a harrowing—" I checked my chrono "—ten hours. Can we get a hot meal and some rest?"

The audio went dead, and on the other side of the window, the white-coated experts argued. I put Liam's crate on the floor and threw myself down on the bed. Unida found a water pac and tossed it to me.

"Thanks."

Finally, the audio pinged again. "Explorer Unida, please lie down in the med pod, as Cadet Kassis is doing, so we can do a complete scan. Then we'll let you get food and rest." As Vardel spoke, the hood of the med-pod lowered over me. I dropped the half-drunk water pac into the convenient drawer beneath the bed and got my fingers back inside before the pod snapped shut.

I stared at the opaque cover arching over me, then let my eyes drift closed. Liam curled up in the curve of my neck, and we both went to sleep.

SOMETIME LATER, the pod pinged and opened. I squinted into the gloom, reluctant to open my eyes. My stomach growled, and Liam chittered in response. With a grunt, I sat up.

The room was gloomy. Light from the observation window revealed Dr. Vardel speaking to another white-coated woman. The sound was turned off, so I couldn't hear what was said.

Beneath the window, Unida sat up. He looked around, then reached over the retracted pod cover to knock on the window. The two women startled, then turned to look at us.

Unida raised a hand. "Hi. Can we get a meal? Or at least a snack?"

Vardel's voice came through the audio. "How are you feeling?"

"Hungry." I slid off my bed and stalked across the room. As I moved, the lights came on, dim at first but brightening quickly.

"Other than that?" Vardel snapped.

I crossed my arms and stared at her. "We can't really tell because we're so hungry. You've poked and prodded us—don't you have enough data to sift through for a while? Let us eat. If Unida suddenly sprouts a second head, you'll be the first to know."

The nameless woman's lips twitched, and she looked away. Vardel heaved a dramatic sigh. "Fine. I'll have the kitchen send in something. In an hour, I expect you to be ready to answer a comprehensive health survey."

"Sure, whatever you want." Unida swung off his bed. "After we eat."

WE SPENT three days in quarantine, answering health questions every four hours, getting scanned twice a day, and basically going out of our minds with boredom. They cut the comms between us and the rest of our team for reasons that were never fully explained.

Finally, on the morning of the fourth day, Dr. Vardel stomped up to the window. We'd been awake for several hours after our oh-six-hundred health survey but had ignored her because we'd learned it pissed her off. Sometimes it's the little things that give joy.

The audio pinged. "You're free to go." Her voice echoed sourly through the module.

I jumped off my bed. "We can go back to work?"

Unida sat up more slowly. He regarded Vardel over the retracted hood of his bed.

She glanced at him, then focused on nothing in the middle of the room. "Yes. You are cleared to return to duty. The sector you were exploring has been quarantined, so you'll be assigned another location." The audio snapped off.

"Duh." Unida swung his legs down and jumped off the bed. "We were done with that sector."

"What if we hadn't noticed the snails?" I whistled to Liam, and he flew to my shoulder.

"It's our job to notice everything. Once we do our survey, the vids are reviewed by the biological and environmental teams. They probably would have flagged the lack of debris on the ground, or maybe they would have noticed something in our snail vids. They send a phase 3 specialized team to look at anything they flag. Someone else from Foxtrot would have noticed them if we hadn't spotted them first."

We picked up the little bits and pieces we didn't want to leave behind —unopened items from our meal pacs, the drawings Unida had been working on, the little bed I'd made for Liam from a thin blanket. With a last look through the module, we left.

Team Foxtrot had already been deployed for the day, so we stowed our stuff.

"They haven't added us to the duty roster, so we get the rest of the day off." Unida tossed his stuff in his locker.

"Aren't you bored? I've had too much time off." I thrust the extra rations into the new survival bag that had appeared in my hammock. Presumably, my previous bag had been destroyed during decon or was being taken apart by scientists. I opened my locker and stowed the bag.

Unida grinned. "When you've been on a phase 2 team as long as I have, you learn to take advantage of every hour you're off duty." He tossed his new survival bag into his locker. "I'm headed to the gym."

I followed him into the sunshine, shivering a little. After three days in a temperature-controlled box, the regular Qureshi weather had a bite.

I didn't feel like lifting weights. Unida and I had established an exercise routine in quarantine to maintain our physical fitness, but he loved lifting heavy things. I preferred team sports. I wandered across the open space between the modules. Liam took off from my shoulder to play with the two other gliders currently in camp.

I rounded the corner of the kitchen mod. A short woman, moving fast, slammed into me—Major Bellincioni.

I rocked back on my heels. She jumped to a crouch, hands up in a fighting stance.

I held my hands away from my sides. "Good morning, Major."

She blinked and drew herself up. "Cadet Kassis. You're out of quarantine? Good. I need you." She pushed past me and trotted across the compound. We reached the decontamination tent, and she ducked inside. "You know how to program drones, correct?"

"Yes, sir. Of course." I hurried across the empty tent to a small booth enclosed in clear plastek. "Plebes have a whole term of mission equipment familiarization, and I did an advanced programming sequence as a senior. Unida checked me out on the current equipment before we discovered the death snail."

She waved that away. "Wasn't part of the curriculum when I went through. Drone driving was an enlisted specialty. Still is. Not sure why the Academy insists on teaching officer candidates." She sized me up, as if that were my fault.

I opened my mouth to defend myself but snapped it shut when she went on.

"All the drone guys are out in the field—that snail you discovered has caused quite the dustup. All of Foxtrot and half of Gecko are in quarantine. We're having trouble with the decon routine, and I was hoping you could fix it."

I frowned. "The decon routine uses drones?"

She waved her hands again. "Drones. Bots. They're the same thing. Automated tech that does a single job. If we had an AI to run all this stuff, I wouldn't need cadets to fix things. But—never mind. Here's the control panel—get it running again."

I stared at the code on the holo-screen in front of me. "I don't have any practical experience with this style of bot. Maybe one of the guys in quarantine could—"

"They're outside my purview. Anyone in quarantine belongs to Vardel, and she reports directly to Admiral Zehr. That's why you couldn't connect to your team channel—you were temporarily reassigned away from Team Four."

"That seems like—"

"Fix it." She tapped the control panel and whirled away.

CHAPTER EIGHT

"How am I supposed to fix a decon bot?" I swiped up the code and ran the diagnostics. Although some of the error codes matched what I'd learned in class, most of the information was Gagarian to me. If Chymm were here, he'd have it fixed in no time.

Which gave me an idea. I scrolled through the comm list for the Qureshi team, looking for anyone I knew. Sarabelle Evy, now a major, caught my eye. As a pilot, she wouldn't be any help on this project, but maybe I'd get the chance to say hello if she flew into our base.

Finally, I found what I was looking for. Ensign Threndish Elsinore. He'd been a year ahead of us at the Academy and in a different flight, so we hadn't had much interaction. But I'd heard Chymm mention his name. I tapped his comm link.

A blond man with a round face and pale blue eyes appeared. "Elsinore."

"Hi, this is Siti Kassis. I'm a friend of Chymm Leonardi di Zorytevsky. I need help with a bot program, if you have time."

"Any friend of Chymm's is a friend of mine." Elsinore's cheerful voice made me smile. "What's that old rascal up to?"

"He's on his senior tour on Harawi. I was wondering—"

"I remember my senior tour like it was just last year. Maybe because it was. I went to—"

"Look, sorry to cut you off." I swiped my screen and pulled up a sharing app. "But the major said this decon bot isn't working properly, and she wants it fixed now. I don't know much about programming bots."

"Have you tried turning it off and on?" His nasal laugh grated on my ears. "That's a tech support joke. It's funny because it's true."

"It's off now." I switched the system on and was greeted by a red icon on the screen. "System error 423."

"Send me the code. Programming bots is my middle name. Or it would be if it wasn't Orson. Ah, yes, I can see exactly what the problem is! If you give me a minute, I can tweak this and send you a loop to overwrite what you've got."

"And that will fix it?" I held my breath while I waited for him to reply. And waited.

I tapped his contact link, but it was still active. "Ensign Elsinore?"

"Call me Dish. That's got it!" He chuckled. "What a pickle. I wonder how that got so messed up? It looks like someone inserted a rogue loop."

"You mean on purpose? To sabotage the system?"

"I couldn't speculate on their intentions, but that was the effect. I recommend you install this security protocol, as well."

My holo-ring vibrated, and a blue icon flashed. I downloaded the files he sent and opened them. "Do you have time to walk me through the code?"

"No problem!" Elsinore stepped me through each line of code, describing in detail not only its function but also the etymology of the programming commands, his first encounter with each, and other commands that could have done a similar job but would have resulted in a microscopic decrease in efficiency.

I made notes as he spoke, hoping I could explain a fraction of this if Bellincioni asked. When he finally reached the end of his tutorial, I thanked him profusely for his help and promised to give him credit for the job.

"My pleasure. Any friend of Chymm's is a friend of mine."

"Yes, so you said." I flicked the files into the loading queue and ran the start up. The system rebooted, and the red error code disappeared. "It worked! Thank you so much, Ensign."

"Call me Dish. And call me any time. Programming bots is my middle name."

"I thought it was Orson." I smirked.

"Why yes, it is. How did you know?"

I thanked him a few more times, told him a couple of "Chymm saves the day" stories from senior year, and promised to call him again if I had any more problems. Finally, I signed off.

I toggled my comm system and sent a message to Maj Bellincioni. "System repair complete. Sabotage may have been involved."

I stood and stretched. I hadn't realized how long that programming session took until I checked my chrono—well past noon. Odd that I hadn't heard anyone going to lunch. Was the tent sound-proofed?

The sound of footsteps on gravel disabused me of that notion. The tent flap swung up and the major appeared. "What's this about sabotage?"

I flicked the highlighted code Dish had sent. "This section—"

"Start the system. Want to see it running while we talk. Always multi-task the no-brainers, cadet."

"Yes, sir." I flicked the virtual switch and showed her the error-free startup screen.

"Don't want to see data. Show me activity." She waved at the empty tent.

"Sorry, sir." I scrolled through the commands and found a demo screen. A couple of swipes started the bots running. The far end of the tent accordioned open, and a platform like the one Unida and I had ridden on slid into view. Gear bins swung into place on either side.

"Now, talk."

Her narrowed eyes followed the progression of the panel and the decon system as I told her what Dish had said and pointed out the faulty code. Her gaze flicked to me when I mentioned sabotage again, then went back to the bots. "Who was logged in when the file was uploaded?"

"Oh." I swiped through the interface and pulled up a system log. "The rogue loop was loaded four days ago. There was one user logged in—" I stared at the screen in horror.

"Who, cadet?" Bellincioni's pale gray eyes snapped to mine.

"It says Cadet Siti Kassis."

CHAPTER NINE

I closed the log and opened it again. My name still showed in small black letters. "That's impossible! I was out with Senior Explorer Unida." I tapped the time stamp. "We were discovering the plastek-eating snail."

Bellincioni held up a hand. "Saboteur isn't going to use their own login. You share your credentials with anyone?"

"No, of course not. Besides, this isn't me." I opened the log entry and pointed. "My account uses my full name. This entry says Siti." I logged out, then swiped my hand through the login sequence again. "See—I log in as Serenity."

"Someone is using your name. Must be someone who knows you."

"Or someone who's heard of me. Thanks to my dad and our trip to Earth, I'm not exactly low profile."

Her narrow eyes burned into me. "Good point. Easy enough for anyone to find out you're on this mission. Question is—why sabotage the decon sequence? Are they trying to damage this mission or hurt you?"

My stomach twisted. "You think someone is targeting me?"

"Haven't seen any outsiders on this mission, have you? Corporate spies hoping to steal Qureshi away from the CEC?"

"Why would they want Qureshi? We haven't found anything of value here. I thought the CEC expected to use it as a forward base to watch Gagarin."

"Exactly." She pointed a finger at me. "No point in squashing the mission—and this would hardly stop us anyway. They're after you. You made any enemies?"

I bit my lip. Derek Lee hated me. He and Felicity had never *said* they blamed me for their mothers' downfall, but the rest of the Academy had made it clear they gave me credit for the bust. I'd even gotten a commendation for my part on Sarvo Six. As had everyone in Charlie Blue.

"Spill it, cadet." Bellincioni leaned against the console, fully focused on me as the machinery moved behind her in perfect synchronization. "If someone on this mission is on a vendetta, I need to know."

"I don't know, sir." I clamped my lips shut. If Lee was out to get me, I'd find a way to pin it on him. But I wouldn't carry tales on a fellow cadet until I was certain. Even as skeevy a cadet as Lee Derek.

The major's eyes narrowed to slits and she pointed her finger again. "If you know anything, I need that info."

I shook my head. "I could speculate, but that's not fair." In fact, the more I thought about it, the less likely it seemed. Lee didn't have the tech skills to modify these bots, I was sure. He could have gotten the code from someone else. If that was the case, he'd need to contact that person again before his next attempt. If there was another attempt.

"True enough." Bellincioni stood, dusting her hands together. "Just have to make sure no one has time for this kind of nonsense. Go get some chow. Leave this to me."

I hesitated.

"Chow, cadet. Now."

I turned away, then turned back. The major needed to know who had fixed their system. I didn't want her to find out later and accuse me of stealing credit. And I certainly didn't want her asking me to fix anything else. Maybe Bellincioni would write a commendation for Ensign Elsinore. "About the code."

She pushed her hand out, palm toward my face. "We're done, cadet."

"Yes, sir." I turned away and marched out of the tent. I'd write a report and send it to her, making sure Dish got the credit. And maybe Dish could help me find out who was impersonating me on the system.

I GRABBED a bowl of noodles and sat on the deserted patio. Liam dropped to my shoulder for a brief snuggle, then leaped into the rafters again. I toyed with my food and stared into space.

"You going to eat that?" Unida dropped onto a bench opposite me, his tray overloaded. Now that the camp had been running for a few days, meal offerings were getting more varied and better tasting. His tray held a sandwich, a noodle bowl like mine, three flat breads with piles of toppings, a bowl of fruit, a huge salad, and an enormous rectangle of something brown and moist—cake or bread.

I took a deep breath, and the aroma of cinnamon and chocolate filled my nose. "Where'd you get cake?"

"It helps to know the chef." He grabbed a knife, cut the chunk, and dumped half on my tray. "Stevers can make cake out of anything."

I sniffed again. "I actually smell it. The stench is gone!"

He sucked in a deep breath. "Right so. Do you think we've gotten acclimatized or they've learned how to filter it out?"

"I'm taking bets on that very topic," a familiar voice replied.

I squinted against the sun. "Rico? What are you doing on Qureshi?" I jumped up.

"That's Senior Explorer to you, cay-det." Rico came around the table and gave me a bear hug.

"Congratulations on the promotion." I turned to Unida. "Do you know Senior Explorer Rico Waldroon? Rico, this is Rafael Unida."

The two men bumped fists.

"You want some chow?" Unida indicated the kitchen.

"Already ate on the ship." Rico pointed at the sky. "I brought Doc A-J down to check out your discovery."

"You're assigned to Li?"

"That's Dr. Abdul-James to us." He winked. "You aren't a dependent anymore." He turned to Unida. "I babysat young Siti on the mission to Earth."

"You did not. *I* kept *you* out of trouble."

Unida rolled his eyes at our bickering and worked his way through his food.

"I don't understand why Li—Doc A-J—is here. She's an environmental scientist, not an alien zoologist." I paused to slurp up noodles.

Rico dropped onto the bench beside me. "I just follow orders, and my orders said bring the doc to the planet. We got redeployed from Goryu when they heard about the apocalyptic snail of death. Are they going to name it after you?"

"Gaw, I hope not. It's bad enough being the daughter of the Hero of Darenti Four. I don't need to be the Death Snail Girl, too. Besides, they should name it after Unida."

Unida looked up. "No, thanks."

"The Unida-Kassis World Eater." Rico waved both hands across the sky, as if imagining a giant holo. "I'm putting credits on that."

"Fantastic." I picked up my tray. "I'm going to go find Li. Unida, whatever you do, don't make any bets with Rico. He always wins."

Unida, his mouth full, nodded his thanks.

"Now that you've unfairly bollixed my new prospect, I'll come with you." Rico jumped up. "I'm not sure they'll let you into the lab without me."

"Thanks." I dumped my tray and followed him across the camp.

While we'd been isolated, three more modules had been installed. Rico opened the door to the second one and waved me inside. We stood in a narrow room that spanned the width of the module. The interior wall was transparent, allowing us to see the scientists working inside. They all wore white coveralls, with hoods and face shields.

"If that thing eats plastek, how is any of that helping?" I asked.

Rico muttered under his breath for a moment, then looked up. "I told her you're here. She said she'll meet you for dinner—she's right in the middle of something."

Inside, one of the scientists lifted a hand, and I waved back. "I should have realized she'd be busy."

He opened the door. "They take breaks, so it was worth a shot."

"Can you smell the stink?" We settled down on a bench outside the module.

Rico drew in a deep breath. "The faintest hint. I heard it was really bad here."

"It was when we landed. I guess they figured out how to adjust the dome. Or maybe setting it to a higher strength to keep the snails out did the trick."

We sat in silence for a few minutes, soaking up the sunshine.

"The Earth kid was flying the shuttle." Rico's voice was lazy, almost slurred. He leaned against the side of the mod, his eyes closed.

"Earth kid?" I asked.

"Big, muscular kid. Dark skin. Long, curly hair."

"Joss. We all got basic shuttle training at the Academy, but he wants to be a pilot."

"I heard you've done pretty good there."

"Better than you might have expected of a spoiled brat."

"You weren't spoiled—just kinda whiny."

I slapped his arm. "At least I didn't bet my way through the mission."

"I made a lot of people happy. Petty gambling is entertainment for the masses." He paused. "I don't do that anymore."

"Make book? You don't?"

His head moved side-to-side. "Gotta prove I'm sergeant material. I straightened up and made senior early."

"Wow. I guess we've both grown up."

We sat there until a shadow passed overhead, blocking the sun. I blinked sleepily upward. "Shuttle landing. Who's coming in now?"

Rico jumped up. "More scientists, I imagine. I gotta return to the ship. I'll see you around, kid."

I gave Joss and Peter's stock answer. "Not if I see you first."

He laughed and punched my shoulder. "Didn't know it was talk like a caveman day!"

"Go away, Rico." I looked around, but no one was nearby, so I gave him a swift hug.

Across the camp, the deep blue force shield sparkled and paled. The shuttle settled to the ground like a leaf on the wind, and the shield brightened behind it. The quiet engines stopped, and the rear wall hinged down to form a ramp. A group of people streamed out.

"I'm out!" Rico raised a hand as he wove through the small crowd and entered the shuttle.

Unida had disappeared from the patio, so I headed to the barracks module, my cold fingers tucked into my pockets. The heavier force shield kept more heat in, but it also filtered out some of the warmth from the sun. If anything, today was colder than the day we'd landed.

A loud whoop stopped me in my tracks. I turned to see Joss running toward me. "Did you see that?"

"What?" I turned, scanning the horizon for threats.

"My landing!" He reached me, flinging up his arms, palms out. "I landed that shuttle."

I slapped his hands, as expected, and he gripped my fingers, shaking me a little. "I stuck it. Lt Ling said it was perfect. And I haven't even been to pilot training yet." He whooped again.

I pulled my hands away. "You'll be an awesome pilot."

"I *am* an awesome pilot." He flung an arm over my shoulders. "Where are we going?"

I shrugged.

He steered me toward the barracks. "I gotta move. Let's hit the gym."

CHAPTER TEN

AFTER A LONG SESSION of weightlifting and hand-to-hand sparring, I finally escaped. I don't mind working out, but Joss's preferred brand of exercise was not my favorite.

The patio was packed when I arrived, my hair still damp from the showers. I found Joss, and we grabbed food, then looked for empty seats.

"Siti!" An arm waved from a table surrounded by people in civilian clothing.

I poked Joss's arm and started toward the table. "That's Li. She was on the Earth team."

"I think I met her once." Joss pointed across the patio. "I'm going to catch up with Morse and Leng-wei. I heard they might be playing poker later."

"You'll lose your shirt."

Joss flexed his arm in a body builder pose that was marred by the tray in his other hand. "Just the way I like it. But I'm a lot better than I used to be."

"Derek Lee was playing with them on the flight. He'd love to fleece you."

Joss snorted and angled away.

"Siti, over here!" Li called as I neared the table. "Move over, guys. Make room for Siti. She's the one who discovered our little gem."

I sat next to Li and wrapped an arm around her in a brief side-hug. She introduced me to the sea of scientists, but most of the names slipped away. I could always look them up later with the camp's directory app.

Li pushed her tray to the center of the table and leaned an elbow in a puddle of cold coffee. "Tell us about finding the snail."

I handed her a napkin. "We noticed a frond had fallen from one of those spiky trees and went to look. And there it was, eating the edges. A bunch more showed up and we tried to bag one. Did you call it a 'little gem'?"

Her eyes sparkled and several of her colleagues nodded. "It's going to be a game-changer if we can figure out a way to contain it. Plastek is easy to break down and reuse, but it does require energy. A creature that eats it could be a huge credit-saver."

"As long as it only eats stuff you want it to eat." I tapped my spoon on my bowl. "If it gets loose in the camp, it will eat everything—furniture, dishes, modules."

"There are only five of them in the lab, and they're in transparent aluminum containers. Their slime has no effect on trans-lu."

"You're the experts. What have you been doing since I left Earth?" While Li told me about her more recent assignments, I ate. The others finished their meals and cleared their dishes.

"And then they sent me here." Li finished her story and looked around at the empty table. "I need to get back to the lab—we're working extended hours. It was really good to see you, Siti." She dashed away.

I stacked her forgotten dishes with my own and took them to the recycler. As I dropped the bowls into the chute, "Dish" Elsinore popped into my head. Maybe he could help me track down my impersonator.

"I've set up what we in the business call a watch-n-sting." Dish spoke through a haze of holograms as he swiped and poked faster than I could follow. "If anyone attempts to activate that account, it will remotely initialize all available cams in the vicinity. They will record the guilty party, the recording gets sent to me, and I'll send it to you."

"Thanks, Ensign—I mean—Dish. If I can ever repay the favor…"

"A friend of Chymm—"

"—is a friend of yours. I remember. But I like to help my friends, too."

He tapped his temple. "Noted and logged for future reference, my friend. I shall call upon you in my time of need."

I bit my lip, trying not to laugh at his awkwardly pompous phrasing. "I hope you do. Thanks again. Kassis out."

"Who was that?"

I swung around. "Joss, you startled me! Why are you creeping around the camp?"

Night had fallen. Three of the four moons—Sagan, Hira, and Piazzi—hung at different points in the sky, their various crescents providing little light. The largest, Saha, would rise later tonight, but it was much farther away, and even full, it would appear smaller.

We stood on a corner of the shuttle landing pad. Bright bars of light shone from each camp module, leaving the main paths between the buildings well lit, with stripes of darkness between. The approach lights glowed softly—they'd automatically brighten if a ship arrived.

"A friend of Chymm's." I explained about the fake login. "This is all hush-hush, so please don't mention it to anyone." Why had I said that? Maj Bellincioni hadn't told me to keep it secret. But if we were going to catch someone in the act, we'd have to make sure they didn't know we were watching.

"No worries. You wanna play poker with us?"

I shook my head. "I might—" I broke off as my holo-ring vibrated. It was Dish. "That was fast."

He grinned, but it looked strained. "Yeah, that is not a good thing. My sting-n-watch has already alerted forty-three times in seven different camps. Someone is using versions of this account to access systems all over the planet. I've alerted the rest of the security team, and we are attempting to block the accounts. Whoever set this up has managed to give themselves a back door—"

"Who are you talking to?" a voice in the background came through Dish's audio.

"It's Cadet Kassis, sir—the person who told me about—"

"Cut that link!"

"I gotta—"

Dish's voice cut off.

"Kassis."

I swung around. Maj Bellincioni stood in the dark between the closest path and the landing pad. Behind her, three large explorers waited, their faces in shadow. "Come with us. Both of you." Without waiting to see if we'd comply, she turned and marched away.

I exchanged a glance with Joss, and we followed the major. The three explorers closed in behind us.

I stretched my steps and caught up with Bellincioni. "What's going on, sir?"

She held up a hand to forestall questions and angled around the patio. A handful of explorers sat around a table playing a card game. Derek Lee looked up as we passed, his eyes following us. He said something, and the other players turned to watch us. I flipped my braid over my shoulder and ignored him.

We stopped at the back of the kitchen module, and Bellincioni waved the door open. This module followed the standard configuration: kitchen in the front, with command offices and VIP quarters in the rear. Bellincioni waved us toward an open door. "In there. Wait."

Joss and I took seats on the far side of the conference table. Two of the guys following us filed into the room and took up stations by the door. The third did not come inside.

"Are we in trouble?" Joss whispered to me.

I shrugged and flicked on my mission directory. I took snap of the higher-ranking guy and looked him up. There. "Excuse me, Explorer van Kerick?"

Van Kerick made eye contact but didn't say anything.

"Are we being detained?" I stood and took a step forward.

"Sit." Van Kerick's hand moved to the holster strapped to his leg.

I sat. "I'd say that's a 'yes.' What are we supposed to have done?"

"That's easy. You broke into a bazillion systems around the planet and destroyed stuff, remember? I got caught up in your wake." Joss made wave motions with his hands.

"I did not do any such thing! You know it wasn't me."

He chuckled. "Duh. I was joking."

"Don't say things like that, even as a joke. You know they're recording everything in this room." I looked at the ceiling, facing the far corner. That was the most likely location of a camera. "He was kidding. I didn't do anything."

The guards snapped to attention. Joss and I jumped to our feet as Commander Jankovic entered, Bellincioni on his heels. He eyed us for a few seconds, then yanked the chair away from the end of the table and dropped into it.

"Wait outside," the major muttered.

The two guards pivoted toward each other and marched, single file, through the door, their broad shoulders barely clearing the opening.

"At ease, cadets." Jankovic dug his heels into the carpet and pulled his chair up to the table. He flicked his holo-ring and tossed a file onto the conference table projector. Line after line of red code scrolled up into the ceiling. Here and there, a line flashed and turned green, then scrolled away. "Care to explain this?"

I bit my lip. "I'm not sure what I'm looking at, sir."

"This is the havoc your unauthorized logins created." He flicked his fingers and the file stopped scrolling. A quick swipe pushed that file off-center and another took its place. "Team Two's labs lost power—during a sensitive experiment. Team One's landing pad also lost power. Our decon system went down—again. Team Three has had a glitch in their force shield for days. All caused by your account." His eyes bored into me.

"Sir, I told Major Bellincioni—that's not my account. I have no idea who—"

"What about this Ensign Elsinore? What is his role in this mess?"

"He helped me fix the decon system. It's in my report to Major Bellincioni. I asked him to check on the phony account—and he said it's being used all over the planet. I was talking to him when the major brought us here."

Jankovic's eyes swung to Joss. "What about you?"

"He has nothing to do with this, sir—"

"I wasn't talking to you, Kassis." Jankovic didn't even glance my direction. "Cadet Torres, what is your role in this event?"

"None, sir."

"You're saying you know nothing about the destruction your teammate instigated?"

"I'm saying Cadet Kassis would never do anything to damage a Corps mission."

"That isn't what I asked you, Torres."

"Yes, sir. But it's true."

Jankovic beckoned Bellincioni forward. The two officers held a muttered conversation, then Bellincioni went to the door.

Jankovic stood. "Kassis, I'm sending you back to the ship."

"Sir, no!" An explorer who had been sent to the ship would never be assigned to a planet again. For me—a cadet on my SenTo—it spelled the end of my career before it even started.

CHAPTER ELEVEN

THE WIND PICKED UP. Joss and I stood with our personal gear on the corner of the landing pad. Liam wound his warm body around my neck, warding off the chill.

The enormous van Kerick and his companion—whose name I hadn't had time to look up—stood behind us. The poker players had dispersed, so there was no one to witness our humiliation. At least not in person. I was sure they were watching through the windows or via the surveillance feeds.

"I'm sorry you got caught up in this," I whispered to Joss. "I can't believe they're sending you back, too."

"That's what happens when you tell the commander he's being an idiot." Joss pulled his hat down over his ears. "I don't regret defending you."

"You shouldn't have gotten involved. You know we've lost our commissions, right?"

"I was never really sure I wanted to do this explorer thing anyway. It was Pete's idea. I came along to keep an eye on him."

I pulled my collar up. "Right. That's why you endured three years at the Academy. To keep an eye on Peter."

He shrugged. "The Academy was fun. Most of the time."

"Yeah, it was." Angry tears burned my eyes. I blinked them back. "I'm going to find out who did this to me—to us—and make them pay."

"Good luck with that." Derek Lee sauntered up to the landing pad, a survival pack thrown over one shoulder.

"What are you doing here?" Joss stepped forward, but van Kerick put a hand on his shoulder.

Lee smirked. "Flight training. I get to fly you kids back to the ship."

I turned away and closed my eyes. Bad enough that we'd been dismissed from the mission, but to have Derek Lee participate in our humiliation was too much.

"What's wrong? Has the great Siti Kassis fallen from grace? Now you see how it feels."

I spun around, advancing on Lee. "Did you do this? Is this your idea of payback?"

Van Kerick stepped between me and Lee, blocking the light now blazing from the landing pad. "The shuttle is landing. Stand back."

The spacecraft swung over our heads and hovered over the pad, then descended through the blue fuzz of the shield. The landing gear touched down, and a few minutes later, the rear hatch opened. A pair of officers in flight gear swaggered down the ramp. The taller one made a comment to the shorter. The two laughed, and the taller one stalked away toward the kitchen mod, a bag over his shoulder.

"You my cadet?" the shorter pilot asked. "You'll fill in for Nabiyev—he's staying dirtside."

I recognized the voice: Major Sarabelle Evy. I put a hand over my face as the hot tears pricked again—this time equal parts anger and humiliation. The only thing worse than an enemy like Lee seeing my failure up close and personal was having a friend witness it, too.

Evy jerked her head toward the shuttle. "We're on a quick turn—run the checklists, cadet." As Lee hurried inside, she turned to us. Her eyes widened when they landed on me. "Siti, what are—you're not my cargo, are you?"

I lifted my chin. "I am. I've been framed and railroaded, and they're sending me back to the ship."

"There must be a mistake." Evy turned to the two guards. "Who ordered this?"

"Commander Jankovic." Van Kerick stood at ease with his hands behind his back.

She eyed him. "Where is he?"

"I don't know, sir. Probably his quarters."

Evy crossed her arms. "Why don't you take me to him? Don't worry about the cadets. They aren't going anywhere. Your hulking friend can watch them." She waved at the path. "Lead on."

The nameless explorer nudged me with a rock-hard elbow. "Into the shuttle, cadets."

I picked up my gear and my survival bag. On a phase 2 mission, even a shuttle flight to the ship was considered hazardous duty, so survival gear was required. I slung the two bags over my shoulders and trudged up the ramp into the ship.

We stowed our gear on the pallet next to Lee's and strapped it down. This shuttle was configured for cargo—the troop seats had been removed. We picked a couple of jump seats and folded them down from the wall.

I dropped into mine and fastened the restraints. A couple of explorers loaded a pallet of boxes and crates, not making eye contact with us as they did. They probably feared our humiliation was contagious.

"Maybe we should wait for the major to return." Joss stood beside me.

"I don't think we have to jump to attention when she comes in. What are they going to do? Send us back to the ship?" I laughed bitterly.

Through the open cockpit door, Lee looked over his shoulder and smirked.

"No, I mean maybe she can talk sense into Jankovic, and we won't have to leave." Even as he said it, his face fell, as if he realized how unlikely that would be. He dropped into the seat.

"I don't think the commander is going to be swayed by Evy. He's made up his mind." I darted a glare at Lee and lowered my voice. "Or has been paid off to get rid of me."

"Really?" Joss scoffed. "You think this is aimed at you? Why would anyone go to so much trouble to get rid of a cadet?"

"You heard Lee, and you know he blames us for his mother's court martial. Maybe his buddy LeBlanc helped. *He* definitely hates us—and he's got the credits to do whatever he wants." Micah LeBlanc had been expelled from the Academy after our plebe summer. He'd been sent to a rehabilitation facility—a plush summer camp for the unruly children of the ultra-wealthy—and supposedly cured of his psychotic behavior. My father had made sure he didn't return to the CEC.

Joss grunted noncommittally.

"What?" I demanded.

"I think that's a lot of trouble and expense just to get you kicked out of the Academy. If Lee—or LeBlanc—really wanted to hurt you, I'm sure they could find easier and cheaper ways to do it than taking down an entire CEC phase 2 mission."

"When you put it that way…" I fiddled with the loose end of my seat harness. "But Jankovic and Bellincioni can't really think I'd be stupid enough to use my own name on a login credential that crashed multiple systems. No one would be that dumb."

"I guess they do." He jerked his head toward the rear of the shuttle.

Evy pushed past the hulking explorer still watching us from the ground, her face like thunder. She stomped up the ramp and flicked her holo-ring. The back ramp began to rise, rotating into position. The guard leaped back, and the ghost of a smirk crossed Evy's lips.

The internal doors slammed shut followed by the bang of the ramp locking into place. She stalked across the echoing cargo hold to us. "What did you do to piss him off so much?"

"I didn't do anything!" I tried to jump to my feet, but the harness held me in place. I reached for the buckle.

Evy waved me off, dropping into the next jump seat. "He's convinced you sabotaged the unit. He was raving about how you took down the whole planet."

"Someone created a login credential under my name and used it to cause all kinds of mayhem."

"That should be easy enough to trace." Evy drummed her fingers against her lower lip. "The system should have biometric markers in the account. If it wasn't you, then the markers won't match."

"I don't think they've cared enough to check that." I bit my lip, and the treacherous tears prickled my eyes again. "I had a friend looking into it, but I haven't heard anything. We were cut off when Bellincioni took us in." I flicked my holo-ring but nothing happened.

"I'm sure your comms have been isolated." She leaned forward to address Joss who had slumped into his seat on my far side. "What's your role in all this? Did they target you, too?"

I spoke before Joss could open his mouth. "He tried to defend me. He said some inadvisable things."

"Inadvisable? That might be harder to overcome than this." Evy waggled her fingers at me. "If Siti's been framed, it can be proven. Insubordination—in any circumstances—is a tough one to beat."

Red stained Joss's dark cheeks. "I know. But there was no real evidence. And he was so certain...I tried to be polite."

"Starting an accusation with 'with all due respect,' doesn't automatically make it polite." I bumped my shoulder against his, so he'd know how grateful I was.

"Yeah, I know."

Evy got up. "We'll have to sort this out later. I've got to get back to the ship, and you two can't stay here." She wheeled away and raised her voice. "You got that checklist done, cadet?"

Lee mumbled something.

"We'll get this fixed. Don't worry. We gotta fly." Evy slapped my arm and hurried to the cockpit. The door slid shut behind her.

A few seconds later, the shuttle rose from the ground. We rotated, then shot away from the ground, the acceleration pressing me against Joss's side. The shuttle bounced a couple of times, rattling us in our seats. Then the pressure eased, and our bodies lightened. My braid lifted off my neck. Liam launched himself into the air, somersaulting to the ceiling, then pushing off again.

"At least someone is enjoying the trip," Joss muttered.

Evy's voice came over the speakers—she must have been right about our comms being out. "Transit time to the ship is about two hours—they're orbiting beyond Saha. You can unbuckle if you want."

We unlatched and spent a few minutes playing in the weightlessness. After a few spins and flips, the gravity of our situation dragged me down.

I pushed off, spinning in a lazy circle, my mind spinning much faster as I tried to see a way out of this predicament.

"I can't believe they made Lee a pilot candidate." Joss pushed off the bulkhead near the cockpit hatch. "He ralphed on the way to Qureshi."

"Dad says it's a control issue—pilots are fine as long as it's their hands on the stick."

He grunted. "I never had that problem. I hope he isn't barfing all over the control panels."

The door slid open and Evy's head poked through. "You two want to come up front?"

"Cool." Joss hit the bulkhead with flexed knees and pushed off again, aiming at the door.

"Is that allowed?" I snagged a nearby handhold and shoved myself toward her.

"My ship, my rules." Evy gave a little push and drifted out of the doorway as Joss passed. "You'll have to go back to cargo before we land."

"Has Lee barfed yet?" Joss tucked into a ball and kicked off the overhead to spin. After three or four revolutions, he hooked his feet on the back of Lee's seat and stopped. His body swung forward, but he used his muscles to stop the motion. Then he nudged the ceiling and dropped into the empty seat behind Lee.

"Freefall doesn't make me barf, showoff." Lee twisted around to glare at Joss.

"It did on the way down." Joss fastened a harness loosely across his lap.

"Sit down, Cadet Lee." Evy drifted past Joss, swatting him in the head as she went. The movement propelled her to the front of the cockpit, and she grabbed her seat as she coasted by.

Joss grinned but didn't say anything else.

I took the remaining seat, glancing at the unusually spacious flight deck. "Is this the VIP shuttle?"

Evy pointed a finger at her chest. "SFO gets to fly the good bird." She turned to Lee. "SFO is senior flight officer—the highest-ranking pilot on flight duty."

"Yes, sir, I know." Lee ground his teeth.

I hid a grin. Trust Evy to have my back, even if the only thing she could do was bait Lee.

"Actually, I expected them to give me bravo-14, which is a pile of junk, because this baby was in maintenance. Plus, flying a pair of cadets back to the ship doesn't usually require the VIP shuttle. But she was ready in time."

"Yay, lucky us." I turned to look out the side windows. If I leaned forward, I could make out the curve of Qureshi behind us. The huge front screen provided a much prettier view—stars sparkling behind the moon Saha, which grew as we drew nearer. It glowed white and green on the daylight side. "What's up with that moon? It looks almost like a planet."

"It *is* almost a planet." Evy swiped a control, and the view zoomed in. "It has a thick atmosphere and weird plants."

"If stuff is growing there, it must be warmer than Qureshi." Joss rubbed his hands together as if they were cold. "Why aren't we exploring there instead?

"The atmosphere is breathable but contains several compounds that would be hazardous to long-term residents." Evy pulled up a file on her holo-ring and flung it onto the front display. "Qureshi is cold because we're on the outer edge of the Goldilocks zone. Saha's atmosphere is thick enough to retain a lot more heat, and the core is apparently much warmer —and more active. It also has strange electromagnetic properties that make communications difficult—like on Qureshi. Altogether, the whole system is a poor prospect. We don't usually colonize borderline planets— we aren't that desperate. But this system is beautifully located to monitor the Gagarian Empire."

For the next two hours, Joss, Evy, and I watched the moon grow larger and talked about our time on Earth and what we'd done since we left. Lee pretended to ignore us, but it's hard to look busy on a shuttle flying straight ahead.

An alert flashed red with an accompanying warning blare.

"Sir, there's a failure in the main drive." Lee swiped the warning away and silence fell.

"Crap. They were supposed to have fixed that." Evy pulled up the diagnostics. "We're off course, too. What did you do, cadet?"

Lee's head snapped around. "I didn't do anything, sir."

"You didn't notice that the programmed correction burn didn't initiate? Didn't I ask you to watch that?" Her hands flew across the control screens.

"Yes, sir, but I was dealing with the drive failure." Lee's olive skin burned red.

Joss leaned across the aisle. "Dealing with it? All you did was report it."

"Are we supposed to be getting that close to the moon?" I pointed through the main screen. Saha had grown huge, as if we'd started a descent.

A quiet pop reverberated through the cockpit. "Sir, we've lost the starboard thruster." Lee's voice shook.

"It's going to get rough." Evy pulled a helmet from under her seat. "Lee, helmet on." The two of them snapped helmets over their heads, the visors down. Her voice spoke over the speakers. "Siti, Joss, get to the back and suit up, then strap in. Now!"

CHAPTER TWELVE

Joss launched himself backwards, the door barely opening before he hit it. I unlatched my belt and followed. We found emergency suits in a clearly labeled compartment. Joss pushed one at me, then started donning his own.

I whistled as I thrust my legs into the suit. "Liam, where are you?"

The little blue and white glider arrowed toward me. I caught him with my free hand and set him on my shoulder, then pulled the suit up over my waist. Liam scrambled down my chest and squirmed into my pocket as I shoved my arms into the suit and fastened the front.

"Get strapped in!" Joss pulled down a jump seat and used the restraints to pull himself into it.

I secured my helmet and pulled myself into the nearest seat. The heavy gloves made my hands clumsy, but I managed to get the straps into place and the buckle latched.

"Controls are not responding." Evy sounded calm through the suit's internal comms. "Are you two secure?"

"Yes, sir," we said together.

"The main drive is out, the directional controls are dead, and we're headed for that moon. We're going to have to land. Brace for impact. Lee, contact the *New Dawn*."

The audio cut out. Long narrow hatches opened at the top of the bulkheads, and automated webbing shot out. It snapped into receiving slots on the decking and tightened around us and the tiny luggage pallet.

The ship rocked and rattled. We plunged, then popped back up. The straps bit into my shoulders until we dropped again. The webbing tightened. I turned my head, but the straps held my helmet in place. I tried to grab Joss's arm, but my hand was immobilized. We slammed down, then up, then down again. I clenched my teeth and tried not to bite my tongue.

The ride smoothed. The comm interface crackled, and Evy's voice came through again. "We're through the roughest part—until landing. We've got the wings deployed, so we'll be able to steer. Looking for a safe landing spot."

"Sir, I'm still not getting through to the *New Dawn*," Lee said, his voice high and shaking. "They aren't responding to my hails."

"Are you sure you're on the right frequency?"

"Yes, sir, I've check it three ti—" His voice cut out.

"What's happening?" I yelled.

"I think I'm the only one who can hear you," Joss said.

I tried again to turn my head, but my helmet stayed stubbornly in place. Despite the continuous rattle of the shuttle, my heartbeat sounded loud in my ears, and my lungs felt tight. Probably the returning gravity. I tried to breathe slower, counting in for four and out for seven.

"I wish—"

I never heard what Joss wished.

CHAPTER THIRTEEN

WE SLAMMED SIDEWAYS. The ship bounced wildly, rattling our teeth. My head hit the top of my helmet and stars danced before my eyes. My mindful breathing went out the air lock.

Under the rattling of the shuttle, Joss chanted a string of swear words over and over like a mantra.

The latch to the pressure suit cabinet gave way, and the remaining suits spilled out into the cargo area, helmets bouncing like badly programmed rev-balls. I winced as one came straight at me. It slammed into the netting over my body, then rebounded away.

One of the straps broke, and our survival bags flew into the air, slamming down again the next second. It was like being inside a jar of dice at a pilots' bar when drinks were on the line.

After an eternity, with more items breaking loose from the netting, the shuttle seemed to slam into something immoveable. We tumbled, tail over nose, two or maybe three times.

Then we stopped. Airborne items dropped to the overhead—we'd landed upside down.

"Siti, are you okay?" Joss called, his voice barely audible through both helmets.

"I think so. You?"

"I feel like someone beat me with a bag of rocks, but yeah."

"We need to check on Evy and Lee. Do you know how to work the comms?"

The helmet speaker clicked and popped. "Kassis, Neanderthal, I need help."

"Is Evy all right?" I fumbled for my buckle.

"You want help, and you call me Neanderthal?" Joss growled.

Lee ignored him. "She's not responding. I can't reach her."

"Why not?" I got the buckle unlatched and dropped into the webbing. "Is there a way to retract the safety nets?"

Lee muttered and grunted a few times. The nets unlatched from the floor—which was above my feet—and retracted into the slot by my head, the loose ends snapping at us as they rocketed past. "Hey!" I fell forward, landing face first on the cargo hold's overhead.

Joss thumped down beside me on his hands and knees. "Good thing the gravity is low. That woulda hurt."

"We're coming," I told Lee as I patted my side where I could feel Liam's tiny, warm body. "You okay, buddy?"

Liam wiggled, chirping quizzically.

"I think we crashed." I climbed over the conduits strung across the overhead and headed for the front bulkhead.

"You think?" Lee's sarcastic voice was tinged with hysteria.

"I was talking to Liam, not you. He can't see what's going on." As I spoke, Liam squirmed again, then crawled up the front of my jacket. His damp nose brushed against my neck as he pushed his head into my helmet. "I don't think this is a good place for you, Liam."

"I can't reach the door release." Joss stood at the bulkhead, stretching his arm to full length. The access panel was a good meter above his head.

"Lift me up."

His brows knitted together. "I'm pretty strong, but—"

"Yeah, I know I'm not a lightweight, but Saha has a fraction of Earth gravity, remember? You could probably *toss* me up there if you wanted."

"Sure. I could do that in Earth gravity." His voice shook, destroying his intended comic arrogance. He laced his gloved fingers together and braced his legs.

I stepped into his hands and pushed off.

"Wow, you weren't kidding. If you need more reach, you can climb on my shoulders." He lifted me higher.

"This is good. Hold still." I slapped my gloved hand against the panel. It lit up, and I tapped the open icon. The door slid halfway and stuck. "Crap. Can you move to the left? No, my left."

Joss shuffled a step to the side. The top edge of the door hit me about mid-chest.

"I'm going to pull myself up." I grabbed the edges of the door.

"I'll give you a boost."

I bobbled as Joss flexed his knees, then I flew upward. "Hey, easy!" I yanked at the edges of the door and ducked my head, curling through the opening. My shoulder banged against the half-open door. I fell forward and landed on my hands and knees. Fortunately, the cockpit overhead was lower than the cargo compartment, thanks to the sleeping quarters above. Or beneath, now.

Joss snickered. "Oops. Don't know my own strength."

I struggled to my feet, the baggy, one-size-fits-most pressure suit hampering my movement.

"Stop messing around and help me!" Lee cried.

The cockpit's ceiling was smooth underfoot. I stepped over a jumble of protein bars, empty wrappers, water pacs, a tablet, and a broken stylus. Lee and Evy hung from their seats at the front of the small compartment.

With a grunt, Joss heaved himself into the cockpit behind me.

"Grab the first aid kit." I pointed at the small white case with a blue star strapped to the rear bulkhead and turned to Lee. "Why aren't you moving?"

He slammed a hand down on the crumpled flight console. "I'm pinned. These things are supposed to be built to protect the pilots. It shouldn't have moved."

"When we get back to the ship, you can file a complaint." I peered through Evy's face shield. "Evy? Major Evy? Sarabelle!"

She didn't respond.

"Check life support. Can I take her helmet off?"

Lee poked a few controls. "All green." He reached for his helmet.

"Good idea, you test the air first." Joss held out the white case.

Lee froze with his hands on either side of the helmet. "You think the system is wrong?"

"How would I know?" Joss leaned around Lee's upside-down chair to peer at the crumpled looking console. "I can't believe it's working at all."

Lee flicked a few more controls. More lights came on, some green. More red.

I moved to the far side of Evy's chair. "Would you two stop wasting time?" With a quick twist, my helmet popped, and I pulled it off my head. Liam squeezed his body through the neck of my suit and jumped to the underside of the flight console.

"Smells okay to me." I hung my helmet from the loop on my hip and released Evy's. "She's breathing." I snapped the med kit open and pulled out a ScanNSeal. "Check the manual and tell me how to attach this thing. I can't reach her arm unless I take her suit off, and we can't cut it off—we might need it later."

Joss flicked the med case and activated the manual. A vid walked us through placement of the sensors and activation of the device. It hummed for a few minutes, then pinged softly.

"She's got a concussion—not lethal, but she'll need additional medical care. The device can administer medications and bring her around." I tapped the stabilizer button. "It doesn't report any back or neck injuries, so we should probably get her out of the seat."

"Me, too," Lee whined.

"I vote we leave you there until the *New Dawn* sends a SAR team. Keep you out of the way." Joss moved into the aisle between the two pilots' chairs. "Good thing this is the VIP shuttle. The regular cockpits are so cramped."

"How do you know, Neanderthal?" Lee had removed his helmet and was pushing at the console that held him in place.

"Can you lift her a little, Joss?" I reached for Evy's harness buckle. "Release the pressure on the straps. I'm going to unlatch them."

Joss braced his feet, put his hands on either side of Evy's waist, and pushed upward. I snapped the buckle open. Joss grunted as her weight fell on him, but he didn't drop her. He lowered her slowly to the overhead while I guided her legs past the crumpled control console.

"How'd you get her out?" Lee demanded.

Joss laid Evy on the overhead. "I know what a shuttle cockpit looks like because I've done a few student rides, too. You aren't the only student pilot here." Joss stood and reached under Lee's seat to yank something.

The chair slid back, and Lee thudded to the ground.

"You stupid cave—"

"Lee, shut up." I put every gram of authority I could find into my voice. "Call the *New Dawn* and find out when they're sending the SAR."

Lee's eyes narrowed, and he turned to look at the console. "That would have been easier when I was still up there."

"I can put you back," Joss growled.

"Joss, shut up." I kept it conversational this time, since I knew Joss would listen. "Evy's coming around. Major Evy, can you hear me?"

Evy's eyelids fluttered, and finally she opened them. "What happened?"

"We crash landed on the moon—Saha," I said. "Do you remember?"

She raised her hand to her head, staring at the black glove she wore. The pilots' pressure suits were more streamlined and better fitting than ours. Even Lee's student pilot gear was made to fit.

She grunted. "We had a bunch of malfunctions. When I get back to the ship, the maintenance crew is going to—"

I cut her off. "We aren't getting back any time soon. The ship is upside-down. Lee is trying to reach the *New Dawn* to report our condition and get an ETA on their Search and Rescue team."

"I'm not getting anything," Lee said. "I still can't get through to the ship."

"Electromagnetic interference," Evy whispered. "That's why we didn't explore this moon."

"That and the dangerous atmosphere and the volcanoes of death."

"Volcanoes of death?" I swatted Joss's arm. "Not helpful."

"The distress beacon should still work." Evy licked her lips. "Do we have any water?"

"Here." Joss grabbed one of the pacs on the floor and tossed it to me.

I popped the top and held the spout to Evy's lips. "The ScanNSeal says you've got a concussion. You need to rest. The bunks aren't really accessible, so—"

Evy struggled to sit up. Joss stood behind her, so she could lean against his lower legs. She looked around the cockpit, taking in the crumpled control console, the crushed front screen, and destroyed bulkhead behind it.

"Is the ship airtight?" she finally asked.

"As far as I can tell, sir. The life support system reports no problems." Lee slapped the seat hanging beside his arm. "It's the only thing that reports all green."

"And the beacon?" Evy's eyelids drooped.

I pulled up the manual for the ScanNSeal again. Wasn't there something about not letting concussion victims sleep? Were the drugs it administered making her tired? They wouldn't recommend a medication that caused drowsiness if she wasn't supposed to sleep, would they? I found the relevant screen and started reading.

"I can't confirm that it's working, sir." Lee's words came out fast and uneven.

"No, how would you?" Evy's head turned slowly, her expression dreamy.

"Sir, what should we do?"

Evy blinked a couple of times and leaned forward as if to stand. "Keep trying to call them. I should do an EVA to check our current location and status."

"No, you aren't going anywhere." I pushed her back to a prone position. "The ScanNSeal says you need to rest. I'm going to climb up into the bunks and throw down a mattress. Lee, see if any of the external cameras are working. Joss, check the inventory—if we have any drones, we can send one out to do a recon."

Lee crossed his arms and stuck out his chin. "Who put you in charge? You're in disgrace, remember?"

"I put me in charge."

"And I'm backing her up." Joss took a step closer to Lee.

"I'm in charge," Evy said faintly. "And I'm telling you to do what Siti says. She's got a good head on her shoulders." Her eyes sagged shut.

I made a rude gesture at Lee as I moved to the rear of the cockpit. A hatch in the overhead—now the floor—led to the small bunk room. Normally it would slide open in response to the access panel, but that relay appeared to be fried. I used a handle to pull the hatch open. It protested loudly.

When the opening was wide enough, I lowered myself through. The low gravity made that much easier than it looked. My baggy, one-size-fits-most pressure suit caught on the handle.

"Joss, can you give me a hand?"

He crossed the cockpit, his own suit stretched tight across his chest. Looking down, he burst out laughing, then grabbed the back of my neck and hauled me up a few centimeters. I pulled the loose material off the handle, and he let me drop.

The lights flickered on as I descended. I landed softly, flexing at the knees. The small compartment had been built to withstand turbulence, so most of the fixtures were still firmly in place. The mattresses had fallen to the top of the bunks, and an open cupboard had spilled its complement of plastek cups.

I took a second to look in the attached lavatory—which could have been a huge mistake if anything had broken. Fortunately, it was solid.

"One of you grab this, will you?" I shoved one of the mattresses through the hatch above my head. It went up easily in the light gravity but was too wide to fit through the hatch.

Lee folded the end of the mattress and dragged it through. I riffled through the remaining cupboards and loaded the front of my baggy suit with high-end meal pacs and a handful of single-shot spirit pacs.

The underside of the bunks provided foot holds, and I levered myself through the hatch. Back in the cockpit, I spilled my treasure onto the floor beside Evy. "Look what I found."

Lee snatched up one of the spirit pacs. "Booze?"

"This is the VIP shuttle, remember? There's a guest book down there—it has the signatures of some high-level government types." I snatched the pac from him. "Let's save this for emergencies."

"Party emergencies?" Lee grimaced and stomped back to the communications panel.

"Sure. Once you get confirmation the SAR team is coming, we'll celebrate." I scooped up the spirit pacs and tucked them into the med kit. They fit as if the bag had been designed to hold them.

Maybe it had.

"I sense sarcasm, but I think that's an excellent idea." Joss stepped through the half-open cargo hatch.

"How'd you carry all that stuff up here?" I pointed to the armload of straps and boxes. "And more importantly, why? I thought you were getting drones."

Joss grinned. "I found the grav belts." He handed one to me and another to Lee. "And this cargo hammock. If we need to move, we can put the major into it—mattress and all—and attach that to our belts like we did on Sarvo Six."

"Brilliant!" I fastened the belt around my baggy suit. "But why would we need to move?"

"You know you can adjust that suit, right?" Joss ignored my question and tapped a setting on my wrist comp. "Stand up straight. The sleeves and legs have this folding bit—" He tapped the controls a few more times.

The legs of my suit accordion folded down into the tops of the boots, stopping with just enough tension to be comfortable. The arms did the same into the cuffs. Then the body, folding vertically instead of horizontally.

"Why didn't you show me that before?" I slid a hand over my now trim middle.

"It was funny to watch."

Lee cackled.

Joss swung around. "Did you contact the ship, giggle boy?"

"Listen, Neanderthal—"

I stepped between the two of them. "Stop. We are on a hostile planet with an injured teammate. Both of you—all three of us—need to put our personal differences aside until this is over." I glared at Joss, then turned the glare on Lee. "We can go back to hating on each other after we're rescued."

Lee ran his tongue over his teeth, then nodded. "Agreed. Truce." He held out a fist.

Joss pursed his lips. He looked at Evy and shoved a hand through his hair in an unconscious imitation of his dad. Finally, he knocked his gloved knuckles against Lee's. "Truce."

I fist bumped both of them. "Truce. Now, Lee, any word from the ship?"

He looked away. "No. Still no response."

"Joss, did you find the drones?"

With the click of a magnet, Joss pulled a small tablet from his pant leg. "I've got three of them in the airlock."

"Perfect. Lee, monitor life-support. We need to know if the inner doors are compromised. Joss, open the ramp and send our fliers out."

While Lee brought up the status controls, Joss lifted off and flew back into the cargo area. I shifted so I could watch him through the internal door. He hovered near the rear of the ship, then inverted himself and tapped at the rear door controls.

"Can't you read it upside down?" I called.

"It's easier this way."

"If you say so."

The light over the door turned red, and a grinding reverberated through the ship.

"That doesn't sound good." I edged around Evy and tapped the controls in front of her seat. They would definitely be easier to read upside-down, but I tilted my head sideways and found the right icon. The camera in the airlock flashed up on the small screen. "It's moving very slowly."

"It's almost wide enough…there."

On screen, the first drone—one of the larger non-stealthy recon drones—lifted off and flew through the narrow opening. A new image flashed in the lower corner of the screen, and I tapped it. The view from the drone filled the screen. Upside-down, of course.

I tapped my holo-ring through my heavy glove, and a screen popped up and connected to the ship. "Hey, this thing is working again. Did you do something, Evy?"

She didn't answer. I peered around the chair—her eyes were closed.

"Probably the interference." Lee poked at the communications board. "It's blocking your block."

"Do you have any idea what you're talking about?" I flicked the holo and swiped the drone view to my palm.

"Not really. I'm a pilot, not a nerd."

"Nice."

"It's true—I can't make heads or tails of most of that tech stuff."

I glared at him through the hologram, but he looked sincere.

Then he ruined it by puffing out his chest. "But give me a shuttle, and I'll fly you anywhere."

"Next you're going to tell me you're a 'pressure-suited space god.'"

He grinned. "If the label fits."

"Would you two stop flirting and look at this?" Joss flew through the hatch. "We have a problem."

I glanced at the holo in my palm. "Oh, crap."

CHAPTER FOURTEEN

THE DRONE FLEW AROUND the shuttle, the camera focused on the ship. Strange red and purple plants lay crushed under the twisted pile of metal and ceramic shielding. The muted sun, low in the sky, glowed through the heavy cloud cover, casting long shadows that made the details hard to make out.

Except one detail, which was immediately obvious. The ship had landed on the lip of a crevice. The rear of the ship sat on the flat ground, but the front end—the part we were currently standing in—hung over the abyss. The bow of the ship nosed against the far side of the crevice.

Lee hit the controls of his grav-belt and lifted a few centimeters.

"Slowly!" Joss held out a hand. "I don't think it moved. It looks like we're wedged in."

"What's that?" I zoomed in on the section of the cliff beneath the nose of the ship. A trickle of rock and dirt fell away from the underside of the ship. "Did we drop?" I gulped and rose off the deck.

Joss swiped his tablet, and a second drone view popped up over his palm. "I'm sending this one to the other side."

We watched, hardly breathing, as the drone exited the airlock and circled the shuttle. It rotated a few degrees at a time, taking in the ship and the surroundings. Thick purple and red plants grew along the edge of the cliff, with vines hanging over the edge. The fissure widened on this side, expanding to a rocky valley several hundred meters below. Deep in the valley, a sluggish river of lava oozed in a crooked red and black line.

"I think we need to evacuate." I drifted toward Evy. "Toss me that hammock, Joss."

"Where are we going to go?" Lee asked. "The air is toxic."

"I'd rather take my chances with long-term health effects than fall to my death." I stretched the hammock out beside Evy's mattress, then leaned forward to put her helmet back on. "We'll move to the rear of the ship and see what we can take with us."

Joss squatted to move the mattress on top of the hammock. "Lee, see if you can open that hatch wider—this is going to be a tight squeeze." He tossed a metal bar at the other man.

"Watch it!" Lee jumped out of the way and the crowbar clattered to the floor.

"Nice catch." Joss hooked the hammock end to his grav belt.

Lee grabbed the tool and waved his empty hand. "Gotta protect the money makers."

Joss rolled his eyes. "Learn to catch, then the money-makers wouldn't need protecting."

"Boys." I glared at them as I connected the head of Evy's hammock to my belt. "Lifting in three, two, one, lift."

We lifted the hammock off the deck, holding our breath as we did.

"No movement." Joss stared at his holos. "At least, not as far as I can tell."

Lee turned sideways and shoved his boots under a handrail near the door. He tried to tuck the crowbar into the door. "There's no way to get any leverage with this thing." The tool clanged to the deck. Lee positioned himself in the opening, his back against the door jamb and his feet against the partially open door.

He grunted and pushed. With a shriek of metal, the hatch gave way, crashing into its housing. Lee panted and grinned. "Easy."

"Good job." The words fell grudgingly from Joss's lips.

I restrained myself from rolling my eyes. "Let's go. Grab that crowbar, Lee—we might need it later."

I backed through the opening. Joss followed, pulling Evy between us. I don't know about the others, but I held my breath as we lowered her to the overhead near the rear exit.

"This should make us more stable, not less." Lee smirked—he must have noticed my trepidation.

"Unless our weight was holding the nose in place, and now it's loose."

I glared at Joss. "Thanks for that." I disconnected the hammock. "What have we got in the way of emergency supplies?"

Lee flew to the front of the compartment. He opened a panel revealing a meter-high white cube with the letters HLP in red on the side. "Every shuttle has a HLP." He pronounced it "help." At his touch, a panel on the side lit up, and he tapped. "The hostile condition landing package has a force shield generator, an air tank and oxygen extractor, emergency comm system, and rations."

The cube slid out of the bulkhead. Lee pushed on one corner to rotate it upright. As he crossed the cargo bay, it bobbed along behind, tethered to his belt.

"Let's grab our bags, too." He swooped up to the pallet still locked to the floor above us and unlatched one of the retaining straps. My duffel fell loose, but he snagged it, then picked up the survival packs.

"There's more food in the back." The voice issued softly from my helmet, still hanging from my hip.

I lifted it and put my face into the opening. "Was that you, Evy?"

"Yeah." Her voice sounded thin and dreamy. I looked at the woman on the mattress. Her eyes were still closed, but her brows were drawn together in concentration. "Near the airlock. Green symbol."

I located the green icon—a slightly curved line with pointed ends and a few pointed oblongs sticking out on each side. Someone—probably Aneh—had told me the universal sign for food was meant to be a piece of grain. I unlatched the door, and a pile of meal pacs fell out of their inverted bin.

I grabbed the bin before it hit the floor and scooped the pacs back into it. "There's enough for several days. Plus, water for a week, if we're careful. Grab one of those straps and let's lash it to the HLP."

"Is that everything?" Joss tested the straps holding the crate in place. "We shouldn't count on being able to come back in here."

"Are we going to fit through there?" I pointed through the window in the rear doors. The external ramp had opened about ten degrees—barely wide enough for the drones to exit.

"If not, we might be able to override the automated system and open both doors." These shuttles were designed primarily to deliver people and cargo to locations that could sustain life. The system tested for external contaminants and would automatically enforce use of the airlock if the atmosphere was unsafe.

The boys put on their helmets, then Joss tapped the controls by the door. The ramp shuddered but didn't move. The motor whined. With an ear-splitting shriek, the ramp slammed closed, the sound reverberating through the shuttle. The whole vehicle shook.

Liam leapt to my shoulder and squirmed inside my suit. I snapped the helmet over both of us and twisted it to lock.

"Did the front end move?" I pointed at the holo still floating at Joss's shoulder.

"Maybe? We should go. Now." Joss hit the controls.

The airlock cycled, and the inner doors slid aside. As we lifted the hammock, the rear ramp started to hinge up.

"Why is it doing that?" I asked. "It's not supposed to open in a toxic atmosphere."

"Maybe the external air sensors are damaged." Lee flicked his holo-ring and started swiping through screens. "Or maybe the airlock override was engaged." He glared at Joss.

The other boy held up both hands. "I didn't do anything. Maybe the air isn't as toxic as we thought."

The shuttle shook again, and the front end dropped.

"We need to leave. Now." I hit my belt controls and lifted.

Joss flicked his controls and shot forward, dragging the foot of Evy's hammock with him.

"Wait for me!" I lunged after him into the airlock.

The ramp ground to a halt. Joss and I ducked through the triangle of open space on the right side of the ship. Evy's mattress caught in the narrow opening, but we yanked her free. We rose, looking for a safe place to land.

"I'm stuck!" Lee hung a meter above the ground outside the stalled ramp. The setting sun glinted off his helmet, momentarily blinding me. "The HLP won't fit."

"Take her—I'll help him." Joss pulled the hammock end loose from this belt and tried to hand it to me.

"I can't hold both ends!"

He growled and pointed. "Put her here." He dropped—too quickly.

I slapped my controls, setting the lift to zero. At this altitude, in this gravity, I shouldn't fall too fast. I hit the ground harder than I expected, and my legs crumpled under me. Joss kept Evy's hammock from crashing beside me.

"Stay there!" Joss took off, arrowing toward the rear of the shuttle.

Oh, please, like I'm going to listen to him being all Neanderthal.

I disconnected the hammock and launched myself after him. The whole ship seemed to shift as I drew closer. The rear ramp trembled as the door motor tried to lift the heavy plate. Normally, it rotated down, but with the ship inverted, it was trying to push the door upward and was pressing the ramp against a fall of rock. The system wasn't designed to open that way.

I inspected the pile of boulders. Maybe we could move them, so the ramp could open. The boys stood in the gap between the stuck ramp and the ship, trying to shove it wider. "Joss! Lee! This isn't going to work. There's stuff in the way."

The shuttle shuddered again. The boys pushed harder.

Joss tried to wave me off. "Siti, what are you doing here! Get away—Evy needs you."

"I'm not leaving you to go down with the ship."

"Don't worry, if it starts to go, I'm out."

"Hey, what about me? I'm trapped!" Lee shoved frantically against the door. Inside the helmet, his face looked gray.

"You're not trapped." Joss resettled his feet and tried again. "If the ship starts to fall, release the tether on the HLP."

As if in response to his comment, the ship shuddered. Lee reached for his belt controls. "Not yet!" I yelled. "We need that thing. Releasing is a last resort. But this isn't working." I lifted away.

"Where are you going?" Lee called.

"I have an idea. Be ready to pull the HLP free." I lifted above the ship. It looked like a dead bug, with the landing gear sticking out of the body, feet flat against the sky. I flew to the front, hovering just above the underside of the cockpit. "You guys ready?"

"What are you doing?" Joss asked. "I don't like being in the dark."

"I'm going to put a little weight on the front of the ship. That should lift the back and give you a little more space to open the ramp."

"What about the stuff in the way?" Joss asked.

"The boulder holding the ramp closed isn't very tall—if I lift enough, you'll have plenty of room."

"If you push the front down, the whole thing is going to fall into that crevice!" Lee's voice cracked.

"I won't push that hard. You only need a meter. Joss, you'll push the ramp up. Lee, you pull the HLP out. On my mark. Three. Two."

"I don't like—"

"One. Mark!" I set my feet against the nose of the ship. Nothing happened; I didn't have enough mass on my own. I bounced. "Did it move?"

"A little. We need more." Unlike Lee's, Joss's voice remained calm. Which was impressive, since he was the one who could get sucked into the void by the ship. Lee was probably already as far from the ship as his tether would allow.

"On it." I dialed my grav belt to heavy, slowly increasing the pressure on the nose of the ship. It rumbled. My legs burned as my weight increased. The ceramic plates under my feet cracked from the pressure. This wasn't working. I snapped the belt to off.

Biting my lip, I scanned the underside of the ship. "The good news is the ship isn't falling into the hole. The bad news is it doesn't seem to be moving at all. My legs aren't strong enough to set the gravity any heavier." A rectangular outline on the bottom of the ship caught my eye. "Hey, is there an emergency air lock in the cockpit?"

Unlike the regular shuttles, there was no hatch directly from the cockpit to the outside. VIPs were expected to walk through the cargo area—usually empty or decorated with a red carpet—and exit through down the ramp. But safety required a second exit, right?

"Yeah, it's through the floor. Emergency egress only," Joss replied.

"I'm going to see if I can get it open." I lifted off the ship and flew the few meters to the hatch. "It looks like a standard access." I put my hand against the control panel. It lit up red. "I'm not authorized."

"Of course not," Lee said. "You're a prisoner. They aren't going to let you open the emergency exit."

"What if there's an emergency? Like now?"

"I'm coming. Here, Torres, tether this thing to your belt."

A trickle of fear dripped down my back. Lee wouldn't hesitate to put Joss in a dangerous situation to save his own sorry rear end. "Wait."

"Got it."

A few seconds later, Lee flew into view and pushed me aside. "I should be able to—Hah!"

The access panel turned green, and Lee spun the wheel. The bolts retracted, and he pulled the hatch open. When he let go, the hatch tried to swing shut. "Hold that."

I grabbed the edge. "What are you going to do?"

"I'm going to open the inner hatch, then your boyfriend is going to bring the HLP through the ship and out this way."

"Why does he have to do it? You're the one with the access. What if he can't get through?"

Lee crossed his arms. "We can leave it. Wait until the ship falls to the bottom of the cliff, then try to retrieve the HLP. If it isn't melted into slag."

"I got this." Joss's voice came through my helmet. "This is less risky than trying to push the ramp open. I'm not touching anything. I'm in the cockpit. Get that inner airlock door open." Contrary to his words, his voice sounded strained. Why wouldn't it be—he was trapped inside the ship and completely at Lee's mercy.

Fortunately, Lee needed the HLP as badly as the rest of us. He dropped through the tiny airlock and pushed his hand against the internal controls.

"Are you sure that HLP will fit through this airlock? It's tiny." I hovered a few meters above him, staring through the narrow tunnel.

"That would be a pretty stupid design if it doesn't." The panel turned green, and Lee spun the inner wheel.

"That didn't answer my question."

"Stand clear." The inner airlock slipped out of Lee's fingers and hinged downward, swinging wide.

Joss yelped.

The ship shuddered.

"Get out!"

Lee surged out of the opening, slamming into me and shoving me away.

The shuttle lurched. The front end dropped.

Joss shot out of the airlock. The ship tilted farther and seemed to pull Joss backwards with an invisible rope.

"Cut the tether!" I screamed.

CHAPTER FIFTEEN

THE SHIP TILTED BENEATH US, the front end dropping into the deep crevice. Joss rocketed upward, the HLP popping out of the airlock in his wake like a cork from a bottle. He flew over our heads, the cube hurtling after him.

The ship teetered, then stuck in the gap.

At the top of the arc, Joss regained control. The boy and box dropped slowly.

"See?" Lee pushed me away. "Nothing to worry about."

"Then why'd you slam into me like that?"

"I was trying to push you clear—just in case."

"Calm down, children. Let's get back to Major Evy." Joss changed directions, angling toward the rear of the ship.

I'd almost forgotten about the injured officer. Guilt washed over me, making my stomach sour. I tugged my jacket down and straightened my helmet as we skimmed over the ship to the clearing behind it.

Evy lay where we'd left her. She'd rolled half-way off the mattress, and her eyes were open. "What kind of trouble have you been up to?" She tried to sit up.

"We were getting the emergency supplies." I gestured to the cube Joss lowered beside her. "Is all the other stuff still there?"

Joss patted the top of the bin lashed to the HLP. "Good thing we put the lid on. We should set up a camp and get the emergency beacon going."

"If the ship's emergency beacon isn't working, what makes you think this one will?" Lee slapped the side of the cube.

"It might not. But if we don't activate it, it definitely won't work." Joss lifted off the ground. "Lee, why don't you stay here with Evy, and Siti and I will take a look around."

"Oh, you'd like that, wouldn't you?" Lee put his hands on his hips. "You think you can escape from us that easily?"

Joss and I exchanged a befuddled look.

"How would we escape?" I waved my arms wildly. "We're on an uninhabited moon with no communications and no vehicle. None of us are going anywhere."

"I don't trust you two. How about the caveman stays with the major, and I'll go with Kassis?"

Joss opened his mouth, but I cut him off. "Fine. The sooner we get this done, the faster we can get Evy settled somewhere safe." I grabbed my emergency backpack from the pile beside the cube and settled it over my shoulders. "Joss, set up the emergency force shield and the beacon."

He flashed a thumbs up and started opening the HLP.

"Stay together," Evy whispered through the audio connection. "Don't split up on an unexplored planet."

"Yes, sir," Lee and I responded automatically.

I lifted to thirty meters. "We'll fly a wide grid at half-klick intervals, looking for water."

"I'm in charge of this sortie." Lee pulled up beside me.

"Fine, be in charge. What do you want to do?"

"We'll start here and fly half-klick intervals in a wide grid."

"Great plan." I swiped my holo-ring and pulled up a distance counter. "How far do you want to go?"

"We'll start with five klicks in that direction." He swung his arm over his head and brought it down to point toward the rising sun.

"Bearing eighty-seven degrees." I turned on the tracker and matched his vector. "I'm mapping—you scan for water."

He glared but didn't say anything as we rose from the crash site, lifting to the top of the lush canopy.

"Or whatever you want to do. Sir." I added the last word in a flat voice.

He ground his teeth and opened the scanning app.

We located three water sources in the first ten minutes. Tall red and purple tree-like plants formed a thick canopy below us. At the first alert, we dropped through the leaves. The trees grew very close together, their thick branches entwined in an impenetrable net. We twisted and wove between the limbs but couldn't reach the ground, so we gave up and moved on.

"Maybe we should have gone on foot from the landing site." I stared down at the thick leaves. Strange chittering and squeaking filtered through the plants. Liam rubbed his face against my cheek, his paw resting on my ear.

"We want to be in a location that's easy to evacuate when they come to pick us up." Lee flicked a file and scribbled in some data.

"Like the rocky cliff where we crashed."

Lee nodded. "We should stay close to that edge. Let's swing around and do a two-klick semi-circle." He angled north.

I pointed. "What's that? It looks like a clearing, but it—there's something wrong about it." I squinted into the distance. "We should send a drone."

"Why bother? We're looking for a safe place to wait for rescue, not running a full-on phase 1 exploration."

"It's weird—too regular. Look at the jungle around us. Why isn't that space overgrown, too?"

"Maybe it's like the cliff where we landed. These weird plants are thinner in the rocky areas."

My internal comm buzzed, but no one spoke. "Hello? Who's there? Joss?"

"What does the Neanderthal want?" Lee swung around and flew backwards so he could glare at me.

The system clicked a couple of times, then a voice spoke. I didn't understand the words, but I recognized them.

"Drop, now!" I hit the altitude release on my belt and fell through the heavy purple canopy below us.

"What?"

I flicked the internal comm to off, then looked up. Lee hovered just above the thick leaves. I reached out and grabbed his ankle. "Get down here. Don't use the comms."

He shook his foot, trying to dislodge me and said something I couldn't hear through my helmet.

I dragged him lower and pressed my helmet to his. "There's someone here. Turn off your comms." I rummaged through the pouches on the outside of my suit and found a cable. By plugging one end into each of our suits, we could hear each other without yelling or using the comm system.

"What are you doing? Let's get their attention!"

"No. Listen." I flicked my ring and played the recording.

"What is that?"

"Gagarian. There are Gagarians on this moon."

"Good one, Kassis. Where'd you get this recording?" He reached over and flicked my ring to play it again.

"Joss sent it to me. That sound at the beginning is a signal to hide. It's something they used on Earth. Then that burst of Gagarian. That clearing we saw—what do you want to bet it's a Gagarian base?"

"That's ridiculous. There's been no indication the Gagarian government has taken an interest in this system. And if they had, we wouldn't be here. You know the treaty says whoever lands first gets control."

"I probably know the treaty better than you." I dropped lower, holding his arm to pull him with me. The foliage wasn't as thick here, and we were able to fight through to the ground. The thick canopy created deep shadows, as if it were dusk rather than morning. "But I also know Gagarin doesn't always play by the rules. Since we didn't know they're here, I'd guess we landed on Qureshi first, and then they snuck in to Saha."

"Why would they want to land here? With that weird electromagnetic field, the communications suck. This moon is useless as a base."

"Why did we want to land on Qureshi? Comms weren't great there, either. But we wanted to spy on them. Maybe they're spying on us." I tested the ground around the base of the tall trees.

Vines dropped from the branches overhead and burrowed into the dirt, like auxiliary trunks. We had landed in a relatively clear area between two larger clumps of plant. "Stay on the roots. The ground here looks really soft."

"Why not stay aloft?" Lee hovered beside the nearest vertical vine.

"How's your charge? Mine's down to sixty percent. And if we have to stay below the canopy, we aren't going to get any sunlight to recharge."

"Then we should go back up. We can fly low where they won't see us. We need to get back to Evy and the caveman."

I fingered the cable. "I hope they're still there. If the Gagarians investigated our crash site, they'll have figured out we survived, and they'll be looking for us. They might already have Joss and Evy in custody."

He unplugged and lifted, the cable trailing behind. I followed him into the thick leaves. Around us, the creaking and chittering grew louder, as if the creatures had decided we weren't a threat. Or maybe they were in league with the Gagarians and trying to draw attention to us. I resisted the urge to shush them.

Liam chattered softly and rubbed his body against my face.

The light grew brighter as we reached the higher levels of the canopy. Finally, Lee stopped. He made a "come here" motion and plugged the cable into my helmet again. "Let's wait here until our suits change colors. Change your settings to camouflage."

CEC uniforms were made of a chameleon material that blended into the surroundings, but these emergency suits appeared to be older models. "Are you sure this suit has that setting?" I flicked the small screen built into the arm and tapped the icon. "I've got low vis and high vis. Low it is."

"We should have had you and Evy trade suits." Lee watched me like a hawk—probably waiting for the color change. "The suit is getting darker, but it's not matching the purple."

"That's probably good. The purple is on the underside of the leaves. We want to be green." I pulled the end of the closest overhead leaf down so he could see the top. "Move over here."

He shifted closer to me, and his suit began to transition from deep purple to the dark green of the leaf tops. Sunlight glinted off the top of his helmet.

"You might want to dim that." I squinted at him.

He flicked his holo-ring and adjusted the controls. The helmet shifted to a matte finish and darkened to green.

My own suit was another matter. The emergency gear that came with the shuttle didn't have the complexity of the individual issued stuff. After a few minutes in the sunlight, my gray pressure suit had darkened to a mottled green and gray.

"Is the helmet okay?"

He tapped the hard top of my head. "It's not as pretty as mine, but it will have to do. Stay low—let's try to keep to the top layer of leaves."

He lifted slowly past the leaf I still held. When the communications cable pulled taught, I grabbed his leg and let him pull me higher. "Can you see anything?"

"There are a lot of leaves here. Why are you hanging on me?"

"The comm cable." I tapped my belt controls and rose until our heads were level, holding the slack in my gloved hand. "I don't need you jerking me around by this. You might break it."

He growled but didn't reply.

Our heads pushed through the last of the overlapping leaves. Sunlight made me squint. It was dimmed by the heavy layer of clouds but still bright compared to the twilight beneath the canopy.

"I don't see anything moving."

I turned in a small circle, lifting the cable over my head so I wouldn't get tangled. The jungle stretched out for kilometers in every direction, flat except for a group of oddly symmetrical hills about five klicks from our landing zone. In the distance, low mountains formed a ragged horizon.

Nearby, a flock of birds—or other winged creatures—lifted out of the thick canopy, squawking. They swirled upward like a drift of leaves in the wind, then plunged back into the foliage.

Our crash site was a huge, rough scar. Our ship had cut a wide swath through the lush jungle, leaving crushed and broken trees in its wake. Even from this distance, the devastation was obvious.

Between us and the distant mountains, green and purple rippled like waves in the wind. The rectangular clearing—its clean edges and right angles obviously man-made—sat in the sun, along the edge of the same rift where we'd crashed. Small, badly camouflaged cubes stood in a neatly ordered grid. It looked like every CEC base—and every Gagarian base—I'd ever seen holos of.

"Do you have any tech that will allow us to see farther?" I patted down my own suit, but I'd already inventoried the few pouches and pockets. Besides the comm cable, I had a small stunner, a single ration pac, and a water pac.

Lee didn't answer but pulled out a thin curved device and attached it to the front of his helmet. "There's movement by our landing site. I make five—no six—people with grav belts."

I spun and stared into the sun. As we watched, two more people rose, lifting a hammock between them. "Crap, they got Evy and Joss."

CHAPTER SIXTEEN

"Now what?" I resisted the urge to drop lower into the leaves. If we didn't move, our camouflage should protect us at this distance.

"Now we stay away until we're sure they've finished searching, then we try to rescue Evy."

"Just Evy? I know you hate us, but you can't leave Joss with the Gagarians—"

"Relax. They didn't get Torres. At least not yet. I only saw Evy." He frowned. "Actually, that's a bad thing." He lifted a hand to cut off my angry retort. "They'll know Evy wasn't alone, so they'll be searching for her crewmates. If they'd caught Torres too, they might have thought it was just the two of them."

"But she was in a hammock—it takes two people to lift a hammock."

Lee shrugged. "You're probably right."

"We need to find him, rescue Evy, and steal a shuttle."

Liam cheeped in agreement.

"Sure, no problem. We'll steal a Gagarian shuttle. Do you know how to fly one?"

"No. You're the pressure-suited space god."

He gave me a dirty look. "I could probably figure it out if I had a translation program. But I don't read Gagarian. I think we'll have better luck trying to piggyback on their communication system."

"You think theirs works any better than ours?"

"They must've made it work. They'd hardly put a base here if they weren't able to communicate with their headquarters."

"For all we know, they send space pigeons with scrolls back to Gagarin."

That startled a laugh out of him. As we talked, we'd been slowly moving toward our crashed ship, staying low, with only our heads sticking out of the tallest foliage. It meant our progress was slow but relatively stealthy. If they were actively looking for us, they might spot the disturbance in the leaves, but the endless breeze ruffled the leaves in random patterns, so we were probably safe.

Or not. I grabbed Lee's arm and set my belt to drop. "They're going to be looking for us. They'll guess we have grav belts, so they'll set a wide search perimeter. They probably have heat mapping. If we're lucky, they'll think we're animals they haven't catalogued yet. But they'd be stupid not to check. We need to find cover."

"Where? *Our* tech would find us easily. Just fly over and scan. We have to assume they have similar. Gagarin is good at copying Commonwealth tech."

"Then we either need to get far away or hide where their tech can't find us. Caves would probably work." A shiver of discomfort went through me at the thought of hiding in caves. The last time I'd been in a cave system, I'd been with a Gagarian spy. A double agent who'd pretended to be my friend.

"How about that crevice we almost fell into?" Lee dropped a couple of meters into the trees, then pulled up a map on his holo-ring. He stretched it about a meter wide and zoomed in. "This is the scan I pulled from the shuttle before we left. It's not very detailed because the CEC didn't spend much time on this moon, but it's better than nothing. You can see that crevice opens into a valley down here." He swiped his finger through the bottom of the map. "We can go south and work our way around to the mouth of the valley and hide in these cliffs."

I drew a line across the map with my fingers. "Or sneak across here and jump over the side."

"Or that. It depends on how many people they have searching for us."

"Can you access any of the drones from the shuttle? Joss had a tablet, but since your holo-ring was connected to the ship, you must—"

"Brilliant." He swiped the map away and opened another screen. "The two micro-drones were still in the airlock when we left the ship. With any luck, the Gagarians will have entered the ship through the cockpit airlock rather than the cargo doors. Maybe they won't have found the drones yet."

He flicked a few more things and another screen opened. "Got it."

I peered over his shoulder, as he activated the drone. The camera flickered on, showing a dark area with a slash of light. "Can you tone down the contrast? Sunlight coming through that gap is making it hard to see anything."

"No worries. I'll take it out." The view swooped a little as the drone lifted off, then it zoomed toward the bright triangle. As soon as it was through, the system compensated, and the view cleared. "I'm taking it straight into the trees. Hopefully they won't even notice it."

"They're pretty quiet. Maybe they'll think it's a bug."

"I haven't noticed any bugs, have you?"

"Wasn't looking."

The drone zipped into the thick bushes at the edge of the crash site. Once undercover, it turned one hundred and eighty degrees.

"Move closer." I jiggled his arm.

"Wow, I wish I thought of that." Lee played with the controls, and the drone pushed through the leaves, stopping as soon as we got a clear view.

Two people stood in the clearing created by our ship's crash, near our HLP. They wore dark uniforms with no rank or patches visible.

"Does this thing have audio? I want to hear what they're saying." I leaned over Lee's shoulder.

He swatted my hand away. "It has audio. Hang on." He flicked a few icons, and I heard a deep voice speaking a fluid language. "Do you understand Gagarian?"

I pressed my lips together at his smug tone and then laughed. "Actually, I do. Or at least I have a translator." I flicked my holo-ring and brought up a translation program I had loaded locally. I still wasn't sure why I'd installed the thing—we certainly weren't expecting to meet any Gagarians. I turned it on and then dialed up the sensitivity. The system translated the man's voice into text which appeared in my holo.

Voice one: —set up this emergency force shield and then left her. Don't worry, we'll find them.

Voice two: I'm not worried. Tell <unintelligible> to set up the lights. <unintelligible> they'll return here once it gets dark.

Voice one: You don't want to set a trap for them?

Voice two: You know what the wildlife is like around here. They'll come running for the lights before planet-rise.

<laughter>

In the holo, the taller person stalked across the clearing and out of sight. The shorter one—a woman—tapped on the control panel on the HLP.

"Wildlife?" Lee squinted through the dim light. "Why is it getting dark already? It was morning when we crashed."

The shadows in the clearing had grown long. "Yeah, the rotation on this moon must be way shorter than a normal day. See if you can find a place to set the drone down, so it can watch the camp. That'll save power. I'll set the translator to notify us whenever it has comments to translate. They can't get into that thing, can they?"

"The HLP? Sure. They aren't password protected. They're emergency shelters—designed to be easy to activate so anyone who survives a crash has shelter. I wonder why Torres didn't set it up. He should have at least activated the force shield."

I'd been wondering the same thing. I'd told Joss to do that when we left. "They said the force shield was up. Could the Gagarians deactivate it?"

"Yeah—it's intended to protect you from the environment or animals, not people. There aren't any locks."

"We need to find Joss before they do."

"How do you propose we do that?"

"I'm working on it. Let's find somewhere to hide. Did you get the second drone out?"

"I'm flying it over the cliff, so we can see what's what." A new hologram showed a rough rock wall rising as the drone dropped. He rotated the camera to point downward, but in the darkness, nothing was visible except a sluggish red glow. Lee tapped and swiped, and the view changed. "Night mode."

The faint glow grew brighter as the drone descended.

"Is there a heat sensor on that drone?"

"Ooh, good call." He flicked through the settings. "Holy crap, that's hot. I gotta—" The hologram fizzed and went black. "It's not responding."

I smirked. "Did you just melt CEC property?"

"I didn't see you doing anything to stop me."

"Whatever. I think the damage to the ship trumps the dead drone. And you get the blame for that, too."

"I did not crash the shuttle! That was an equipment ma—"

Liam tweaked my ear and chirped a single, urgent sound.

"Sh!" I pressed my hand against Lee's face plate.

We held our breath, listening. Around us, the wildlife noises chittered and droned on. No audible human noises.

"Is there another drone?"

"The bigger one the caveman was using." Lee grabbed my arm. "That's how we find Joss. If he's still free, he probably has the tablet that controls that drone. I ought to be able to get a message to him at least."

While Lee swiped through screens, I unplugged and stuck my head above the canopy to check on the Gagarians. The light had faded to the point I could no longer see their base. Points of light shone in the distance—presumably the scar we had created when we crashed. Nothing moved above the trees.

I slid back down to Lee's side and clicked the cable into his helmet. "Anything?"

"I can see that the drone is active, but I can't control it. The tablet has precedence. And there's no messaging capability. If his comm wasn't locked, we could call him."

I gritted my teeth. "Yeah, so much could have been avoided if he and I weren't under arrest."

"Technically, you aren't under arrest." He snapped the holo closed and rose.

"That makes me feel so much better about our forced radio silence."

We continued moving toward the cliff edge, stopping to listen and watch for observers. If they were really looking for us, they would find us eventually. We had to hope they were hot on Joss's trail, and not expecting anyone else.

When we reached the edge of the rift, about two klicks south of the crash site, we stopped. I released my helmet's airlock so Liam could get out. The air smelled crisp and felt cool against my face. I snapped my helmet back on. According to the reports, the compounds in the air wouldn't cause problems after brief exposure, but I didn't want to take any chances.

Lee dropped over the edge of the crevasse to see if there was anywhere we could hole up for the rest of the night. We hadn't encountered any dangerous creatures, yet, but anticipation made me nervous. I hoped Liam would warn us if any approached.

Lee appeared suddenly in the darkness.

I bit back a yelp. "Don't sneak up on me like that." I took a deep breath to bring my heart rate back to normal.

He dropped to the ground beside me and plugged in the comm cable. "Sorry about that." It sounded almost human. "There's a ledge about twenty meters down."

"Sorry? You getting soft on me?" I nudged him with my elbow.

He rolled his eyes and opened an app on his ring. "I'm just tired. Also, I wanted to check something I remembered—" He flicked the drone screen and enlarged the feed. With a triumphant yell, he pointed at two people standing in the shadows at the edge of the clearing. "They aren't wearing helmets."

"What?" I leaned closer to see the holo. "Can you get a better shot of those two?"

"I don't want to move the drone. They haven't noticed it yet, and I want to keep it that way. But I think I can zoom in…"

The view changed, and the two shadowy figures grew larger. In the darkness, it was hard to tell if they wore helmets or not. "They probably have personal shields, even if they don't have helmets." I tapped my suit's control panel. "I don't have the power to generate one of those right now. We need sunlight to charge up the batteries."

Lee got to his feet and reached out a hand. "Come on. Let's check out that ledge as a hiding spot. Then we can start looking for Joss."

"We might want to get some sleep first." I took his hand and let him pull me up. He misjudged the low gravity, and I flew into him, knocking us both to the ground.

"Oof."

"Sh!" Lying flat on his chest, I put my gloved hand against his helmet. "I heard something." Our voices wouldn't carry, but our movements might alert someone. Or some*thing*.

Lee lay on the ground, his eyes wide and staring up at me. We froze for an interminable time, our eyes locked on each other. It occurred to me I had no idea what color his eyes were, and in the darkness, I couldn't tell.

After a few moments, I slowly rolled aside. "Did you hear it?"

"What was I supposed to hear?" He sat up, moving as quietly as possible.

"Not sure. Might have been something pushing through the trees." I pointed into the thicker bushes behind us. "Let's do the ledge thing."

We got to our feet, moving slowly and carefully. Liam leapt down from a nearby branch and landed lightly on my shoulder. He didn't give his usual cheerful greeting which worried me.

Lee unplugged the comm cable and handed the end to me. I bundled it into my chest pocket. I held it open so Liam could climb in, but he ignored the invitation. He stood on my shoulder, nose up and sniffing, his tail wrapped tightly around his feet.

After a quick peek through the foliage at the top of the cliff, Lee crawled out, staying low. He tapped his grav belt and dropped over the side.

CHAPTER SEVENTEEN

I watched for a few seconds, but nothing happened. No dangerous animals attacked from the trees, no people burst out with lights blazing. I ducked through the thick leaves and stepped off the edge.

With the lower gravity, I dropped slowly. My belt kicked in a few meters below the lip of the cliff and halted my fall. I paused, my gaze raking the rocky wall in front of me. I couldn't see anything in the darkness.

Then I remembered the low-light setting on my suit. I tapped the control panel and activated dark mode.

Everything around me brightened. The rough cliff came into sharp relief. The wind or water had carved smooth eddies and whirls into the cliff. Just above my head, a circular opening had worn through a vertical wedge of rock. Off to the right, an oblong of impenetrable darkness might have been a cave. Finally, I spotted Lee a few meters below my feet, waving. I dropped to his ledge and pulled out the cable.

Liam jumped off my shoulder, exploring the rocky alcove while Lee plugged his end of the cable into his helmet. "It's not really a cave—more of a wide spot. That other cave looked like it might have occupants."

"Occupants?"

"Animals of some kind. Maybe birds? There was an old pile that might have been a nest and little pieces that might have been bones. It looked disused, but I didn't think we should take any chances."

I swallowed. "Good plan."

"We can get some rest here, and the overhang means they shouldn't spot us from above."

"Unless they send a drone with a night cam. Or drop into the fissure to look." I lowered myself the ground, leaning against the rocky wall. The meter-wide ledge sloped gently down in the back. Above our heads, the stony outcropping provided protection from the elements and prying eyes. Heat wafted up—presumably from the lava fissure that had melted our drone—making our pressure suits uncomfortably warm.

Lee sat beside me, our feet in front of us and almost level with our eyes. "This might not be very good for sleeping."

"One of us can lie down while the other stands—or sits—watch." I tapped my grav belt and turned it off. "And we can power down our gear until sunrise."

"Any idea when that will be?" He shut his grav belt down and checked his battery. "I'm still at eighty percent."

"I'm down to thirty. These emergency suits are a lot less efficient." I reached for my helmet. "I'm going to take this off and eat."

"You sure that's a good idea? We can use the goo packs."

I gave a dramatic shudder. Goo packs were built into pressure suits. At the press of a button, water mixed with a dry powder and the resultant goo could be slurped via a nipple. "Have you tried goo? It's disgusting. The reports on this moon say the toxins are dangerous at *prolonged* exposures. A few minutes eating a protein bar is worth the risk in my opinion."

"Besides, those Gagarians weren't wearing helmets." Lee unfastened his own helmet and attached it to the loop on his leg. Keeping vital equipment attached was one of the first lessons CEC explorers learned. No telling how quickly we'd need to move.

"I told you, they have shields."

"If it only took a shield to protect from this atmosphere, the CEC wouldn't have blackballed this moon." He took a bite of a protein bar and closed his eyes while he chewed. "Even if we had to maintain shields outside, this would be a better base than that iceball."

"You forgot the comm problems. But maybe the reports were wrong. Or maybe the Gagarians have tech we don't."

He snorted. "Not likely—they steal everything from us."

Liam jumped to my shoulder and rubbed his body against my cheek. He cheeped softly—so quietly I almost didn't hear it.

"I think Liam wants us to stop talking," I whispered. "There must be something out there."

With my helmet off, the night air cooled my heated cheeks. I ate the protein bar as quietly as I could. The crinkle of the wrapper sounded loud.

Beyond our ledge, the creaking and chittering of daytime had been replaced by different sounds. The wind moaned—probably blowing through the weird rock formations. A low rumble off to our left increased in volume and pitch until it became a roar.

"Not too close," Lee whispered. "But I don't think we want to attract its attention."

I shoved the last of my bar into my mouth and lifted my helmet. Liam crawled into the neck of my suit. I tucked in my messy braid, slid the helmet over my head and clicked it into place. "Safer to use the comm cable."

"Good idea. Who's on first watch?"

I checked the chrono on my suit. "Sunrise should be in about six hours. I'll do the first three—you take the second." I pushed myself up on my hands—easy in this gravity—and shifted to the right to give him room to lie down. My tough emergency suit grated loudly against the stone. I cringed, but it wouldn't tear—they were built for this kind of use.

"Before you go to sleep, can you give me access to the drone cam?"

He flicked his ring, the light flaring brightly in the helmet. I must have made a sound because he dimmed it quickly. "That wasn't bright—your low-light settings magnified it. Here's the feed. With the lock on your comms, I can't give you control of the drone, but you can watch."

"I don't suppose you know how to deactivate the lock?"

He chuckled. "Not likely."

"What's that supposed to mean? Not likely that you'd know, or not likely that you'd do it if you did know?"

He waved his hand, the holo-ring leaving trails on my retinas. "If I knew how, I'd fix it. We're in this together—we need every advantage we can get." Lee rolled onto his side, the top of his head a few centimeters from my hip. In the darkness, his suit almost blended into the rock.

I flicked my night-vision back on, but I couldn't see his face from this vantage. "Maybe we should surrender."

I'd said the words quietly, but Lee jerked upright. He propped himself up on one elbow and craned his head toward me. "Surrender?"

I shrugged, not sure if he had his night-vision activated. "We crashed on this moon. According to every treaty ever, they have to rescue us."

"Yeah and throw us in prison for entering Gagarian space without clearance."

"This isn't officially Gagarian space. They've laid no claims to this system—if they had, we wouldn't be here." In the distance, the low rumble started again. Was it closer—whatever it was?

Lee waited for the rumble to grow into a shriek and cut off. "They found our shuttle. And they're here illegally. Do you really think they'll help us? For all we know, they've already killed Evy and Joss."

I resisted the urge to grab my chest—that hurt like an arrow to the heart. "But the CEC will come looking for us. They'd be better off to help us."

He didn't answer for a few seconds. Another rumble started, this one cut off by a louder and closer shriek. Maybe it was two animals fighting, not one sounding a challenge? My heart ticked faster, and my chest tightened. Something about that primal scream spoke to the ancient cave dweller deep inside me and scared the crap out of her.

"Even though I wasn't able to send the distress signal before we crashed, the *New Dawn* knows we disappeared. They know our comms don't work. How could they not? But without a distress beacon, they have no idea where we are. Searching an entire moon for one officer and three cadets—two of them disgraced—isn't going to be high on their priority list."

"But—"

"Listen to me. If they could hear our beacon, they'd come. Without it—they might do a quick flyby of the moon to check. But we can't count on them. We need to rescue ourselves."

"How do you propose we do that?"

He dropped to his side, pillowing his head on his arm. "We steal a shuttle and go."

"I thought you didn't read enough Gagarian to do that?"

"We'll figure it out." He was quiet. I almost didn't hear his last, sleepy mutter. "We have to."

When he started snoring, I unplugged the comm cable. I watched the drone footage, but the Gagarians had left the crash site. The lights still burned, offering an illusion of safety. My inner cave-woman begged to go there, but I ignored her.

Shadows prowled the edges of the clearing. A creature—about a meter high with four or maybe six legs—moved with stealthy grace through the darkness, reminding me of vids of the tigers of Earth and the *vildmacska* of Armstrong. The feline stopped and raised its muzzle. The rumbling scream rolled down the valley.

My analytical side tried to convince the cave-woman that creature couldn't reach this ledge, but she wasn't buying it. I pulled the tiny stunner out of my belt pouch and set it my lap. I didn't know if it would take down a creature that size, but better safe than sorry.

I leaned against the warm rock, grateful for the volcanic heat wafting upward as the temperatures dropped. The suit provided protection, but fear chilled me from inside.

But a person can only maintain fear for so long. After a while, the state becomes the new normal, and the edge of adrenaline wears off. The screams died out, and more common night-time sounds took over—or at least the droning and creaking sounded more normal to me. I found myself nodding off about two hours into my shift. I got up and paced the tiny ledge—barely a meter each direction before I reached the end of the road or Lee's head.

When my alarm went off at the end of my three-hour shift, I nearly leaped off the ledge in surprise. I leaned against the back wall, breathing heavily, and slapped the alarm button. It cut out, mid bleep.

The cliff walls, reddish gray through the night-vision, looked farther away. High in the sky, Qureshi glowed in a thin crescent of white, offering no real light. The insects—I hoped they were just insects—creaked and droned.

Something grabbed my ankle.

I choked back a scream and banged my helmet against the overhand. "What the crap, Lee?"

He sat up and handed me the end of the comm cable. "Sorry. I didn't mean to startle you."

"And you thought grabbing my ankle would be the way to not startle me?"

"What would you recommend I grab next time?" Laughter threaded through his voice.

I tucked my stunner back into my belt pouch and patted it as I sat. "You grab anything, you know what you're going to get. I am going to sleep."

"I really am sorry." He groaned a little as he stood. "Get comfortable. It's not as bad as it looks."

I snapped the comm cable out of my helmet and settled into the corner. The warm rock cradled my body, but the helmet didn't provide any support for my head. I twisted around, then sat up and unfastened the helmet. "I can't sleep with this thing on."

He replied, but I couldn't hear it. Then he activated his external speaker and dialed it to low. "You shouldn't breathe the air for that long."

I fastened the helmet to my leg and snuggled back into the corner. "I looked at the stats again—we'd have to be here for weeks before it's really dangerous."

Lee didn't answer. He stood staring out at the darkness, the comm cable dangling from his helmet. He should be able to hear me through his external comm pickup. "Did you hear me?"

He jerked, then turned. "Sorry, yeah. You're probably fine, then. Good night."

"Good night." I pillowed my head on my arm and closed my eyes. Liam snuggled against my neck, warm and comforting, and I went to sleep.

When I opened my eyes, it was still gray but not completely dark. Liam had deserted me—probably off investigating something. The cold air against my neck might have been what woke me.

I took stock of my surroundings. The hard rock at my back and beneath my shoulder was still warm, but no longer comfortable. The pillow under my cheek felt almost as hard.

Pillow? I reached up and patted the smooth, rounded surface.

"You're awake?" Lee whispered. The pillow moved under my head.

My head was on his leg. I jerked upright, my cheeks hot. "Yes, I'm awake. What time is it?" Maybe if I pretended it hadn't happened, he wouldn't say anything.

"Sunrise in a few minutes. It's a good thing my pressure suit is waterproof. You drooled on my leg."

So much for that hope. I sat up, mustered my dignity, and turned to face him. "Then maybe you shouldn't have put your leg under my head."

His lips quirked, and the light breeze blew his dark hair around his face. I felt like I'd slept on a rock ledge, and he looked like he was modeling for an adventure-wear catalog. At times like this, it was easy to see how he'd charmed all of Delta Black to do his bidding. "I had to stop the snoring."

And then he had to say something like that. I pressed my lips together. "Where's Liam?"

"Out catching bugs, I think. He went that way." He pointed to the left.

In the brightening light, a flash of blue and white caught my eye. Liam jumped and soared along the side of the cliff, alighting on the fantastical wind-blown rocks, then leaped away again. The heat from the fissure below must have provided extra lift—he flew upward instead of just soaring down.

"What are the Gagarians up to? Did they catch Joss?"

"I haven't heard anything to indicate that." He stretched the hologram in his palm to a larger size. "There's been no activity since you went to sleep. At least, no human activity. I think there were animals around the crash site last night." He pointed to what might have been pawprints.

As I ate a protein bar, I told him about the felines I'd spotted. "They were the ones making all the noise last night."

"What noise? The only thing I heard was your snoring."

We finished breakfast and made our plans. With the dying wind, the heat had intensified, and our ledge became less comfortable. I whistled to Liam, hoping the sound wouldn't carry beyond the narrow valley. As he flew toward us, I slipped my pressure suit off my shoulders and down to my waist.

"What are you doing?" Lee stared at me, his face going a bit pink.

"I'm getting my jacket out so the solar panels will recharge, so it can generate a personal shield. I wish I could connect to the pressure suit like you can. Or get rid of the suit all together." I wrapped the jacket around my backpack, with the solar panels arranged across the top. Then I shrugged the suit back on and zipped it shut.

"Let's not get rid of anything until we're sure we won't need it." He tossed his helmet from hand to hand. "I really don't want to put this back on."

"If you're not careful, it will fall over the edge and you won't have a choice." I slid mine over my head but didn't twist it into place. Liam, having declined to ride inside, perched on my shoulder. "But you could probably just use your shield. That's what I plan to do as soon as I have enough charge to sustain it."

"You don't mind? I didn't want you to resent me for not having to wear it." He hooked the helmet to his leg, and the faint sheen of his personal shield flickered over his head and face.

"Who are you? Don't get me wrong, I prefer this Derek Lee to the arrogant *terkvard*, but why are you being so nice?"

"I'm not a bad guy!" He held up both hands. "I got in with the wrong crowd at the beginning, but that was almost three years ago. Can't we start over?"

My eyes narrowed. "I don't know. Maybe." He'd done some really bad stuff—or at least tolerated it. And I wasn't sure this wasn't a trick. "We'll see how this all turns out. Ready?" I latched my helmet.

He nodded, and we launched up the side of the cliff.

CHAPTER EIGHTEEN

We paused below the rim, scanning the foliage above us. Thick plants hung over the edge, with trailing vines digging into the narrowest cracks in the stone. We shimmied under the vines, burrowing through the green and purple leaves. Then we worked our way deeper into the jungle.

Hovering a few centimeters above the ground, we stretched out flat and snaked through the thick vines and trunks, pausing every few minutes to listen. Nothing moved. Our drone cam showed no people at the crash site.

A creeping feeling crossed my shoulders and shivered down my back. Something was wrong. Why weren't they looking for us? Was it a trap? Without the connecting cable, I couldn't talk to Lee without risking someone overhearing. With a grin, I grabbed his ankle.

He jerked, then turned to look over his shoulder.

I smiled. Turnabout was fair play, right?

He stopped, and we settled to the ground, sitting close together. He snapped his helmet back on and connected the comm cable.

I explained my thought process.

"I was thinking the same thing." He flicked his holo-ring and brought up the drone vid. With a swipe, he reset the timeline to sunset, then flicked the triple speed playback.

"Stop." I pointed at the feline shadows. "Those are the screaming creatures."

Lee shuddered dramatically. "Don't want to run into any of those." He started the feed moving again. "Wait, what's this?" Two men and a woman appeared on the cam, their faces lost in the shadow.

"Do you have audio?"

He nodded. The sound kicked in. Gibberish rolled through my helmet. I turned my translator on.

Voice one: ...him. This isn't a standard commonwealth uniform.

Voice two: It says 'colonial explorer corps.'

Voice three: That's a cadet uniform. Take him back to camp.

Voice one: Look for the others.

Voice three: Why do you think there are others?

Voice one: A single officer and one cadet on a shuttle? It's possible but highly unlikely. What would they have been doing?

Voice three: It's not unlikely at all. They sometimes use these <unintelligible> for cadet training. A simple run to the planet and back—maybe they dropped off a VIP or are headed to the ship to pick up equipment.

On the vid, two people marched Joss out of the broken branches and into the clearing.

Voice three: Take him back to base.

"Let go of me, you goons. I'm a victim of a shipwreck. I demand sanctuary under the Inter-Colony Treaty of 2430."

"That's the wrong treaty, colony boy." A female voice—voice three, I thought—said that in standard. A short woman stepped in front of the camera, her back to us. "Take him back to base."

The woman watched the three figures fly away, then moved toward the shuttle. The two men followed her.

Voice two: I'm more interested in the hammock.

Voice one: What do you mean?

Voice two: If they were using the hammock to carry the injured officer, then obviously there are more—

Voice three: Not necessarily. The cadet probably attached the hammock to the HLP and tethered it to his belt at a two-meter trailing distance.

The voices grew quiet as the speakers moved away.

"That's a good idea," Lee said. "We should have thought of that."

"They got Joss."

"I know. And now they think they've picked up everyone, so it's safe to go back to the crash site and…" His voice trailed off.

"Do what? You can bet they took the HLP with them—that means our food supply is gone, too. I still think we'd be better off showing up on their doorstep and demanding sanctuary."

"You're crazy. You heard what they said to the caveman." He folded his arms, his face set stubbornly. "I say we go to the crash site and see if we can salvage anything. Then we go after Evy and Joss and hijack that shuttle."

"Good plan." I hoped he could hear the sarcasm through the comm cable, but I was too tired to argue. Maybe we'd find something useful at the crash. "If it were me, I'd set up surveillance, just in case. Let's watch the rest of the vid."

He scrolled through the recording, slowing down whenever anything appeared on cam. We spotted the felines again, then nothing for a long stretch. The light intensified as the sun rose. Something flickered at the corner of the screen and disappeared.

"Was that a drone?" I made a back-up motion.

"Can't tell. It could be a bug." He ran the vid back and forth a couple more times. Then he shrugged and shut it down. "I say we assume it was a drone."

We sat in silence for a few minutes. Lee took off his helmet.

I unfastened mine to let Liam out. "Any suggestions on how we avoid it?"

Lee shook his head. "The HLP is still there."

"Probably a trap."

Liam jumped to my knee and turned to face me. He chittered earnestly, his little arms gesturing as if he were giving a presentation.

"Is he—is he talking to us?" Lee asked.

"Obviously."

"Do you know what he's saying?"

"Not a clue." I held out my hand, and Liam jumped to it. He scampered up my arm and rubbed against my face. Then he launched himself into the thick jungle, leaping toward the crash site.

"He's going to draw the drones away from the crash site." Lee pressed his belt controls and rose off the ground. "We need to get over there while he's got them distracted."

I stared at the little glider. He clung to a low branch, staring back at me. "What?"

Lee swept a hand in Liam's wake. "He's going to draw the drones away."

I opened my mouth, then closed it. I bit my lip, then tried again. "How much experience do you have with sair-gliders?"

"None. I don't like the little rodents. But yours is different. And he was clearly telling you he'd take care of the drones."

Liam popped out of the foliage and chittered at me, as if agreeing with Lee. Then he scurried away again.

"You think he understands Standard?" I stared at Lee.

He shrugged, his face going pink. "I've heard of weirder things. Didn't you claim he found a piece of senidium for you on Sarvo Six? Why wouldn't you believe this?"

I set my belt altitude to one meter and thought it over. Why didn't I believe it? Liam was smart—way smarter than the average glider. He'd proven that over and over again. He'd been living with me for three years—maybe he understood what we said.

Or maybe the senidium had been a coincidence. But there was no reason to ignore the opportunity to take advantage of another coincidence.

"Either way," Lee said, "he's going to distract the drones. Let's use that."

"Good point."

We followed Liam through the thick undergrowth. In places, we had to skirt around dense thickets of aerial roots, but the little glider waited for us. Finally, he stopped, perching at eye level on a convenient branch. He made eye contact with me and cheeped. Then he made the same noise at Lee.

"Go for it, buddy," Lee whispered.

Liam chirped and took off down the branch. He leaped into the space between two big green and purple leaves. Sunlight glinted off his white stripes, making them appear almost metallic. He called out in his high, chirpy voice.

"Let's go." Lee dropped to an altitude of half-a-meter, stretched out flat above the ground. The guy must have abs of steel.

I slunk down beside him, pushing myself along with my feet to keep my screaming muscles quiet.

We reached the first broken branches and ducked under a half-fallen tree. I peered around the edge of a massive leaf. Some of the crushed foliage had started decomposing already, leaving patches of slime on the jagged trunks and branches. Lee's nose twitched, and he pressed his fingers against his face as if to stop a sneeze.

The tangy smell clawed at the back of my throat and tickled my nose. Water dripped from a nearby leaf—it must have rained here. Either the overhanging cliff had protected us, or the weather was as erratic as the wind.

On the thought, a gust blew through the clearing, ruffling broken leaves on one side of the crash zone. The rest were dead still. A broken bough fell, revealing a corner of the HLP.

A flash caught my eye—Liam jumping from a shadowed branch into sunlight. He leaped through the disaster area, pausing on the HLP to sniff and investigate, then disappeared into the trees on the far side.

Immediately, three tiny devices rose from the crushed plants on the ground and took off after him. Luckily for us, Gagarian drones were larger and clumsier than ours.

Lee put his feet down and started to rise. I grabbed his arm. "Wait," I breathed.

Liam leaped back into view. He ran across the top of the ship's inverted hull, then disappeared back into the trees. The three drones followed, and two more lifted off in his wake.

Lee raised an eyebrow at me.

I shook my head and held up a finger. Somehow, I knew Liam would be back for one more round.

Minutes later, the little glider appeared again, the five drones buzzing behind him. Liam frisked about through the devastated undergrowth, then darted away at ground level. The five drones arrowed after him.

I snapped my helmet back on, and he followed suit. "Now," I mouthed.

CHAPTER NINETEEN

Lee started toward the newly revealed HLP.

I grabbed his arm again. "Trap." He couldn't hear me, of course, but he got the idea.

His gave me a scathing look. "Duh."

I plugged our comm cable in. "Then why are you going toward it?"

"Liam got the drones."

"You don't think they left a stationary one watching the HLP? I would. We need to check the ship."

"Not a problem. I've got a bit of tech that's—well, you remember Laghari, from Green flight back at the Academy?"

"The hacker?"

"Yeah. He gave me an app that first summer—before I got shunned—" He looked away as if the memory was painful. "Anyway, it messes with the cams."

"Oh—we had one of those. Chymm built it."

He chuckled. "I think every flight has a tech guy—they do that on purpose. If we were here with our team, there'd be someone who could build one. Luckily, I keep the app on my ring." He flicked his device and swiped at an icon. "They're now offline."

"But if you disrupted their cams, they'll know we were here. We didn't need to bother with chasing the drones away." I hurried toward the HLP. "They'll probably send someone to check as soon as they notice the glitch, so we'd better hurry."

"Naw, this app doesn't glitch out the feed—it records a loop and feeds it back to the cam." He opened the crate strapped to the top of the HLP and dumped the meal pacs onto the ground.

"That's highly illegal." I scooped the food into my backpack.

"No kidding. But who cares?" He filled the crate with rocks and laid empty meal pac wrappers on top before closing the lid and strapping it back into place. "At least we won't starve any time soon."

"Let's make a quick trip through the ship." I lifted off and flew toward the crashed shuttle. Still connected via the cable, he was forced to follow.

"Are you kidding? That thing is unstable."

"It hasn't moved since we left. And we'll use our grav belts. Don't touch anything without warning me." I unplugged and dove through the open hatch headfirst.

A couple of centimeters of water covered the overhead inside the cockpit. "It must have really rained here." I unfastened my helmet and turned to Lee as he slid slowly through the hatch. "What might be useful—is there another HLP?"

"No, why would a shuttle have two of them?"

"You try the comm gear again. I'm going to check the back." I slid through the open hatch into the cargo bay. The overhead was dry here—the lip of the hatch had kept most of the water inside the cockpit. Dropping to the inverted ceiling, I poked my head into the bunk area now under the cockpit. I'd pulled one of the mattresses earlier, but maybe there'd been something I'd missed.

The place had been tossed. The Gagarians had obviously done a full search, although they hadn't been too careful. I found a couple more bottles of liquor and another meal pac.

In the cargo hold, I found a survival bag and the shuttle's emergency beacon. It had been smashed—obviously the Gagarians were taking no chances of attracting CEC attention. Which meant Lee was probably right about what would happen if we got captured.

It also meant we needed to rescue Evy and Joss. Immediately. I looked for weapons.

"Comm gear is dead." Lee lifted through the hatch and dropped to hover in the middle of the cargo hold. "You got anything?"

"A couple of small things—are there any weapons on this ship?"

"I checked the armory in the cockpit. Picked clean." He moved to the rear of the ship. "There's usually a couple of weapons here, too." He pointed to a door hanging from smashed hinges. "Guess they got here first."

"Figures. I have the stunner that came with this suit."

"I have a stunner, too. Evy had a blaster, which means the Gagarians have it now."

I'd been thinking about this. "Wouldn't she have given it to Joss? He was going to set up the HLP, then scout around the area. She wouldn't need protection once the force shield was on, and she was kind of out of it anyway."

He shrugged. "Then they got it when they captured Joss."

"Maybe. What about the other pressure suits?" I lifted a crumpled heap from the damp overhead and shook it out. A quick search revealed another mini stunner in the pocket. I held it up in triumph. "Check that one."

Lee grabbed a suit draped across the conduits that ran the length of the cargo bay's overhead. "What was that? Did the ship move?"

I snorted. "No, Nervous Nelly, the ship is wedged tightly into place. But even if it was balanced on the edge of the cliff, the weight of one suit wouldn't be enough to tip it over the edge."

"Fine. Let's get out of here, though. It would be easy for them to corner us here." He drifted into the open airlock and checked our drone's cam—no one in the clearing.

"Coming." I swung the extra survival bag over my shoulder—good thing the gravity was so low—and followed him through the narrow opening near the ground. I removed the second bag to get through, then pulled it out after me.

"Let's get out of here." Lee lifted off the ground and turned toward the cliff.

"Hang on—let's see if we can figure out where Joss got captured." I flicked my grav belt controls and flew over the broken foliage into the thicker trees on the far side of the crash zone.

"Why do you care where they caught the Neanderthal?"

I gave him a death glare as I dropped to a convenient root. "If he had the chance, he would've left the blaster for us."

Lee dropped beside me, his feet hovering a few centimeters above the mud. "You think he heard them coming, hid his weapon, and surrendered?"

"Joss is not stupid. And he's been fighting armed goons most of his life. If he knew they had caught Evy, then he knew they'd be looking for all of us. By letting himself be captured, he could convince them the crew was only two people and give us a chance to rescue them. Pull up our surveillance drone and see if you can tell where they got him."

"I can figure out the general direction. But we have no way of knowing how far away he was. Too bad he didn't have a tracker on. I'm going to make that recommendation when we get back—all prisoners should be tracked." He grinned at me as if this were hilarious.

"We weren't prisoners."

"You were being transported back to the ship in disgrace. Your comm system had been muted. If that doesn't say prisoner, I don't know what does."

I ignored him because I'd had a brilliant idea. I flicked my holo-ring to pull up a tracking system Chymm created three years ago during our exercise on Sarvo Six. He'd been able to track the holo-rings of every cadet in the field—or at least those within a few klicks. It worked without the standard comm mini-sats, which obviously weren't in orbit around Saha. I had no idea if the app would work here, but it was worth a try.

I dug through my unused apps and found it. "Crap. Not downloaded."

"What are you looking for?" He had pulled up the drone footage. He turned in place and pointed into the woods. "They brought him from that direction."

As we wove through the trees, I explained about the tracking app. "But I haven't used it in so long, it's not in my local memory."

"That would've been way more useful than fumbling around in the woods." He flung out his arms. "They could've caught him anywhere. He was wearing a grav belt, so there's no way to track his movements."

"Let's go back to the clearing."

"We should be going to their camp, to figure out how we're going to break the others out."

"That'll be a lot easier with a blaster. I'm sure Joss figured out a way to leave it for us." I went back to the first line of broken branches and paused. "According to the drone footage, they pulled him out of the woods here." I looked behind me. We hovered a couple of meters from the cliff edge, but it wasn't visible in the thick foliage. "If it were me, and I was afraid they were going to grab me, I'd stash a blaster there."

I worked my way through the vines and aerial roots, angling toward the cliff. Here, the vines hung in a thick screen over the stone lip. "This is much more overgrown than our section of the cliff."

"So?" Lee fidgeted nearby.

I spotted a newly broken vine. The ripped ends oozed a little slime. "This was broken recently—more recently than the crash." I lifted the broken vine and pulled away the enormous leaves, revealing a cloth-wrapped bundle. "Ha! Joss's shirt."

"He never misses an opportunity to take his shirt off."

"But look what he wrapped it around." I shook the fabric away, revealing a blaster.

CHAPTER TWENTY

"I KNEW he'd leave it for us." I hooked the holster to my belt and buckled the strap around my upper thigh.

"Maybe I should have that." Lee moved closer and held out his hand. "After all, you're a prisoner."

"Not a prisoner. And I have an expert marksmanship badge. How well do you shoot?"

Lee's face went red. "Whatever. Just don't shoot me."

"You're not making that easy."

We repacked the extra gear we'd picked up in the ship, distributing it between the two of us. I whistled for Liam.

Lee made a chopping motion. "Don't do that. The drones are following him."

"I don't get you. One minute, you're convincing me Liam is a smart as we are, and the next, you're worried he'll bring the drones to us."

"How's he going to get rid of them?"

I shrugged. "He'll figure it out."

We waited. Around us, jungle steamed as the sun slowly penetrated the thick canopy. The broken vine oozed more yellow goo, and Lee wrinkled his nose. "That smell gets you in the back of the throat."

I unstrapped my helmet and pulled it over my head. "Not a problem."

The leaves rustled in the wind, and sunlight fluttered through the vines and branches. I unlatched my helmet and whistled again. Liam's soft chittering answered. "There he is!" I pointed high into the trees above us.

The blue and white glider raced along a vine, a single drone close behind.

Lee lunged behind a screen of vines and aerial roots.

I bit my lip. I was sure Liam would have ditched the tail by now. I sat on the thick roots, not moving, hoping the drone wouldn't see me.

Liam stopped suddenly. He spun on the branch, so fast I thought he might fall, and batted the drone with one paw, hard. The tiny flying cam smacked into the thick branch. Sparks flew out and disappeared before they hit the jungle floor.

Liam made some conversational noises, then zig zagged down a pair of aerial roots to land on my shoulder.

"Nice work." I stroked his thick fur.

Liam agreed, then tapped my faceplate. I lifted the unfastened headgear. The glider darted inside, squirming through the neck opening and taking up residence in my pocket. "I told you he'd lose the tail."

Lee crept out from behind the vines. "Do you think we can risk the comms?"

"Better stick with the cable as long as possible. They're probably still scanning for additional crew members—I would be, wouldn't you?" I snapped my helmet tight and lifted through the trees, not waiting to see if Lee followed me. Sunlight hit my head, warming, and my helmet darkened.

Lee popped up beside me, his uniform darkening to green in seconds. He plugged in the cable. "The base is about two klicks that way. I say we go about one and three quarters, then drop and take the last bit close to the ground."

I shrugged. "Sounds good to me."

We disconnected and flew along the tops of the trees as we had done the previous day, our torsos brushing through the topmost leaves. The sun dropped quickly. A ten-hour day took some getting used to. Maybe that was another reason the CEC had chosen not to explore this moon.

In the lead, Lee lifted a hand, then pointed down and dropped out of sight.

I followed him through the thick vegetation. The trees here were larger, with heavier branches and roots. In places, we had to climb through multiple layers of vines and vertical roots. We fought through the dense mass and finally reached easier ground.

The jungle was thinner here, with sunlight filtering through. A few meters beyond us, the growth stopped. Several buildings—uncannily like our CEC modules—cast long shadows across a wide landing pad. The sun dropped lower, turning the badly camouflaged modules red.

I ducked behind a thick tree trunk, hoping their security system couldn't penetrate the jungle. I tossed Lee the end of the comm cable. "Now what?"

"Now we steal that shuttle." He pointed at a craft sitting in the middle of the otherwise empty field. A hatch in the bottom stood open, and several technicians moved around it, doing whatever maintenance staff does to space craft when they're on the ground.

"You think you can fly that thing? And will it hold all four of us?"

"It doesn't have to hold all four of us. I can fly it to the ship from here. They'll send a team to rescue Joss and Evy."

"You'd leave them here?" I reached for the blaster in my holster. "Abandon teammates?"

He held out both hands. "I'm not talking about abandoning them. I'm taking about getting a competent rescue team here."

"We agreed the Gagarians aren't going to let us endanger their mission here. That means they'll eliminate survivors. We need to rescue Joss and Evy now. Not in a day or two."

"Once we get it off the ground, they'll know the jig is up. Evy and Torres will be safer. It's not just escape—it's a bargaining chip."

"You think? How much do you know about Gagarians?" I crossed my arms. "They aren't going to let us escape. If we try to fly that shuttle out of here, they'll shoot us down—you think they won't?"

"With what? Do they have anti-aircraft weapons?"

"Do you know they don't?"

He held up both hands. "Fine. What's your plan, then? We can try to steal the shuttle and get help—if we survive their ground-to-air defenses. Or we can rescue our friends, then try to escape. I don't think we have a better chance with an injured pilot and a Neanderthal in tow."

"Would you stop calling him that?"

"Why?"

"Because it's insulting!"

"No, I mean why do they call him that? What's his story? You said he's been fighting armed thugs most of his life—I thought he grew up on Earth. Isn't that the land of milk and honey?"

I blinked, startled by the change of subjects. "How about we focus on the rescue? If you can keep from calling Joss names from now until we get them free, then I'll tell you the story." I extended my fist.

He ran his tongue over his front teeth, then nodded and bumped my knuckles. "Deal. What's your plan?"

"I don't suppose you have any more secret hacking software on your ring?" I rolled my shoulders. I'd never spent this long in a pressure suit before, and the pull of the fabric was starting to bother me.

"I've got a couple things, but I don't know if any of them will work. The loop thing was worth the risk at the crash site—we knew no one had been there for hours. But here—" He waved in the direction of the base. "There are too many people. We could end up splicing in a loop with people—people who might be visible elsewhere at the moment."

I sat on a root, unlatched my helmet, and dug two meal pacs out of my bag. He took the second one and settled nearby, opening his own helmet.

I took a deep breath. "The air's not too bad here. I guess it's the broken branches that produce that awful smell."

He ripped open a packet and dumped the contents into his mouth, nodding as he crunched. We ate in silence for a few minutes.

"You still have access to our drone?" I rubbed my eyes. "We probably should have looked for the drone control tablet—Joss would have left that for us, too."

"We don't need it." Lee opened an app, and his fingers flew through the interface. "I can fly 'em both. I didn't try before—didn't want to take it away if the Nean—if Torres needed it. But now that we know he's indisposed, we can use his, too. I'm bringing them here."

"Great. We'll set watch on the base. See if we can figure out where they keep prisoners. If Evy and Joss are still alive—" I swallowed hard. "They'll have to feed them, right? Or at least keep an eye on them."

"I'd lock 'em in a storage room with a cam inside. You could leave someone like that for days without checking on them."

"Did you learn that on Sarvo Six?" Peter and I had been locked in a storage closet by Delta Black's co-conspirators. Luckily, we had a few tricks up our sleeves.

"I had nothing to do with that!"

I stared at him. "You took my friends hostage on Sarvo Six. I was there—remember? Peter and I took you and Herria out. And you accused me of being weak. Before that, you threatened me with a knife during Trial by Fire."

His face went white, and he hung his head. "I didn't want to hurt anyone. My mom told me I should befriend LeBlanc—that I would have a 'golden future' if I worked with him. And he was so persuasive." He glanced at me and looked away. "You don't know what it was like—he was the most important cadet in the Academy, and he wanted to be my friend. All I had to do was follow his lead. I knew it was wrong, but I convinced myself it was no big deal. At TbF, no one got hurt—"

"I got a concussion! And stealing stuff is wrong even when no one is hurt."

"LeBlanc said you were faking—that he didn't hit you very hard."

I stared him down.

"I know. But—he had me so convinced he was right—that everyone was out to get us, and we needed to protect our own." He rubbed the back of his neck.

"Then I got in deeper—and the wrongs we did were more wrong and harder to talk myself around. But you get to the point where changing your beliefs means admitting you were desperately wrong. I couldn't admit that. My mom getting caught and tried was probably the best possible outcome for me. It forced me to see that her plans for me—her way of thinking—was dragging me down, not helping me succeed."

He looked away again. "She wouldn't even talk to me after she was arrested. Like she was disappointed in my failure to be a good criminal."

I felt a strange stirring of compassion. That summer, he'd done bad things—some I'd seen with my own eyes. But the rest of us hadn't been angels. And the Academy review board had acquitted him. After that incident where he took my flight hostage, and I took him out, we both could have been expelled. I suspected my dad thought if he pardoned my behavior—even if it was in reaction to Lee's—he had to pardon the actions that caused it. If only to prevent any appearance of favoritism toward his daughter.

Now I wondered. Maybe he'd seen something redeemable in Derek Lee. The entire Academy had treated him and Felicity as lepers, but maybe I should offer him a chance at redemption.

Or maybe he was playing me.

I'd keep an open mind—and watch him like a hawk.

CHAPTER TWENTY-ONE

WE MOVED a little deeper into the woods and flew the drones to run surveillance for us. Then we took turns trying to get a little sleep while the other watched the vid feeds. By the middle of the short Saha night, neither of us was operating at peak efficiency.

"There." Lee shook my shoulder and flicked a file to my holo-ring. "I think they're in there."

A man in dark, unmarked clothing stood outside a door with a weapon held across his body. When the door opened, he snapped into a crouch, blaster pointed at it. A short woman with curly hair stepped out, and he swung the muzzle away. She closed the door and rattled the handle, then stepped into a puddle of light.

I gasped.

"What?" Lee looked from me to the vid and back.

"I know her. That's Marika LaGrange. She was a double agent on the Earth mission. She escaped with Thor Talon."

"Thor Talon? The G'lacTechNews guy?"

I nodded. "He was embedded in our team and turned out to be a Gagarian spy. Or she recruited him—I'm not one hundred percent clear on what happened. But he's with them."

"I wondered what happened to him. One day he was breaking news from Earth with Aella Phoenix, and the next he was 'on sabbatical.' Then he disappeared."

"I'm surprised you even noticed."

"If I hadn't gone to the Academy, I was going to be a newscaster." He grinned a thousand-credit smile.

That surprised a chuckle out of me. "Probably an excellent back-up plan. Maybe Joss and I should try that. Since our CEC careers are over before they've begun."

"You won't need it. When we get back to the Academy, I'm sure your dad will check the records and clear you of misconduct. It sounds like there wasn't a lot of evidence."

"A couple of hours ago, you were convinced I was a criminal."

"Not really. But it's easy to think bad of people who have everything when you've lost so much." He held up a hand to stop my argument. "Even if it's your own fault."

I grimaced. When he chose to turn on the charm, it was hard to remember he was a *terkvard*. "Yeah, poor you."

He glared.

"Let's stay on task." I poked at the holo still paused in his hand. "I wonder what Marika is doing here."

"Will she listen to you? Will she care what you think?"

I shook my head slowly. "If Joss can't convince her to let him go, I don't have a chance."

He raised an eyebrow.

"They were an item back on Earth. Or at least, they hung out together. A lot. Until she tipped her hand by turning me over to the Hellions."

He nodded. "Right. Personal appeal won't work. What are her weaknesses?"

"I'm not sure she has any. But let's forget her. We know where they've got them. Let's break them out and steal that shuttle." I pointed at the vid still hovering before his face. It showed the closed door and the puddle of light.

"You can bet they've got surveillance, too."

"Use your magic app." I stood and pulled my helmet over my head.

"How long does it take to redo a feed? We can work our way across the base, spoofing the cams as we go, grab them, and get out."

"And what if they aren't in there? What if that guy was guarding something else?" Lee put his own helmet on, plugged in the comm cable, and swiped up a new screen.

"He was there for Marika's protection—he left when she did. They aren't worried about whatever is inside getting out, which makes me think it's Joss and Evy. Probably restrained and locked up. You got anything that'll unlock doors?"

He lifted his backpack and grinned. "No, but I've got a sharp knife and a laser cutter right here. They're supposed to be used for building shelter or cutting firewood, but they work on camp modules."

"How do you know that?"

"I might… Let's say it's a guess."

"Then let's try it." I popped the cable, lifted off the mass of roots, and wove through the foliage.

The trees and vines stopped at the edge of the flight pad. They folded back on themselves, leaving a sharply defined, ruler straight edge. Lee pushed past me, but I grabbed his arm and yanked him back.

"What?" he mouthed.

"There's a force shield. I didn't want you to break your nose. It might derail your newscasting career." He couldn't hear what I said, so I stuck out my hand and stepped forward. Blue sparked and my hand slapped into an invisible wall.

He poked the force field with a finger. Blue flared. Then he grabbed a nearby vine and pushed it toward the invisible wall. The leaves curled back but produced no blue sparks. He plugged the comm cable into my helmet. "What do you think that means?"

"Our gloves are different from the leaves? Doesn't really matter if neither can get through." Liam poked his nose through the neck of my suit and rubbed his face against my cheek. "We could send Liam in, but I don't know what that gets us."

"What do you mean?"

"Liam can get through force shields. Or at least he could get through the one on Sarvo Six." I popped my helmet long enough to let the little guy out.

"Not possible."

I shrugged. "I didn't think so either—then he did it."

"How? Did he phase through?" Lee watched the glider leap from my arm and scamper along the edge of the clearing. "Where's he going?"

I shrugged again. "Maybe he doesn't want us to see how he does it. Or maybe he can't get through this one. And even if he does, what good does that do us? It's not like he can turn the thing off."

Liam disappeared over a wide leaf, then scampered back into view on the edge of the tarmac.

Lee started, pulling the comm cable free.

"See?" I smirked as my furry friend gamboled across the pad. Lights flared on and sirens blared. Liam scurried up a drainpipe on the side of the closest building and over the edge of the roof.

The lights strobed. The siren cut off, leaving absolute silence in its wake. Then the buzz of grav generators—more felt than heard—tickled the base of my skull. A double handful of men and women in unmarked clothing zipped between the buildings and spread out along the landing pad, followed by anti-spacecraft weapons on straining grav-lifters. The weapons swiveled, searching for targets.

Lee and I melted back into the jungle. So much for that idea.

Lee waved his hand in front of my helmet and made the hand signal for "follow me." But instead of continuing away from the camp, he took us around the side.

The camp sat on the edge of the same cliff we'd crashed on. But here, the other side of the valley was at least a half-klick away. In the bottom of the valley, the sluggish river of red and black poured away. In the gathering darkness, the burning lava cast a weird magenta glow on the cliff walls.

We dropped over the edge of the cliff and paralleled the side for about half a klick. Then we went up. At the top, we looked over the lip. The closest buildings stood fifty meters away. The searchers from the landing pad had spread out through the base, checking the perimeter. A pair of soldiers moved away from us. If we'd risen any earlier, they would have spotted us.

I lifted the comm cable and handed Lee the other end. "Where's the edge of the force shield?"

"I don't know. I thought it would be at the top of the cliff, but they walked right here." He pointed at the rocky edge. "I think we can get in this way."

The siren blared again, and the lights strobed to red. We ducked beneath the edge as soldiers raced past, intent on their destination. A quick look confirmed they were headed toward the landing pad again.

"Now!" Lee yanked the cable from my helmet and launched himself over the lip of the rock face. He skimmed along the ground, his body parallel to the stone. I threw myself after him.

We raced toward the closest building. Every second, I expected to ram into a force shield—surely they didn't think the lava river would stop anyone? But we didn't hit any resistance. My abs and back screamed as I fought to maintain my horizontal flight path. The speed we moved helped, but it had been a long day. My toes dragged against the stone, slowing me and kicking up small rocks and dust. I lifted a little higher and gritted my teeth as we flew.

We darted into a narrow space between two modules, the darkness hitting in an almost physical blow. I collapsed against the wall, out of breath. Lee hurtled away from me, dropping to a crouch at the far end of the building. I struggled to my feet and scrambled closer.

A team buzzed across the narrow mouth of our alley, their feet a meter above the ground. We slammed ourselves against the wall, hoping they wouldn't notice us in the shadows.

CHAPTER TWENTY-TWO

After they passed, I tapped Lee's shoulder and grabbed the cable. "How did they not see us?"

"They're responding to the landing pad alert—no one has told them to search, yet. We need to find a place to hide before they decide to do that."

"Or just grab the others and run."

"There are too many of them. Now that we're in, let's lay low until they settle down. Maybe Liam will trip the shield a couple more times for us. Nothing like crying wolf to get a response team off kilter." He looked around our narrow space, then pointed up. He unplugged the cable and lifted off.

I followed him up the side of the module. We hovered in the shadow of a block device—probably a water collector. At Lee's signal, we dropped softly to the rooftop and crouched, out of sight from the ground. If they conducted a thorough search, though, they'd send people overhead, right?

Lee handed me the cable again. "This is getting really old. Do you think it would be safe to use our comms?"

"In the middle of an enemy camp? Yeah, no. If they have any idea we're here, that's the first thing they'd scan for—unrecognized comm frequencies. This is safer. Although, inside their force shield, it's probably safe to take our helmets off."

"You forget—that whole side of the base is open." He waved at the cliff. "Which makes no sense."

"How'd you know it would be open?" I asked.

"It was a guess. There weren't any bollards. The shield around the landing pad has bollards, like ours do. But there weren't any along the cliff. Obviously, they're trying to keep wildlife out—they weren't expecting enemy combatants to infiltrate." He grinned.

"We aren't enemy combatants. This was the problem on Sarvo Six—you think we're military agents. We aren't. We're explorers. Our job is to visit new planets and check for viability. Not take over camps or steal shuttles. Maybe you're in the wrong service."

His face darkened. "Maybe I am. But after PSW, I was lucky to stay in this one. No one else would touch me. I tried."

I bit my lip. Under the flat statement, a tremor of emotion pulsed—a sense of betrayal and loss. "Maybe you can transfer after you get commissioned. I've heard of people doing that."

"If we pull this off, I can probably take my pick. Be quiet for a minute—I'm going to flip through the frequencies and see if I can hear anything."

I smothered an angry retort at his high-handed attitude. Evy had put me in charge—why did he think he got to call the shots? Because he had better gear? I unplugged the comm cable and lifted a few centimeters off the roof. Moving slowly, I eased around the water collector and crept toward the edge of the building.

I stretched out on the cold plastek, then removed my helmet and set it aside. Pushing with my fingers and toes, my belt keeping me just above the surface, I crept forward to peer over the edge.

This module sat among a row of similar buildings—four on this side with three more across the way. Between the two rows, a wide lane of empty plasphalt formed a walkway. The narrow alleys between each module were also paved—the buildings had been dropped onto a solid pad.

To my right, the landing pad stretched bright and empty. Another squad of—what were they? Soldiers? Agents? Spies? Another squad of Gagarians had spread out to check the perimeter. They scattered to the edges of the paved area, then skimmed above the ground parallel to the barrier. It took about ten minutes for them to check—and double check—the entire perimeter, then they zipped back to the buildings.

A shout rang out. The rest swung around. A straggler pointed into the jungle, and the others converged. I couldn't hear their conversation at that distance, but a flash of blue and white in the brilliant lights clued me in on the cause: Liam.

The sair-glider leapt from a thick branch and soared over the camp, passing through the faint blue haze of their shield. The alarms blared again, and the lights strobed. Liam swooped up and into the bushes.

I didn't need to hear them to understand what happened next. Someone raised a blaster and fired. Someone else yelled as the blaster fire splashed against the inside of the shield. Liam disappeared into the jungle.

"Now they know we're here." Lee dropped beside me.

"Geez, you scared the crap out of me." I turned back to watch the Gagarians return to the larger module at the far end of the row. "And you're wrong. They know a glider is here. They have two CEC explorers locked up—they shouldn't be surprised if a glider is trying to get back to its owner."

"I wonder if they knew gliders could pass through the shields?"

"I'm not sure most of them can. I never saw any of them do it on Earth—not even Liam." As I rolled over to look up at the faint blue fuzz, the lights on the landing pad went dark. The bollards around the edges glowed blue, and the shield brightened. "I guess they've decided to up the power."

The blue and white glider soared overhead and dropped lightly to my stomach.

"How'd it get back in without setting off the alarms again?"

I stroked Liam's silky fur. "He, not it. And who knows. Maybe the Gagarians gave up and turned off the alarms." I lifted Liam off my belly and rolled over. "Now that he's cried wolf a few times, it's time to rescue our friends."

Lee's hand snapped around my wrist. "What's your plan?"

"We're going to fly over there, cut through the roof, and get our friends out."

"Wouldn't it be easier to cut through a wall? That way they don't need grav belts to get out. Or better yet—cut through the locking mechanism on the door."

"That's out in the open. Thanks to your device, the cams aren't a problem, but anyone could walk by. Let's go in through the wall between those two mods." I pointed to the narrow alley between the likely prison and the next building. "I hope we're right about where they are."

We waited another twenty minutes, to make sure the response team was back in bed—or wherever they went when they weren't responding to wildlife alarms. Then we lifted off the roof and zipped across the wide walkway to the other side. Lee pulled out his cutter, and I crouched beside him.

"How loud is that thing?"

He flipped a switch, and the hand-held device began to purr. "Not very." He pushed it against the side of the module.

A rumbling echoed down the alley, ratcheting up into the now familiar scream.

Lee yanked the cutter back.

I snickered. "That was one of those felines. Excellent comedic timing."

While he went to work on the wall, I crept to the end of the alley and peered out. Nothing. I pulled up the drone cams. Lee had set the smaller one to circle the camp, above the shield. Aside from the dim lights on the side of each module and the blue indicators around the landing pad, it was dark. No one moved between the buildings, and none of them had windows.

By running the vid back, I tracked the searchers into the large building at the end. Either it was a barracks, or it was their headquarters. Or maybe both. Either way, we knew most of the people were inside, and people tend to chat. Maybe we could find an air vent and listen in.

Lee's soft voice pulled me around. "I'm in." He'd cut three sides of a square in the wall about a meter on each side. A series of shorter cuts along the shorter side allowed him to fold the section away like a door. "After you."

I ducked through the opening, taking care not to touch the melted edges. They looked cool, but I didn't want to risk damage to my suit. My helmet swung against my leg. I grabbed it before it hit the wall.

As I straightened, the room began to glow, then brightened. I stood inside a small empty room with the front door to my right, one in the wall across from me, and two more to my left. Light shone from three rectangular fixtures embedded in the ceiling. A single uncomfortable-looking chair sat near the external door. The walls were blank.

Lee pulled the cut section close to the hole as if shutting a door. "What do you suppose they use this building for?"

I held my finger to my lips and leaned close. "Hopefully it's a prison for Colonial explorers." I tried the door opposite our improvised entrance. "Locked. Can you cut it open?"

"I can do better than that." He flicked his holo-ring and swiped through the icons. "Laghari gave me another useful app." The door clicked.

I turned the handle and it rotated smoothy. "Why didn't you use that app on the front door?"

Lee's face went blank, then flared red.

I bit my lip to stop the grin spreading across my face and eased the door open a crack.

The rattle of a shuttle launch filled the room. I froze.

"Wow, Torres can snore." Lee motioned for me to open the door farther.

"I'm not sure—"

He pulled the handle from my hand and swung the door wide. Lights flared on. A large, hairy man sat up, rubbing his eyes.

"Crap!" Lee slammed the door shut.

CHAPTER TWENTY-THREE

SOMETHING HEAVY SLAMMED into the door.

"We're supposed to be stealthy!" I dragged the stunner from my pocket and yanked the door open again.

The man—obviously in the process of crashing into the door again—hurtled through the opening, barely missing me, and slammed into the wall opposite.

I fired my stunner, hitting him square in the back. He collapsed to the floor.

"Not a prison for explorers." I crouched to check the man's pulse. Strong and regular. "Now what?"

Lee checked inside the room. "It's pretty bare in there—this guy could be a prisoner, too." He stared down at the man.

The guy wore a sleeveless top and tight underpants, both more gray than white. Dark hair grew thick and bushy on his shoulders. I gingerly grabbed his equally hairy arm and rolled him onto his back. It was harder to do than I expected—the guy was a solid mass of muscle under a layer of fat. The white shirt rode up, exposing his furry belly.

"Did he have clothes in there?" I tried to focus on his face. He was older—probably late forties or early fifties. His hair was cut short, with a lot of gray in the brown and a bald spot on top. His slack face had heavy jowls and puffy eyes. "He doesn't exactly inspire confidence in the Gagarin military."

Lee did a more thorough check of the room. "There's a pair of pants and a shirt on the floor. No other clothes, no equipment, not even a toothbrush. And the bed doesn't have a blanket—it's just a plain mattress. And get this—there's no handle on the inside of the door. Definitely a cell."

The man snored again, his rank breath expelled in a loud rumble.

I waved my hand. "I'm guessing he's here to sober up. I wonder why they don't just give him a dose of BuzzKill."

Lee shrugged. "Maybe they figure a hangover is part of the punishment. Let's put him back in, shall we?"

I stood and unlatched my grav belt. "Help me get this around him." I adjusted the belt to full length and stretched it out next to him. We rolled him on top then pulled and yanked to get the belt around him. Fortunately, these generic models were designed to be used by anyone in an emergency—all shapes and sizes. With a grunt, I got the clasp latched.

A few taps lifted him off the ground, with his head and feet hanging low. It would be wildly uncomfortable if he were conscious. We pushed him into the cell and dumped him onto the mattress.

A brief struggle got my belt free, and Lee shut the door. "Do we check the other two rooms?"

"You got a better idea?" I checked the stunner. "I've got one more shot before I need to recharge this thing."

"Let's make it count, then." He grabbed the next door handle in his right hand and counted down with his left. On one, he flicked the unlock code and jerked the door open.

I lunged forward, stunner aimed into the dark room.

Nothing moved.

I waved my hand inside the door, and the lights came on. "Evy!" The major lay on a mattress on the floor, her face covered in sweat. Shoving the weapon into my pocket, I hurried inside and checked her pulse. "She's got a fever. Don't they treat prisoners' medical conditions?"

Lee tossed me the medical kit from his backpack. "Any bets the next one is Torres?"

I shook my head and went to work on Evy. The ScanNSeal clamped around her arm and checked her vital signs. Her quick breathing seemed to slow as the machine administered basic medications. The screen blinked red. "Med pod treatment required asap."

"Tell me something I don't know." I pressed the acknowledge button and pulled the cuff off her arm.

"Siti." Lee's soft call caught me by surprise. "We have a little problem. Could you come here?"

"In a minute." I pulled an emergency blanket from my pack and tucked it around Evy.

"No, now would be better." He sounded odd—uncertain and nervous.

With a last glance at Evy, I stood and walked into the third room.

"Crap."

CHAPTER TWENTY-FOUR

"Hello, Siti." Marika LaGrange, my first Explorer Corps friend and self-confessed Gagarian agent, sat on the cot in the last room. She held a blaster, pointed squarely at Lee's chest. Lee stared at her, the thumb of his right hand rubbing nervously against the middle finger.

I reached for my own weapon, but Marika's swung to me. "I wouldn't. Take off your weapon and drop it on the floor."

"Where's Joss?"

"Stop stalling. Take off the weapon." She rose from the narrow bed and took a step forward.

I stumbled back, trying to get out of range.

Marika jabbed her blaster at Lee again, pointing at his head. "Drop the weapon, Siti. Then take off the pack. And the grav belt while you're at it. Your friend has already complied." She kicked a grav belt by her feet.

"Or what, you'll kill Lee?" I stood completely still. "Go ahead, he's a *terkvard*."

Marika blinked. "That's not very nice. You aren't usually so callous."

"You obviously haven't spent any time with Lee." My heart pounded. I didn't like Lee, but that didn't mean I wanted him dead. Surely, she wouldn't shoot him in cold blood. "Where's Joss?"

"Give me the blaster, and we can talk." She waved her weapon at Lee again.

I released a breath I hadn't realized I'd been holding. "Fine." With trembling fingers, I unbuckled the belt and set the holstered gun on the ground.

"Slide it to me—with your foot."

I pushed the holster with my toes, shoving it across the tiny room.

Without taking her eyes off us, she stooped and pulled the blaster out of the holster. One-handed, she squeezed the release, and the charge pack dropped to the bed. The weapon landed on the opposite end of the mattress. She lifted the charger and tucked it into a pocket. Then she pulled out a stunner and holstered her own blaster.

"In." She backed into the corner of the tiny room and waved the stunner from us to the mattress. "Sit."

Lee and I exchanged a look and sat.

"Where's Joss?" I asked again.

"He's fine. None of your concern. What are you doing here?"

"We crashed. Didn't you see our ship?"

She backed around to the door and leaned against the jamb. "Right. You just happened to crash on *this* moon."

"You know the CEC is exploring Qureshi—the ice planet." I waved at the ceiling, as if she could see it. "We were on our way to the ship when the shuttle malfunctioned. I don't know what happened—I'm not a pilot or a mechanic. But we ended up here. Do you think they'd send an officer and three cadets to investigate your camp?"

"That's pretty much what Joss said. Why were you going back to the ship?" Her expression convinced me she knew the answer to this as well.

"I got in trouble. It's my specialty." I shrugged as if I didn't care.

"No, your specialty was getting out of trouble. Daddy wasn't here to help this time, though." Her lips pressed together. "Now what am I going to do with you? You shouldn't have come."

"I told you, we didn't have any control over that."

"No, I mean you two shouldn't have come *here*. To the base. I convinced my superiors there were only two people on board, not four."

"We weren't going to leave Joss and Evy locked up." I surged up from the bed.

Marika swung her stunner around and fired at Lee. He collapsed to the bed, his head landing where I'd been sitting. The muzzle was aimed at my face before I could blink.

"Next time, that's you." She pointed at the bed. "Sit down."

I pushed Lee's upper body toward the wall and perched in front of him on the edge of the bed. "What do you want?"

"I wanted to let you go, but that's not going to happen now."

My heart lurched. "It can totally happen. Joss and I can carry them. We've got grav belts—we just—"

"It's not going to happen because they know you're here." Her head jerked, indicating the other side of the base. "If you'd stayed away, you'd have been safe—they weren't looking anymore. Heck, if you hadn't cut that hole in the wall, I might have been able to let you leave, but how do I explain that?"

"You would have let us leave?"

"No."

"Stop messing with me, Marika. What's going to happen to us?"

She rubbed her forehead. "I don't know. If the CEC comes looking for you, they'll find us, and we obviously don't want that. Did your ship broadcast an emergency beacon before you landed?"

I thought quickly. If the CEC didn't know we were on this moon, the Gagarians could ship us off to Gagarin—or kill us outright—with no repercussions. "I'm sure it did. I'm surprised they haven't already come."

"That's a pretty good indication they have no idea what happened to you." Marika sagged against the doorjamb again. "That's not good, Siti, not good at all. For you. It's great news for me."

"Look, if you're just going to taunt me, why don't you go away?"

"Believe it or not, I'm trying to help you." She pinched the bridge of her nose. "But I'm not going to do anything to put myself—or my mission—at risk."

"What is your mission?"

"That's none of your business. How'd you get on base?"

"I have secret override codes for all Gagarian force shields."

She chuckled. "You wish. How'd you do it? Did you come in from the lava river?"

"Of course. I can't believe your people left the whole side of the base open. And what about the toxic air?"

"We weren't expecting human visitors." She tossed the stunner from one hand to the other. "And the reports on the atmospheric composition might have been erroneous."

I leaned forward, ready to spring up.

She held up her free hand. "Don't bother. I'm faster than you and completely ambidextrous." She glanced at a device strapped to her wrist. "Sunrise in forty minutes. I need to decide what to do with you before then."

My eyes narrowed. "You're the only one who knows we're here, aren't you? Why haven't you told anyone about us?"

"I like you. I always have. You were a good friend, and I don't want to see anything happen to you. If you would take your buddy here—"

"Not my buddy." Although I wasn't completely sure of that anymore. He was definitely a better friend than Marika.

"Fine, if you would take your enemy and go away, I'd let you do that. I could blame the hole in the wall on Ferken—the drunk in the first cell. I could probably come up with some story—but it doesn't matter because you won't take that deal, will you?"

"You want me and Lee to leave? Not without Evy and Joss." I crossed my arms.

"I was afraid that would be your answer. If you won't promise to stay away, I can't let you go." She pushed herself upright and stepped backward out the door. "I'm going to lock you both in here."

"Wait! What about Evy? Put me in with her, so I can take care of her!"

Marika shook her head. "The med team is treating her."

"They aren't doing a very good job!"

"They'll be back in twenty minutes. I don't want to explain why you're here."

"Then you'd better get our first aid kit out of that room."

Her eyes darted to the other door, then back to me. "Good call. If you're smart, you'll stay quiet. If they know you're here, I can't help you anymore."

I surged off the bed, but she closed the door in my face.

CHAPTER TWENTY-FIVE

"Where'd the redhead go?" Lee rolled onto his back, holding his head. "She was cute."

"She stunned you."

"Cute and aggressive. Just my type."

"Go back to sleep, idiot." I shoved his legs off the mattress so I could sit. "Look what I found!"

Lee sat up. "What?"

I held up the blaster Marika had dropped on the mattress. "She took the power pack, but she left the gun. Do you have a spare?"

Lee patted his pockets. "Sure, I carry a spare SK-175 power pack in my shorts, in case I need one."

"SK-175s will run on any power pack, as long as it has enough juice for the job. What d'ya got?" I held out my hand.

He pulled out his stunner. "She left me this, but I don't know if it's going to help."

"She left mine, too." I took his stunner and peered at the power pack. "It's not strong enough on its own, but maybe we can daisy chain the two of them."

"Do you know how to do that?"

"No, but it can't be too hard, right?" I pulled the battery off the stunner and tilted it into the light.

"She left your holo-ring." Lee pointed at my hand.

"So? I can't do much with it, remember? My comms were quarantined, and my local apps frozen."

"You can control the drones."

"No, I can't."

He looked away. "Yeah, you can. I lied when I said your comm lock would prevent that."

"What the heck, Lee? I thought we were supposed to be partners? What happened to the truce?"

"I was afraid you might—" He broke off. "Never mind. Try the drones."

Afraid I might what? Leave him here? The idea was looking more attractive. "The drones would be helpful if we could get out of this room." I flicked the ring and opened the drone app. The drones were still in place. One watched the HLP in the clearing where we'd crashed while the other circled the base. I zoomed in on the center of the camp. "There's no one outside. It would be great if we could open the door."

"Let me use your ring." Lee held out his hand. "I'll fly the little drone inside this building, so we can see what's in the outer room."

I hesitated. Even though my ring wasn't much use right now, giving it to Lee seemed like a bad idea. On the other hand, if he was managing the drones, I could work on this power pack. I twisted it off and handed it to him. "That's not gonna fit your fat fingers."

Lee raised his left hand, slid the ring on his pinky, and wiggled his fingers. "My fingers aren't fat—they're muscular. And my lightning quick pilot reflexes will save the day."

I rolled my eyes as hard as I could. He wasn't paying attention. With a sigh, I slid the covers off the charge packs, exposing the connectors. "You got any wire?"

Without responding, he reached into a pocket and produced a small toolkit.

I opened the kit and pulled out a cable with a universal connector. "Marika is really slipping. I can't believe she left any of this in here."

"Not much of a spy, is she?"

"No, she's very good. Which means she did all of this on purpose." I shook my head. "She's trying to help us without helping us. Think. There's gotta be a way to open that door." I stood and pressed my hand against the flat surface. "Did that move?" I pressed the door again, with a short, hard jab.

The door popped open. I stared at it in amazement.

Lee leapt up, grabbed the blaster, and yanked the door open. "Let's go."

I followed him into the outer room. Our gear sat stacked in a corner. "What about Evy?"

"We'll come back for her." He slung his backpack over one shoulder and tossed my grav belt at me.

I caught it, scooped up the ScanNSeal, and tossed it into my bag, then followed him out the door.

WE HURRIED into the narrow alley between the modules. At the far end, a wide stretch of empty plasphalt stood between us and the jungle.

I grabbed Lee's arm. "We can't get out that way. We need to go back to the lava side."

"I'm not trying to get out." Lee shook off my hand. "I'm going to steal that shuttle."

I grabbed his arm again, squeezing hard. The muscle under my hand felt like a rock. "You said we'd come back for Evy. And Joss. If we fly away, we'll never get back in."

"If we fly away, we can come back with the full might of the Explorer Corps behind us. They can take down the whole base and rescue Joss and Evy."

"If they come back in time. As soon as you steal that shuttle, Joss and Evy become liabilities. There's nothing to stop the Gagarians from killing them and dumping their bodies in the lava river. 'We didn't see any other survivors.'" I held up my hands in mock innocence.

"There's more at stake here than rescuing your friends." Lee pulled away and stalked along the back wall of the prison module.

I hurried after him and grabbed his arm again. "What do you mean?"

"Think, Kassis. The CEC doesn't know anything about this base. It's our responsibility to fill them in. I think getting that information out is more important than your friends' lives."

I dropped his arm as if it had burned me. "You really think that? Who cares if they have a base here? Eventually, someone else will discover it. And besides, if we save Joss and Evy, then we can *all* return to the ship and tell them about the base."

"Evy is too injured to walk. And we have no idea where Torres is. But I do know where the shuttle is. I'm going to take it and get the word out. If you want to stay here with your friends, go for it." Without waiting for a response, he darted across another narrow alley and ran along the back wall of the last building to the flight line.

I stared after him, the churning in my stomach making me want to vomit. A small part of me agreed with him, which made me feel even more sick.

On the other hand, him stealing the shuttle would give me the opportunity to look for Joss. I couldn't manage Evy on my own, but with Joss's help, we should be able to escape. The shuttle launch would provide a perfect distraction.

Ducking low, I dashed across the narrow alley and tugged on the hem of Lee's jacket. "How long will it take you to get that thing running?"

He glanced back at me. "No idea. A lot depends on how different it is from our shuttles. Will your translation program work on technical stuff?"

"You can't take my holo-ring!"

"I'll need it to get the shuttle working. It's not going to do you any good."

"I don't have any way to control the drones without it." I grabbed his hand and tried to pull the ring off his finger.

He closed his fist and yanked his hand away. "I need it more than you. You can find mine and use it."

"What did she do with it? Maybe it's in your gear?"

He shook his head. "She put it in her pocket."

"Oh, right. All I have to do is find Marika, stun her, rifle through her pockets, and take your ring. It would be easier to steal someone else's."

"Well, there you go. Good luck."

I grabbed his arm again. "Wait. I'll let you keep it, but you need to help me, too. Wait twenty minutes before you start up the engines. I'm going to need a distraction to get them out of here, and you're it."

He turned and stared down at me. A faint pink glow on the horizon heralded the sunrise, and in the brighter light, his eyes were grave. "You should come with me. Your chances of getting them out of here are minuscule."

"I won't leave them behind. But we'll be counting on you to rescue us."

CHAPTER TWENTY-SIX

I COULDN'T BELIEVE I had said that. I was counting on *Derek Lee* to rescue me? What had the galaxy come to?

His lips twitched, as if he could hear what I was thinking. He handed me his stunner and the blaster. "Maybe you can get that power pack working. I won't need these on the shuttle."

I juggled the three weapons until I could get one of the stunners into my pocket. The blaster didn't work, but it looked wicked. The enemy would have to be very close to see that the power pack was missing, and I didn't intend to let anyone that close to me.

I slung the blaster strap over my shoulder and held it on my left side, so I could carry the stunner in my dominant hand. I nodded at Lee. "Good luck. Remember, I need twenty minutes."

He flicked my holo-ring and pulled up the drones. A team of three people, two in medgear and one heavily armed, marched down the wide center lane between the modules. "That looks like the medical team. Let them work on Evy while you get Torres free. I'm guessing he's in that last module—I saw the redhead go in there earlier."

We stood in silence, watching the team approach the small module and go inside.

Lee leaned close to my ear. "I'll leave the drones in place—hopefully you can access them later. Good luck." His lips brushed against my cheek before he pulled away.

"What was that for?" I hissed.

His brows came down in the center. "I said good luck. You've heard that phrase before, right?"

"I'm not talking about what you said, I'm talking about what you did."

He looked confused. "I don't know what you're talking about."

In the pink glow of the sunrise, it was impossible to tell for sure, but I thought he blushed. I shook it off. I could think about whether Lee had kissed my cheek later when we were all safe. I let go of the blaster long enough to punch his arm, then trotted away.

A chorus of small animal sounds began as the sun rose, the chirping and screeching covering any sound my feet might make. I could have used the grav belt, but the charge was low, and I needed it to carry Evy. I connected the belt to the solar panels in my jacket, which I had spread over my backpack, tying the arms around the bag to hold it in place. It wouldn't do much good until the sun was higher in the sky, but every little bit would help.

I reached the rear of the last module—the one Lee thought Joss might be inside. Modules were made to be lived in on unexplored planets. In addition to solar radiation screens and air purifiers, the thin material provided an excellent sound barrier.

Or at least the CEC modules did. I'd always been told the Gagarians stole our tech and mimicked it, so I assumed these modules would be the same. Pressing my ear against the wall, I heard nothing but the creaking and chirping of the dawn chorus.

The alarms blared, sending my heart into overtime. So much for my twenty minutes. I clamped my hands over my ears and leaned against the module. The building shook as feet hit the floor, and the front door slammed open. Voices yelled, directing each other.

I peered around the corner of the building. The alley between the modules looked darker against the brilliant sunrise. These two modules were closer together, with barely room for me between. I crouched in the shadow, watching the Gagarians whiz by the other end on their way to the landing field.

Something clamped onto my shoulder. I spun around, but no one was there. It was Liam. He chittered in my ear.

"You scared the crap out of me," I whispered as I slid a hand over his soft fur. "Did you set off that alarm?"

The glider explained in detail what he'd done—too bad I didn't understand glider. While he chattered, I crept to the other end of the building. I popped out far enough to look both directions—no one in sight. In the distance, voices called to each other, sounding frustrated. I grinned. "Good work, Liam."

The front door of the module swung open at my touch, into a room with uncomfortable-looking couches and a low table. Three bright bars of light glowed in the ceiling, revealing mud on the floor, threadbare cushions, and dirty dishes on the table. I hurried across the room and listened at the first of three doors.

Nothing.

Pulling the stunner from my pocket, I turned the handle and swung the door open. This room was dark. Light from the main room spilled in, revealing rows of hammocks, all of them empty. The responders obviously bunked here.

I checked the next room. Four sinks lined one wall, with a couple of stalls at the back that probably held showers and toilets. Water dripped, and the place smelled damp and musty.

The third door revealed another bunk room. A series of pillars provided hooks for about two dozen empty hammocks, hanging two high. I ventured inside. The lights flared on. There were no obvious cells—Joss wasn't here.

Liam leaped from my shoulder and soared from pillar to post in a circle of the room. He stopped in the middle, swinging on an empty upper hammock.

"What did you find?" I ducked through the first row of hammocks to reach him. As I approached, the little glider jumped from end of the hammock, diving into the limp center. Seconds later, his head popped above the edge.

I pushed the loose fabric apart. Liam sat in a nest of blankets. "There's nothing here." I reached in to push the cloth aside, and my fingers hit something hard.

I stared at the small rectangle—a power block—my mind a blank.

Liam chittered.

I lifted the battery pack. "This is the blaster charger. How did you…?"

Liam dropped his lower jaw in a glider grin, then jumped out of the hammock and launched himself toward the entrance. He balanced on the top of the door, waiting.

With a satisfying clunk, the charger snapped into the empty blaster. I climbed through the rank of limp hammocks and stopped by Liam. "Can you find Joss?"

He made a soft noise, then darted back into the darker room. Across the outer room, the door rattled. I flung myself after Liam.

The glider landed on the lockers at the rear of the room and ran along the tops. He stopped on the third from the end and tapped his front paws against the door. Voices murmured in the outer room.

I yanked the locker open and climbed into the empty box. My backpack caught on the door frame. I slid the heavy bag from my shoulders and twisted around to face the front. The locker was almost two meters tall, but narrow. The sides pressed against my shoulders. I pulled the bag in, balancing it on my feet, then set the butt of the blaster on top of the bag. Liam swung himself around the top of the frame and landed on my shoulder. Then I pulled the door shut. It closed with a loud click.

Narrow slots in the door provided ventilation as well as surprisingly good visibility. A group of Gagarians straggled into the room, their uniforms sloppy, their hair mussed. Hammocks swung as they climbed and rolled in, some of them obviously complaining, but most moving like zombies. Liam's multiple alarm triggers had worn out the guard.

Marika paused by the hammock in the middle of the room. She felt inside, then froze. Her head turned slowly, taking in every centimeter of the small space. Her eyes raked every surface, pausing, then moving on. As her gaze approached my hiding place, my chest tightened. She would find me. Somehow, she'd sense I was here. She'd yank open the door, or worse, fire her blaster at the locker without even checking.

My eyes squeezed shut, and I held my breath, praying for a distraction.

A voice yelled. A chorus of mutters replied, and the room went quiet.

I opened my eyes. Darkness greeted them—thick and black in this windowless box. Liam rubbed against my cheek, giving me a sliver of comfort. I leaned my head against the side of the locker and listened.

Around us, the Gagarians settled. Even breathing dropped into faint snores. Someone coughed; a voice muttered.

Soft footsteps slid across the floor. Marika—she'd spotted me.

CHAPTER TWENTY-SEVEN

ALARMS BLARED. Lights flared on. I squeezed my eyes against the glare, peering through the ventilation slots. Voices groaned and swore.

Marika spun, heading back to her hammock. Around her, the others rolled out of bed again, moaning and groaning.

The Gagarians disappeared faster than they'd arrived a few minutes before, the door slamming shut behind them.

I counted to thirty, then fumbled for the locker catch. The door swung open unexpectedly, and Liam and I fell out. I caught myself on the backpack, barely keeping my grip on the blaster. Liam pushed off my shoulder and landed on a hammock.

The lights popped on. "I knew you were here." Marika stood beside the door, aiming a stunner at me. "Why couldn't you just leave, like I asked?"

My heart pounded, and sweat broke out on my upper lip. "You didn't ask me to leave." I ducked behind one of the hammocks. It wouldn't provide any protection, but it would make me harder to see.

"I practically gave you a key to the lockup, and I told you to go away. And now your friend is stealing a shuttle. Do you know what the commander will do to me? I convinced her there was no one else on that ship. Thanks for screwing me over."

"Come with me." I ducked low and moved to the end of the row of hammocks. "We can escape together."

"I wouldn't exactly be welcome in the Commonwealth." She shut the door and the lock clicked. Metal rattled, and a hammock fell as she unhooked it from the pillar to clear her line of sight. "The only thing that will save me is bringing you in."

I ducked behind another hammock. Liam launched himself the other direction. He clung to the side of a hammock, then scrambled along the side to the pillar at the end. Another hammock rattled and dropped.

I crouched behind the bottom row of hammocks, moving slowly up the side of the room. The slender pillars provided no cover at all. Another hammock dropped.

In a blur of blue and white fur, Liam launched himself from a pillar across the room, screeching as he flew at Marika's face.

The redhead cried out and flung up an arm to shield her face. I catapulted forward, slamming into the door. "Liam, jump!"

I fired my stunner as Marika turned. Blue static sizzled over her body. The glider leaped away as she went down.

Now what? I needed to find Joss, but I couldn't leave Marika lying here. The first person to trip over her would raise the alarm, and they'd know a fourth explorer was on the base. I needed someplace to hide her. Maybe the lockers?

I tapped the controls to her grav belt, and she lifted off the ground. A gentle push sent her toward the middle of the room, sliding between the hammocks she'd unhooked. I laughed. She'd made it easier for me to hide her.

With a flick, the grav belt raised her higher, and I rolled her into her own hammock. The belt snapped open easily, and I pulled it from beneath her limp body. I unstrapped the device on her arm and patted her pockets —no sign of Lee's holo-ring. Then I slapped a slip tie around her wrists and a piece of tape over her mouth.

When they found her, I hoped she wouldn't be blamed for my escape, but I wasn't going to worry about it too much. She'd kidnapped me and used me for cover back on Earth and tried to sabotage our whole assignment. Of course, she'd given us an escape earlier today, but I wasn't going to let a single good act cancel out all her backstabbing.

I threw the blanket over her still form, stifling concern and regret. She'd chosen her side, and I had mine. I couldn't let affection for the enemy overrule my good sense.

With all these thoughts of enemies and sides, I was starting to think like Lee. Maybe that was a good thing. We were stranded on a Gagarian base with no chance for rescue—a downed-warrior attitude should serve me well.

Time to blend in. I rifled through the lockers until I found a Gagarian jacket that would fit me reasonably well. I shucked my pressure suit, holding my nose as I did so—after this long, it was ripe. I shoved it into a recycler and pulled the plain black coat over my CEC gear. If anyone looked closely, they would know I wasn't one of them, and on a base this small, they probably knew each other by sight. I'd do my best to stay far away from anyone else.

I wrapped Marika's wrist device around my arm and tapped the surface. Nothing happened. I pulled Marika's arm from under the blanket and pressed her thumb to the surface. The device lit up. *Hah!*

Although the prompts were in Gagarian, it was easy enough to find the settings and add my own thumbprint to the activation group.

Liam cheeped at me.

"You're right, we need to go. Find Joss."

Through the Gagarian wrist device, I was able to access the cameras scattered around the base. Lee's loop inserter would be handy, but I didn't have time to search the whole building looking for his ring. Joss was my first priority. Then we could break out Evy and escape to the jungle until Lee sent rescue.

If he sent rescue. I wasn't sure I could trust him to come back for us. He obviously hated Joss, and deep down, he probably still blamed me for his loss of status at the Academy. Leaving us behind might feel like justice to him.

But when he docked on the *New Dawn*, they'd want to know how he got a Gagarian shuttle. And where his copilot and passengers—or prisoners—had gone. They'd have to send a SAR team. I needed to get Joss out and hide.

Or turn myself in.

The thought exploded in my brain like a firework as I crept out of the barracks and slipped into the narrow alley between the buildings. I could walk away and hide in the jungle until help came. The Gagarians were treating Evy's medical problems—I'd seen the med team headed toward her cell. And now that Lee had escaped with the shuttle, they'd know the CEC would be coming to investigate. The Gagarians were squatting here illegally—surely it would be politically advantageous to return healthy prisoners rather than dead bodies?

If I released Marika, I could let her take me to the base commander. I could tell them we'd gotten a message out and that when Lee landed, the CEC would be coming. I was a pretty good schmoozer—I should be able to convince the commander to keep us alive. We weren't enemy combatants or prisoners of war—we were stranded CEC explorers. We should be treated humanely and released.

But if Lee hadn't gotten out, they could kill us all.

Hiding in the dim alley, I checked the cams. The internal walkways were deserted. The perimeter of the base bustled with Gagarians, sweeping along the force shield. A handful of older soldiers—probably officers, although like the others, they wore no rank—stood on the landing pad, talking. I wished I could hear them.

A few swipes brought the device's setting menu up again. I cursed under my breath, wishing I still had my translator program. One of these settings would probably pair my audio implant to the device, but I couldn't tell which one. I needed to get closer.

I turned my head and spoke into Liam's silky fur. "Can you go up on the roof? See if there's anyone above the base."

Liam chirped, then flung himself up the wall behind me. He scrambled up the side and disappeared over the top. I slid down the wall across the alley, resting my back against it as I crouched, watching the top. I fiddled with the wrist device while I waited.

Liam's head popped over the edge, and he whistled, mimicking the local creatures. I tapped my grav belt and rose, stopping below the top of the wall. A quick peek confirmed Liam's assessment—there was no one on top of the buildings and no one hovering above. Their stupidity was my good fortune. I rose a little higher and rolled onto the flat roof.

The modules were badly camouflaged. The mottled green, brown, and black contrasted sharply with the darker green and bright purples predominant in the jungle around the base. Combined with the rectangular landing pad, this failure had made the base easy to spot from our landing site.

Luckily for me, the Gagarians' uniforms were equally poorly camouflaged, which meant I blended into the dark roof. Liam, however, stood out like a bright blue light. I reached out a hand. "Get in here."

Liam climbed into my jacket and disappeared inside. His warm body pressed against my side as he squirmed into an internal pocket.

I lifted a few centimeters above the roof and skimmed over it, pausing at the far edge. A quick look revealed no one below, so I crossed the narrow alley and slid across the next building.

This was the module next to the one that housed Evy. I stopped by the air vent, listening, but could hear nothing. Joss could be right below me, and I'd never know. I pushed off again and made it to the last module. I hovered just above the roof and crept to the edge.

Below, the four officers still stood in a loose knot. They wore jackets identical to mine, and only one of them—a tall, broad-shouldered woman—wore the glint of a personal shield. They must have determined the atmosphere—at least inside their camp—was safe. Marika had implied as much. Of course, Gagarian standards were notoriously low, and their lack of care for the health of their citizenry was well known in the CEC.

Still, it was reassuring since I no longer had a helmet or pressure suit. I twisted my jacket so Liam's pocket was not under my body and settled to the roof to listen.

"...have to land. A fifty-klick search pattern should find him easily. Comm is redeploying the mini-sats to cover the area." A tall, thin man waved a languid arm at the sky

"Belay that. We need comm coverage over the whole moon. We have two more units out there, and they'll be in the dark if you redeploy.

Besides, we don't want them to know we've got a problem." This woman was short, with a wide body and dark hair graying in patches.

I scooched forward, the rough surface of the roof grating loudly—at least in my ears—against my jacket. The officers below didn't appear to notice.

It sounded like Lee hadn't gotten the shuttle off the moon—was there something keeping him from achieving orbit?

But why were they speaking Standard? Surely, they'd use Gagarian on their own base. Unless they weren't really Gagarians?

They had to be. Marika was here. And the people who'd investigated our crash had spoken Gagarian. Maybe these officers spoke Standard so the rank-and-file couldn't understand them? But Marika had spoken flawless Standard. I shrugged it off. Whatever the reason, it was good news for me.

A taller woman cleared her throat. "The FlightChief sent three flitter teams—they'll catch up to him in no time. Maybe if we're lucky, he'll crash the thing."

"That would not be good luck. How would I explain the loss of our only shuttle to command?" The short woman's tone was harsh.

The taller woman took a step back. "You're right, sir. But do Commonwealth pilots learn to fly Gagarian shuttles? The chances that he'll crash must be high."

"Our shuttles are very similar in design to theirs. Dirty capitalists have stolen Gagarian Space Force innovations for generations." The tall man laughed, and the others joined him.

I swallowed a growl. Gagarians had been stealing *our* tech for generations, not the other way around.

"Keep a double watch on the perimeter. And conduct a complete search of the base—in case they left something behind. We don't need to discover a bomb the hard way. And I want a constant guard on both the woman and the boy."

The tall woman spoke for the first time. "With the flitter teams and a double guard, I don't have personnel for a full-time watch on both prisoners."

"Then put the boy in with the woman. Interrogation isn't getting anything out of him." The squat woman turned sharply as she spoke and marched toward the wide walkway between the modules. The others followed.

Having Joss and Evy together made my job easier. But the mention of interrogation made my blood run cold.

I waited until the officers had disappeared, then slithered back to the cell module. The sun rose overhead as I waited. The tang of shuttle fuel disappeared behind the almost fruity smell of the jungle. I wiped sweat from my forehead and wished I could remove the Gagarian jacket.

Liam climbed out of my pocket and stretched out beside me, his blue fur glinting in the sun.

"Move into the shade—they'll see you."

Liam didn't move, but his fur seemed to lose its bright sparkle. I stared at the glider. He didn't look any different than normal, but a second ago, his fur had been so bright, and now—

Movement caught my eye. The door of the middle building across the walkway opened, and three people came out. My eyes zeroed in on the center figure—Joss.

He looked bad. His face was gray and pasty, and he had dark circles under his eyes. His hands were secured behind his back, and he stumbled a little as he walked, nearly falling. The two soldiers made no move to help him, leaving at least a meter between themselves and their captive.

Joss stopped, his eyes blinking rapidly as he stared around the base. The soldier behind jabbed the muzzle of his weapon between Joss's shoulders and muttered.

Joss waited a second longer, then stepped forward slowly, deliberately provoking his captors. The guy in back poked him again, but Joss maintained his leisurely pace.

Liam leaped off the roof, soaring overhead.

I bit my lip to keep from yelling and dropped flat, pressing my cheek to the gritty roof, hoping they wouldn't spot me.

The glider banked and dove, swooping toward the three. He disappeared below the roofline. One of the captors shouted, and their weapons cocked. I held my breath, waiting for a shot to be fired.

"Run!" Joss yelled. "They know you're here!"

Something thudded, and Joss grunted. I jumped to a crouch and activated my grav belt. As I turned, I judged the distances, then raced for the far end of the building. At the edge, I pushed off hard and hit the lift button on my belt, hoping to combine my momentum with the belt's internal drive system to get the most speed possible.

The belt whined and went silent. I dropped like a rock.

CHAPTER TWENTY-EIGHT

My face and body stung from slamming into the paving. Luckily, the moon's light gravity meant I didn't break anything. I pushed up on my hands and knees and checked the belt. A dead power pack. I threw myself forward.

Feet pounded and a team of Gagarians converged on me, weapons drawn.

I raised my hands. "I surrender."

"Up." Rough hands grabbed my arms and dragged me to my feet. A man yanked the blaster from my arm and pulled off my backpack, wrenching my right shoulder in the process.

With one soldier holding each arm, they marched me across the tarmac to the main walkway. We met Joss and his captors in front of the building. He looked even worse close up. Both his eyes were bloodshot and deeply shadowed. There was blood on the collar of his jacket, and his hair was matted and greasy.

Of course, after three days on the run, I'm sure I didn't look much better. "Hi, Joss." I tried a carefree smile. "Thanks for the warning. I guess I wasn't fast enough."

His lips twitched. "Least I could do."

The guard holding my arm shook it and pushed me forward. "Move."

A woman opened the door, and they pushed us inside. Joss's captors threw him into the room where we'd found Marika and shut the door. One of them said something in Gagarian to my guard, and they all laughed.

"Strip." The man holding my arm shook it again.

My insides went cold. I took a deep breath and pulled myself upright. "I beg your pardon?"

The man tapped his arm. "Give strip."

The light went on inside my brain. He wanted the wrist device. I unfastened it and handed it to him. "Those things are really bulky. You should get rings like we have."

The man shoved the device in his pocket and regarded me stonily. He flicked his blaster muzzle against my collar. "Off."

I unfastened the pilfered jacket and slid it off. My shoulder protested, but I tried not to wince. I held out the jacket. "Here you go. I don't think it's your size." He made no move to take it, so I dropped it on the floor.

The woman behind me picked up the coat and tossed it to one of Joss's guards. The man said something, and the two left, taking my blaster with them.

"Off." The woman jutted her chin at me.

I pulled on the front of my CEC jacket. "This? You want this? It has nice patches, doesn't it? Do you guys collect them?" When they didn't respond, I took the jacket off, handing it to her with a sigh. My stunner was in the pocket.

The woman stepped closer, staying out of the man's line of sight, and patted down my arms, legs, and torso. Then she spoke to the man and opened the third cell—the one where the drunk had been sleeping.

It was empty now, although the pants and coat still lay on the floor. The male guard jerked his blaster at the door, and I took that as an invitation to move inside. Before I could turn, the door slammed shut, leaving me in darkness.

Another door thudded, but I heard nothing after that.

"Joss? Can you hear me?" I yelled.

His voice came faint and rough. "I can hear you."

"Evy, are you awake?" I tried again.

Evy didn't respond.

I dropped onto the mattress, sliding it with the force of my landing. The rough fabric felt damp under my fingers, in the way cloth does in humid areas. I hoped the drunk hadn't vomited anywhere. I didn't smell anything except the stale scent of his clothing and the faint fruitiness of the jungle.

Now what? If I'd understood the officers correctly—something clicked in my brain. Those officers had been speaking Standard because they wanted me to know Lee hadn't made it off the moon. He'd obviously launched the ship. What had kept him from leaving orbit?

Or had that been part of their plan? Maybe Lee was well on his way to the *New Dawn,* but they wanted me to *think* he'd been forced down. Either way, they'd caught me in their trap. I should have used his launch to escape instead of stopping to listen to them. But hindsight was golden, right?

That platitude didn't sound quite right, but I let it go.

My eyes had grown accustomed to the darkness. An air vent near the floor let in a little light—it must have been hidden behind the mattress before. Based on its location, it connected to Major Evy's room. Using my fingernails, I pried at the louvered cover.

It popped off, and I peered through the slits on the far side. The lights were on, and Evy lay in a med pod. They must have decided her injuries were too dangerous to leave to chance. Maybe the Gagarians weren't going to kill us after all. But that didn't mean I wanted to stay locked up.

I could punch the air vent cover off, but it would wind up in the middle of the floor, which would alert anyone who came in that I'd done it. If it was missing completely, they might not notice. I squinted around the room, looking for anything I could use.

The drunk's uniform caught my eye. Lifting the pants with two fingers, I gingerly went through the pockets. A handful of damp papers—based on the markings, they were used as bets in a poker game. An empty plastek flask. My fingers hit something sticky—a half-eaten protein bar. Ew. I dropped it on the floor.

The jacket pockets netted more poker IOUs, a lip balm, and—unbelievably, one of those wrist band devices I'd stolen from Marika. Probably deactivated—since they'd let him keep it—or maybe they left drunks in here until they were sober enough to figure out how to open the door.

I strapped it on my wrist but couldn't activate it. If it was like Marika's, it would require the drunk's thumb print. Perfect. I fiddled with the buttons and got it to light up. The increased illumination did not make my cell any more inviting.

My stomach growled—it had been a long time since Lee and I ate, and my rations were in the backpack they'd confiscated. I looked at the sticky protein bar. Maybe I could nibble the unchewed end.

I shuddered. I'd have to be a lot hungrier before I tried that. I wiped my fingers on the jacket, stickiness adhering to the thick fabric. An old caper vid I'd watched popped into my head.

"That can't possibly work." I said the words out loud, but they didn't stop me from trying.

I tapped the button on the wrist device and brought the light up to full. Carefully grabbing the corners of the protein bar, I shone the light on the packaging.

There. A huge, smudgy fingerprint. Too big to be mine. Could I use it to unlock the wrist device? I shook the package and dropped the bar onto the ground. Then I held the sticky fingerprint over the screen and moved it around.

Nothing.

I slid my finger inside the package and carefully pressed the sticky bit against the device. The light on the screen changed and words scrolled across. Success!

I couldn't read the Gagarian, so I ignored it and went through the settings as I had with Marika's to add my own sticky thumb print.

Wrist device activated, I wiped my hands on the jacket again and applied a little spit to clean the gunk off the screen.

Now what? Would it open the door? I paged through the screens, trying to decipher the foreign words. Luckily, the functions were very similar to a holo-ring's, so navigating the interface was relatively easy. And many of the icons seemed to be universal—as one might expect from copied tech. It was odd that they used these much bulkier wrist devices instead of holo-rings, but maybe their copycat program wasn't as good as everyone claimed.

The word "Commonwealth" popped up. This would have something to do with us—if I could get this device back to the ship, who knew what espionage information they might find? I pressed the icon. A microphone icon appeared.

"What now?" I muttered.

Two Gagarian words came out of the device. Aha. A translator. Could I get it to go the other direction?

With a little more trial and error, and my limited Gagarian vocabulary (please, thank you, where is the toilet?), I figured out how to make it work both directions. By reading the screen aloud, I was able to decipher more of the device's apps. Which led me to the door release control.

The door swung ajar. I peeked into the outer room, but it was deserted. The hole we'd cut in the side wall had been taped over. The rest of the room was empty. I deactivated the lock on Joss's door. It swung open into darkness.

"Joss?" I whispered.

Something hit me like a shuttle at takeoff. I went down, slamming into the plastek floor and knocking the breath out of my lungs. A man landed on top of me, pinning me to the ground. A huge fist came at my face, almost in slow motion, and stopped centimeters from my nose.

"Siti?" Joss sat back, still straddling my hips.

"I've come to rescue you." I grinned.

"That's 'I'm here to rescue you.'" He pushed himself off me and offered a hand to pull me up. "Only you would get the secret password wrong."

"That's how you know it's really me." I threw my arms around him. He grunted, and I jumped back. "What did they do to you?"

"You should see the other guy." He pressed a hand to his ribs. "I think they cracked one."

"They tortured you?"

"No, I got all this when they tried to capture me." He gestured to the bruising on his face and back at his ribs. "You really should see the other guy—it took three of them to take me down, and I did a fair job on the first two." He flexed, then winced.

"We need to get out of here. I think I can unlock Evy's door." I tapped the wrist device and the door opened. "Too bad we're on a tight schedule—you could use her med pod."

We entered the dimly lit room. The med pod hummed in its corner. The countdown on its cover indicated two more hours of treatment. Evy's clothing sat on the end of the pod. I tapped the screen.

Joss stood sideways in the open doorway, watching our backs. "What happens if you open one of these things early? Will she come out half-baked?"

"Depends on the injury." I scrolled through the medical information, but it was in Gagarian. Maybe my wrist thing had a text translator, too. I tapped the tiny screen. "She might be better off if we leave her here. Since they're healing her, they probably won't kill her outright. Did they question you?"

"They asked why we came here, how we knew they had a base—I told them we didn't. It was all an accident."

"Was it?" The device stubbornly refused to translate the med pod screen. I picked up Evy's jacket. "We can talk about this later. I think we should go. We'll leave Evy here and come back for her when she's healthy enough to keep up with us."

"Where are we going to go? We don't have any supplies or weapons. What kind of rescue is this, anyway?"

"I had two grav belts and a blaster, but for some reason my captors didn't let me keep them." I slid my arms into the jacket. "I'm taking this—no point in leaving it here for them."

"Good call—there's important stuff in that flight jacket."

"What do you mean?" I stuck my hands in the pockets, but they came up empty. "There's not even a meal pac in here."

Joss held a finger to his lips and crossed to the external door. He put his ear against the panel. "Can't hear anything."

"How about here?" I crouched by the hole Lee had cut and listened. "Nothing. Help me get this tape off."

"Why?" Joss came over and started pulling at the thick gray stuff.

"There's a guard out front—I heard them talking about guarding you." I paused. That had been part of the conversation staged on the flight pad.

Maybe it hadn't been true. "They *might* have put a guard on the door. We might have a better chance if we sneak out the side."

The sticky tape pulled away easily, revealing the cut edges of the plastek. I pulled the thin panel inward, and Joss darted a look outside. He gave me a thumbs-up and crawled through. I followed.

The sun had almost reached its apex, and bright light streamed into the narrow alley between the modules. Joss pointed up, then laced his fingers together.

I stepped into his joined hands, and he winced. His ribs must be killing him, but the light gravity made the lift easier. I grabbed the top edge of the wall and pulled myself up. As I rolled aside, Joss pulled himself up, his face contorted in pain. He rolled onto the roof and huddled there panting, a hand clutched to his side.

I pointed at him, then at the roof beneath us, telling him to stay put. He nodded, so I crept forward on my elbows to the front of the small building. A quick look over the side revealed a guard standing on the front step. A pair of Gagarians, fully armed, marched away from us down the wide walkway, heading for the far side of the compound. In the distance, more soldiers patrolled the perimeter.

I twisted around to face Joss, but he still lay on his back with his eyes closed. I probably should have left him behind, too. Now what? We couldn't stay here too long—the medics would be back in less than two hours. I bit my lip and winced as my teeth hit a sore spot.

I looked along the walkway. The two patrolling soldiers had disappeared around one of the modules. It was now or never. If anyone was watching cams, this would alert them to our escape, but Joss needed a grav belt if we were going to get anywhere.

Before I could chicken out, I swung my body over the edge of the building.

CHAPTER TWENTY-NINE

The lower gravity meant landing on the guard's head didn't do much damage. He crumpled under my weight but caught himself before his head impacted the ground. I got an arm around his neck and pulled, tightening my grip with my other hand. The guard struggled, heaving and bucking, then collapsed.

Without releasing my chokehold, I flicked the door lock on my wrist device. I dragged the man through the door, the low gravity assisting me this time. Another unlock got me back into my cell. My captive jerked a couple of times, but I'd been taught that was a natural occurrence in a choke-out.

I dropped the guy next to the mattress and started counting. If my instructors had been correct, he'd start to wake in eight to sixteen seconds. It took me seven seconds to yank off his weapon and his own wrist device. I searched his pockets—four more seconds. My search yielded a protein bar—fully wrapped—and a stunner.

The man blinked and his head moved.

"Sorry." I fired the stunner, sending blue lightning over his prone body. His eyes dropped closed, and his head thunked as he lost consciousness again. I removed his grav belt and jacket. Then I used his thumbprint to activate the second wrist device and add my own login.

Taking my loot, I closed the door behind me. I scooped up the cap my prisoner had dropped on the way in and crawled out through the hole in the wall. Then I used the grav belt to return to the roof. "As soon as they notice the guard missing, they'll be after us."

Joss blinked up at me. "What did you do?"

I removed the belt and shoved it at him. "Got some gear. Put this on. And this." The second "this" was the jacket. He slid his arms into the sleeves and fastened it. I handed him the blaster. "If anyone spots us, pretend you've got me in custody." I tossed him the cap and rolled off the edge of the building, dropping to the ground.

Joss followed, grunting in pain as he landed.

"Use the belt, caveman." I poked the control panel at his waist.

He rubbed his eyes. "Sorry, not thinking clearly."

I tiptoed between the buildings until we reached the broad stretch of empty plasphalt pad that separated the buildings from the jungle. I pointed out the soldiers pacing along the perimeter. They walked around the base at fifty-meter intervals—well within blaster range. "When that guy gets opposite us, take the stunner and fly out there to meet him. As soon as you get in range, take him down, and I'll follow you out."

Joss took the stunner and nodded. "You got it, boss." He handed the blaster back to me. "You might as well have this. As soon as I shoot, my cover is blown. Do you know what the range is on the stunners?"

I grimaced as I slung the heavy blaster over my shoulder. Even in the low gravity, the thing felt unwieldy. "Probably ten meters? That's a guess. Get as close as you can." I pulled the cap lower over his eyes. "If they get close enough to see your features, they'll know you're an escapee."

"What gives me away, my stunning good looks?"

"That and the two black eyes. This is a small unit. They all must know each other." I glanced across the pavement. "Go. Now."

Joss lifted off the ground and zipped away. The guard opposite us noticed him almost immediately. She yelled in Gagarian. Joss tapped his ear, as if his comm wasn't working, and made a "come here" motion as he closed on his target.

The guard glanced at the soldier fifty meters ahead of her, then back over her shoulder. The man behind wasn't visible from here, but he must be within sight of our target. The woman nodded, then moved toward Joss.

The guy to our left came into view as he increased his speed to make up for the woman leaving the perimeter. They were too well organized. "This isn't going to work." I did some mental math. The jungle was forty meters away from the buildings. I could run that distance in about six seconds, but in this gravity, jumping might be more effective. I swung the blaster up to firing position and launched myself forward.

My foot hit the ground about two meters away. Flexing my knees, I let my momentum roll me forward on my sole and shoved off again. Within a few steps, I was flying across the yard, barely touching down long enough to give another push.

Someone shouted. Joss fired his stunner, taking the closest guard out. I flew past him, moving faster than I'd ever run before. My foot hit the ground and I pushed off again, slamming into the blue force shield.

"Ow!" I slammed to the ground. Idiot. Of course there was a force shield. The blue bollards glowed softly, as if mocking me.

Joss yanked the blaster from my shoulder and fired at the soldier approaching from the left. I slapped at my wrist device. Could I deactivate the field before they reached us?

I activated the second wrist device—the one I'd stolen from our guard. Using the first one to translate, I might find a force shield.

"What now?" Joss fired past me, sending the perimeter guard on our right scrambling for cover.

"I'll grab his belt. We can go over the side." I yanked the prone man's belt off and fastened it around my waist. Grabbing his blaster, I laid down a line of fire at the guy to our left. "Follow me."

I cranked my belt to top speed and launched toward the center of the base. The ranks had thinned, since they had people searching for Lee, but as soon as the alarm went up, everyone on this base would be firing at us. I stayed low, shooting between the buildings and across the wide central thoroughfare. A woman yelped and leaped out of the way.

"Keep going! I'm right behind you!" Joss yelled.

I banked hard, narrowly missing the corner of a module, and streaked into the alley between the two larger modules. A quick glance over my shoulder revealed Joss a couple of meters behind me. A handful of Gagarian guards arrowed after him.

Sixty meters to the edge of the canyon over the lava river. I straightened my flight vector, then rolled onto my back. Flying backwards like this was insane—I'd never see an obstacle in time to stop. But unless they'd installed a force shield on this side of the camp in the last few hours, there was nothing to hit. Except the walls sweeping by at eye-watering speed.

I lifted a couple of meters and fired my blaster over Joss's head. I didn't hit anything, but our pursuers ducked away, slamming into the enclosing walls. I flipped back to my stomach.

Joss yelled—something about the altitude and lava.

I burst out from between the buildings and rocketed across the broad strip of stone beyond the modules. With a tap, I increased my speed and rocketed over the edge of the cliff.

And then I fell.

CHAPTER THIRTY

"Crap!" I scrabbled at the grav belt controls, praying I hadn't run out of charge like last time. Heat pressed up at me, like opening an oven door. The fumes nearly overwhelmed me. I should have kept the pressure suit.

Thanks to the low gravity, I fell in slow motion. Hot, sulfur-heavy air blew into my face. Below, the glowing red lava river rapidly filled my field of vision. I curled up to peer at the control panel on my grav belt.

Luck was with me—grav belts were all built in the Commonwealth, so these had standard controls. I hit the altitude button and reset it to twenty meters.

With a stomach-churning lurch, I swooped away from the lava.

With the immediate threat eliminated, I took stock of my surroundings.

Crap.

The far wall of the canyon zoomed at me. I'd flown directly across the deep gorge, but my drop in altitude meant I wouldn't clear the top. But I'd become an expert grav belt flyer during my years on the Academy drill team. I rolled and swerved to my left, my toes brushing against the solid face, and sending a few loose rocks down into the river.

Vector corrected to run parallel to the canyon, I rolled onto my back to look for the enemy. Several of them hovered above the edge of the canyon, swinging their blasters in wide arcs as they tried to find us. Between my precipitous drop into the canyon and the superior camouflage capabilities of Evy's jacket, they seemed to have lost track of me. I zoomed toward the rocky wall.

The heat pulsed at me as I debated my options. The sun had passed its high point, so this side of the canyon was in shadow. The heat below me should mask my body temperature on any thermal scans. Evy's jacket protected me from the worst of the heat, but my legs and face were still vulnerable. I lifted a little higher and edged closer to the cliff wall, slowing my velocity.

I could try to find another ledge to hide on or return to the spot Lee and I had hidden—it seemed like weeks ago now. As I drifted closer to the crash site, I scanned the rocky face for another hiding place and wondered what had happened to Joss. I should have given him the extra wrist device and the coordinates for our ledge.

Far behind me now, the Gagarians lifted higher and scattered, presumably searching for us. They could have already captured Joss—they were far enough away that I'd never hear—

I gave myself a mental head smack and tapped one of the wrist devices. As I floated slowly upstream, I paged through the screens, looking for a communication system. The familiarity of the interface confirmed again the Gagarians' penchant for copying Commonwealth tech. I found an icon that looked familiar and activated it.

Voices shouted. I slapped the mute button. Even with the distance and the ambient noise of nature, I dare not risk alerting my searchers. I swiped and flicked through the screens, looking for a way to connect to my audio implant.

I stared at the tiny screen for three full seconds before realizing the familiar blue icon was exactly what I'd been looking for. I tapped it, then touched the device implanted behind my left ear. A chime sounded, then a voice asked if I'd like to connect.

"Yes." I waited, then tapped the flashing symbol on the wrist device.

"Connection complete. Translator activated."

Translator? In the device?

It didn't really matter. Voices spoke inside my ear in Standard.

"—keep looking. We'll be in deep—" a ping overrode the voice "—if we lose them again."

I recognized that ping—standard CEC obscenity override. Evy's jacket must have a translator built in. I fingered the collar and located the tiny module embedded there. My audio implant had connected to it when I put the jacket on—I just hadn't encountered any Gagarians in a chatty mood since then. I guess I was too busy running—or flying—for my life.

What other goodies might be built into Evy's jacket? Joss had said something about "important stuff" when I picked it up. This jacket was a different style from the standard-issue jacket the Gagarians had taken from me—the translator alone would be worth its weight in senidium. Without my holo-ring, I couldn't activate the personal shield, but maybe I could figure out a way to connect the Gagarian wrist device to it.

As I travelled slowly upstream, I listened to the Gagarians. As far as I could tell, they hadn't caught Joss or Lee yet. I tried changing channels but only had access to a single comm—apparently a general frequency for security personnel. I tried the second device and got the same. The chatter subsided over time as the soldiers settled in for a long, fruitless search. At least I hoped it was fruitless.

As dusk fell, I figured I must be getting close to the spot where Lee and I had hidden before. Without my holo-ring, I no longer had the coordinates to that ledge. If only Liam were here—he could find it, I knew. The Gagarians had said nothing about a glider, so I hoped he'd escaped, too.

I rose a little higher, pausing now and then to search the wall for our precarious outcropping. When I found a likely candidate, I lifted closer. The slanted shelf, the narrow overhang—it looked similar. I dropped to the rock and settled into the angle of the stone. It felt the same. Not that it mattered—I needed a place to rest, and this would serve. And if I was lucky, Liam would find me here.

I reached into my pocket and pulled out the wrapped protein bar I'd taken from the guard. I should have left it in the jacket for Joss. He'd probably gone longer without food than I had. I contemplated the pristine wrapper. There was no telling how long I'd be stuck on this moon without food. I should save it. Besides, these things always made me thirsty, and I had no water.

I settled back in my stony groove, staring up at the stars overhead. First thing tomorrow, I'd have to find water. In a jungle like this one, that shouldn't be difficult, but I had no means to test or purify it. Unless that was one of the secrets of Evy's flight jacket. But without Joss, I had no way of knowing.

Darkness settled in around me. One of the predators screamed. I wrapped my arms around myself—grateful for the warmth of Evy's coat. This ledge was a lot scarier without Lee. My eyes stung, and I fought back tears. I could pretend they were tears of anger—rage against the Gagarians who'd hunted us down and captured us. But I was alone, and even though I was armed and could be dangerous, I was also frightened and exhausted. What if I couldn't find the others? What if Lee never came back to rescue us? I didn't want to spend the rest of my life marooned on an enemy-held moon. Or worse, in a Gagarian prison.

I dropped into an uneasy doze, startled awake each time one of those cats howled.

I WOKE WITH A START, trying to get my bearings. High overhead, beyond the meager overhang, the sky lightened from inky black to deep gray. A splotch of wet dropped onto my face, hitting me square between the eyes—that must have been what woke me. I sat up, stiff from not moving for several hours.

According to the wrist device, it was just after twenty-six hundred hours. Gagarin had a twenty-seven-hour day, so they must be using that instead of local time. Based on the color of the sky, I estimated it was about three hours after midnight—nearly sunrise.

I turned on the Gagarian comm channel again. It was a risk—if they realized I'd taken and activated one of their devices, they could undoubtedly track me. But since they hadn't recaptured me, it was a fair guess they didn't know—or didn't track their nodes as carefully as the CEC did. This seemed like something Marika would have exploited—strange that she hadn't.

But she'd been trying to help us all along, or so she claimed. Maybe she was covering for us again. Or maybe the Gagarians were closing in around me. At that moment, I would have welcomed the company.

I waited a few more minutes, listening to the idle chatter on the device. They were tired—shift change wouldn't happen until twenty-six ninety-nine, which was soon, but not soon enough. Based on their reports, Lee and Joss were still at large. There'd been no mention of Liam.

I rubbed my arms, feeling the chill despite the heat wafting up from the lava fissure. I pulled Evy's coat more securely around me. It was a good thing pilots wore their jackets on the large size—I would not have fit in Evy's normal clothing. The sleeves only reached the middle of my forearms, and it was tight across the shoulders, but it protected me in the night.

Water dripped onto the spot where my head had been, beginning to create a tiny puddle. I dipped my finger into it, wondering if it was safe to drink. Not that it mattered—there wasn't enough moisture collected to scoop up.

I checked my grav belt. The charge hovered around thirty percent, so I'd better get onto solid ground. With a tap of my finger, the belt came to life and lifted me off the rocky ledge. Staying close to the cliff wall, I rose slowly, giving my jacket time to adjust its coloring as I approached the green and purple plants hanging over the edge.

As I lifted, I squinted through the thinning darkness, watching for movement amid the foliage. The screaming cats seemed to sleep in the early morning hours—or at least they stopped screaming. Maybe that was because they were too busy eating whatever they'd terrified earlier.

I tamped down on the twisting tendrils of panic that threatened to overwhelm me and slowed my ascent. I could crawl through that low opening and seek refuge in the brush, or I could continue upward and lift over the jungle. The grav belt's low power decided the issue. I might need a lift later, and there was no guarantee I could recharge the thing. I stepped onto the cliff edge, ducking under the thick branches and pushing through the vines.

I'd taken three steps when something slammed into my chest.

CHAPTER THIRTY-ONE

"Liam!" The tiny bundle of blue and white fur scrambled up my jacket and wound around my neck. I stroked his fine hair, wiping my damp face against him. "How did you find me?"

"Doesn't he always find you?" Joss asked.

I squeaked, biting back my scream before it could escape. "You scared the crap out of me!" I flung myself at him.

He caught me at arms' length, then slowly pulled me closer. Mindful of his damaged ribs, I gripped his shoulders and pressed my face against his chest. "I'm so glad to see you!"

He squeezed me gently, then let go. "I wasn't sure you'd survived the drop into the lava river. I tried to warn you to check your altitude. I don't know why these things even have a relative setting." He tapped the screen on his grav belt.

"It's really useful if you're flying low to the ground. Not so great when you hit a sudden drop off, though. The CEC versions have a failsafe that prevents more than a two-meter change in height. I don't suppose you have any water?"

Joss handed me a water pac. "I snuck into the ship. No food that I could find."

I sipped at the water. "How many of these have you got?"

"Drink up. I found a water purifier, too." He patted his pocket. "The HLP is still at the crash site, but I'm sure it's being monitored."

"How'd you get into the ship without being spotted?" I sipped again.

He shrugged. "Liam found me when I was casing the joint, and he took out the couple of drones that were circling. It was dark, so I took a chance."

I stroked the glider. "He has a very useful skill set." Liam chirped agreement, then jumped away into the dark jungle.

Joss stared into the darkness after the glider. "He's been hunting, I think. Bugs and whatnot."

"That reminds me. I have a protein bar. Do you want half?" I pulled the wrapped package from my pocket. "Or do you think we should save it for later?"

"One bar isn't going to save us. We may as well eat now and keep our strength up." His stomach growled loudly. "And I don't want my belly giving me away."

"If they get that close, we're in trouble." I ripped open the wrapper and handed Joss a chunk. That protein bar tasted better than anything I'd ever eaten. As we ate, I told Joss about my escape and hiding place. "Where did you hide? Did you get any sleep?"

"I had plenty of rest between interrogation sessions. Besides, I was busy—once Liam crushed those two drones, I flew into the ship. No one showed up, so I took the time to really search."

"You weren't worried about the ship falling into the lava river?"

He patted his grav belt. "I had this. Plus, it seemed stable. I figured I'd have enough warning to get out if it decided to fall."

"Did you find anything useful? Besides the water, I mean. Maybe a launchable emergency beacon or an atmospheric escape pod?"

He shoved both hands into his matted hair. "It would be nice if those existed, but no. If we could get the HLP away from the Gagarians, there's a lot of useful survival gear and an extra emergency beacon. I should have launched it as soon as we landed."

"Maybe they're too busy looking for us to guard our crashed ship? We could go get it."

He shook his head. "If we'd thought to grab it as soon as we escaped, it might have worked. But now that we've been gone a few hours, they're going to keep watch. It's the most likely place for us to go. We need that gear, and they know we need that gear. I'm sure they have more of those drones, and we can't rely on Liam to crush them all."

"Then we don't go for the HLP. We circle back to their base and steal gear from them."

"They're going to be watching for that—"

"Hang on." I flung up a hand, cutting him off. "Never mind, just shift change. I've got their security channel on my comm." Perfect. Freshly rested security personnel combing the area for us.

"How'd you do that?" Joss tapped his own audio implant. "I'm not connected to anything, and even if you still had your ring, it doesn't have Gagarian encryption."

I held up my arm, displaying the two wrist devices below my too-short coat sleeve. "I got you one, too. Happy birthday."

I tapped the second device to wake it. Then I showed Joss how to add his thumb print to the system, overwriting the original owner's access. "Now you can put it on. I have a translation app running on this one, but I'm not sure if it will translate incoming transmissions—Evy's jacket is doing that for me."

He nodded. "All flight jackets have translators. One of the reasons I wanted you to take it. Too bad Lee didn't leave us his before he ran back to the CEC."

"He may not have made it to the ship." I explained about the officers I'd overheard. "I know they were trying to draw me out, but that sounded plausible."

"Sounded plausible? He's got more pilot training than I have, and I'd be able to exit the atmosphere." He strapped the device to his wrist.

"In a CEC shuttle, but maybe Gagarian ships are different?" I put a hand on his arm. "I know it's hard to believe he might be on our side, but I think Lee has changed. We should have been more forgiving—he might have—"

"More forgiving? He and his buddy LeBlanc helped kidnap us and tried to get us killed. I can't believe your dad let him stay at the Academy."

"Let's not argue about this, okay? It makes no difference to our situation—we have to assume we need to rescue ourselves. Let's come up with a plan."

"Right. First thing, survival. We have water, we need food. I say we take the HLP."

"You just said you think they'll be watching it."

"Yeah, I do. That's why we need a diversion."

We moved away from the cliff edge, working deeper into the jungle. About five klicks from the base, we reached the first of the steep, conical buttes that jutted out of the jungle. The foliage thinned on the sides, the trees growing shorter and less dense as they climbed. The top of each hill was bare stone.

We hovered under the top leaves of jungle canopy, staring up at the miniature mountains. An observation station stood atop the tallest butte, along with what might be an antenna. I pointed at the tall, thin tower. "Maybe that's why their comm systems work when ours don't."

"I've been thinking about that." Joss tapped his wrist device on the side, to draw my attention, not to activate it. "This thing works fine. I think the 'interference' we were told about is a fiction."

"It's obviously real—our emergency beacon didn't work."

"No, I mean it's man-made. I think the Gagarians are using that antenna to generate the interference. They're blocking our beacon."

"That's against all the treaties—emergency beacons are practically sacred." I stared up at the tower. "Why would you think that?"

"Something I thought I overheard at the camp."

My eyes narrowed. "Overheard how? Since when do you speak Gagarian?"

"I don't speak much, but I understand a fair bit." Faint pink washed over his dark cheeks. "Marika taught me a few words when we were—when she was on Earth. It seems to be related to an old Earth language called Spanish. I was intrigued because some of my dad's ancestors spoke that language. I took some classes at the Academy."

"You've been taking Gagarian at the Academy? How did I not know that?"

He shrugged. "I don't know every class you took. And I only took it plebe year. But that was enough to get me started, and I've kind of continued working on my own time. That's why I don't speak it very well—not much practice."

"Enough history. What did you overhear?"

He pointed at the antenna. "That thing puts out a signal that interferes with communications on all known Colonial Commonwealth frequencies. That's why their comms work—they use a different band than we do. And they've built some kind of—" he wiggled his fingers "—anti interference thingy. Chymm could explain it, I'm sure."

"Did you learn why they're here? Marika said they don't want us to advertise their presence. They've clearly been here a while—maybe even before we landed on Qureshi. But they didn't dispute our claim to that planet. What's their motive?"

His brow came down in an "are you crazy" look. "Obviously they're here to spy on us. Like we came here to spy on them."

"They set up a secret base so they could eavesdrop on our not secret base that's spying on them?"

He snickered at my disbelief. "Exactly. The 'natural electromagnetic interference' is completely man-made. Or woman-made—the current Gagarian prime minister is a woman. Not that she made it herself, but you know what I mean." He grinned. "Here's something else—the 'toxins' in the air are also fictitious. That one I know for sure. Marika confirmed it."

"Just because she said it doesn't mean it's true." I wrinkled my nose. "She doesn't exactly have a history of honesty."

"Yeah, but I believe her. She had no reason to lie about that. And nobody on that base wore air filters—or even personal shields."

"Inside the base, the force shield would protect them."

He touched the faint swelling of his black eye. "No, off base, too. At the crash site when they grabbed us. Those guys I fought with weren't wearing any protective gear."

"Huh." I stared up at the tower again. "Maybe that should be the target for our distraction, then. If we could take the tower down, then maybe we can get a signal off this stupid moon. And steal some survival gear while we wait for rescue."

Joss rubbed his hands together. "Sounds good. What's the plan?"

CHAPTER THIRTY-TWO

Sitting on one of the shorter buttes, hidden in the foliage near the top, we took turns watching the antenna and the small module near it. Two Gagarians moved around the site, flying the perimeter of the flat top. No one entered or left the module. As the sun reached its zenith, a second pair of soldiers relieved the first.

"Shift change—right on schedule with the rest of the base." I gestured to the device on my wrist. "They're sending another wave of searchers out as the current ones return. They don't know where we are."

"No kidding." Joss lay on the ground, eyes closed. "I was wondering why they hadn't surrounded us yet."

Here in our hiding place near the top of the hill, the jungle thinned. We sat in a small clearing with a line of sight to the antenna and the base. Our gear helped us blend into the surrounding colors. As always, thick cloud cover dimmed the sunlight, but the diffused light was much brighter than the constant twilight in the deep jungle.

"Smart ass." I threw a small seed pod at him. Liam, curled up beside Joss, opened his eyes, regarded the pod for a second, then went back to sleep.

"Better a smart ass than a dumb ass." Joss grinned as he quoted one of his dad's favorite sayings.

"Why don't you put those smarts to good use and come up with a plan to take down that antenna?"

"I'm thinking. I'm just doing it with my eyes closed. Too bad we don't have any of those slime snails from Qureshi. They could take that tower down in a few minutes."

My eyes darted to him. "Did you see them, too?"

"Are you kidding? After you discovered them, the whole base had to watch a demonstration. They wanted to make sure we understood the ramifications of letting one of those things inside the force shield."

"It's kind of weird when you think about it."

He rolled onto his side to look at me, propping his head up on one hand. "Weird that Jankovic didn't want us to destroy his camp?"

"No. Weird that it hadn't happened already." I felt my way through the words. "Those things were everywhere, and we were in a phase 2 mission. Why didn't the phase 1 guys find them?"

"Our camp was in a new location—maybe they're local to that area. Not every new planet is a single ecosystem, despite what the old science fiction books said."

"True, and we found them the first day. Still, after seeing the way those things homed in on that downed frond—why didn't they zero in on our camp on the first day and chew it to the ground?"

He dropped to his back and closed his eyes again. "Maybe the force shield kept them out. Or the comm transmissions. Or the shuttle exhaust."

"And none of them ever got inside—in fact, I don't think the decon process ever caught a single one. At least not as long as we were there."

"We may never know. And at this point, it doesn't really matter. Unless you have one in the hidden pocket of your flight jacket."

"Hidden pocket?" I looked at Evy's coat, fingering the open front. "There's a hidden pocket?"

"Two of them. Inside the side seam. Old military thing. If you crash, you're supposed to hide your orders, or your ID or whatever you don't want the enemy to find. You know, stuff you don't want to stash or destroy. Our flight jackets are produced by the same company as the military uniforms, and it's cheaper to use the same pattern."

I pulled off the jacket and spread it across my lap. "Why do you know that? Why don't I?"

He sat up. "You didn't do cadet flight training—it's part of the history we're supposed to learn." He leaned over and tapped the side seam. "Run your thumb along that seam, and it will unseal."

I pressed the side of my thumb against the fold of fabric and pushed it along the length. "You're messing with me, aren't you?"

"No, look." He nodded at the coat.

The seam had unsealed itself, leaving an opening. I slid my fingers through the gap. The pocket was about a hand span wide and ran the full length of the coat. A thin piece of paper crinkled under my fingers. I pulled it out—a faded print of a two-dimensional photo. Two girls—a young Evy and an even younger girl who looked enough like her to be a sister—sat on a low wall in front of a paved plaza. They held ice cream cones and grinned at the photographer.

I handed the picture to Joss. "There's something else in here." Sliding my hand deeper into the pocket, I found a small, hard cylinder. "There's a vial." I pulled out a clear tube full of pink goo.

Joss pulled away, his eyes wide. "Isn't that some of your death snail goo?"

I held up the tube. "Ask and you shall receive? It can't be—it isn't eating through the plastek."

Joss reached out, then hesitated. After a second, he flicked his fingernail against the vial. It rang like a tiny bell. "That's trans-lu, not plastek. Which makes sense—they discovered it was impervious to your death snails."

"They aren't *my* death snails." I ignored his grin. "Why did Evy have a tube of goo?"

"Transporting it back to the ship, obviously." He stared at the goo for a minute, then looked over his shoulder at the tower. "Are you thinking what I'm thinking?"

"That we should destroy their tower with a little pink goo? Oh, yeah."

WE SPENT the rest of the short day planning our op. First, we tested the goo. We considered dripping it onto a leaf, but I worried that might get away from us. It was bad enough we planned to contaminate a nearly pristine moon with the stuff, but dumping some in the wild was further than I was willing to go. I ended up dropping the corner of the protein bar wrapper into the vial. It dissolved in seconds.

"Yes!" Joss held up a hand.

I slapped it. "Nice. Even if the tower isn't the source of the interference, toppling it should provide an awesome distraction. But don't you think they'll be expecting us to do something like this?"

"Maybe not this big, since they don't know we have the goo. But they'll know it's us, which is why we need more."

"More distractions? Or more goo? This is all I got, unless the universe is going to drop more in my lap." I looked at the sky as if expecting a vial to appear. "I get the feeling you were a bit of a hellraiser before we discovered you on Earth."

"Who, me?" Joss widened his eyes in mock innocence. "Peter was the hellraiser. I just got caught up in his mayhem."

"Right. Quiet, studious Peter."

Joss rolled his eye so hard he nearly fell over backward. "No. Peter is an angel. Eric, on the other hand, is a rabble rouser, and when he and Zina started plotting things—" He stopped, a shadow passing over his face. "I wish she was here."

Zina and Joss were twins. Everyone had been surprised when he decided to leave Earth for the Academy, and she stayed behind, but this was the first time in three years I'd seen him express any regret.

"She'd be genius at this." His grin faded, and he glowered at the tube of pink glop. "Too bad we don't have more of this."

"Are you sure we don't? They loaded a pallet of crates on the ship right before we left. Who knows what was in there?"

"Why would Evy have this sample if there was a whole pallet of the stuff in the back? And part of those crates smashed when we landed. If there was snail goo inside, wouldn't it have eaten through the crates? And the ship?"

"If it spilled. I'm sure Li was very careful when she packed it."

"You think your old scientist buddy was shipping samples back to her lab on Grissom?"

"Of course." I held the goo up and looked through it at the setting sun. It glowed with a pinkish light between my fingers. "That's what we do, right? Analyze stuff on site, then send specimens back to the big labs. That's what we were supposed to do on Earth. If we found anything new."

"You mean besides us. Although I'm surprised no one tried to ship Jake or Lena back to Grissom."

"Dad would never have allowed that. HQ doesn't know anything about them." I tapped the side of the vial. "I think we should go back to the ship. Let's use this little sample to take down the antenna. While they're busy looking for us here, we'll sneak into the crash site and look for more goo. Then we'll set up another diversion and grab Evy."

"And send a message through their comm system." Joss stood. "I'm not waiting for Lee to rescue me. Just to be clear, that's because I think he won't."

I nodded slowly. I'd wanted to give Lee the benefit of the doubt, but he should have been back by now. If he was coming.

I held out my fist. "Anyone want to chicken out?"

Joss knocked his knuckles against mine. "Hell, no."

CHAPTER THIRTY-THREE

THE TWO SOLDIERS patrolling the perimeter of the antenna site chatted as they worked. My wrist device connected automatically as we approached. The larger one talked almost constantly, making lewd comments about everything from their commander down to the shape of the butte they were stationed atop. I made a mental note to cut Marika some slack if this was what she had to deal with on an average mission—uneducated, misogynistic thugs.

I turned off the translator.

Surprisingly, there was no force shield surrounding the antenna site. Based on the little bits I'd picked up from Chymm over the years, I suspected a shield would interfere with the signals this station was designed to put out.

"I wish Chymm was here," Joss muttered under his breath.

I nodded as I put my finger against my lips.

We skulked in the thick undergrowth near the top of the hill. On the other buttes, the jungle thinned naturally as it neared the rocky top. On this one, the Gagarians had cleared a full twenty meters. The jungle growth ended in a sheer cut, with bare dirt between that edge and the stony top.

This provided excellent cover for us to observe the soldiers but meant we'd have to get across twenty meters of clear dirt before we reached the tower's base. It would be safer to take the guards down at the outset. That had the potential to blow up in our faces if they managed to get a message back to camp.

The chatty guard floated past us, halfway between our hiding spot and the tower. His companion was out of sight on the far side of the clearing. Our ambush point was in direct line of sight of the base, but that was far away. More importantly, it was in a blind spot between the cameras watching the perimeter. The Gagarians had been careless in their setup. Although, to be fair, they hadn't anticipated visitors.

That was their first mistake.

The big guy disappeared around the side of the small module, his grating voice droning on, interspersed with harsh cackles as he told yet another degrading joke. Or so I assumed. Now I was grateful for my inability to understand Gagarian.

Joss held up his hand. He dropped one finger at a time, counting down. A second after he dropped the last finger, the smaller guard appeared around the edge of the hillside. I waited for him to slide past, my fingers slippery on my stunner. Joss crouched behind me, aiming the big blaster at the man's back.

I lifted off and zipped forward, flying low above the dirt. As the man turned to look over his shoulder, I swung upward and hit him with my stunner. Blue light crackled over his body, and he dropped.

Joss shouldered the blaster and whipped out of the trees. We lifted the man by his arms and legs and carried him into the cover of the jungle. I pulled out the vines we'd twisted into rope and wrapped them around the man's wrists and ankles while Joss shoved a piece of cloth into his mouth.

"When I get to back to the ship, I'm going to put duct tape in my jacket's secret pocket." Joss's his face darkened—no doubt remembering his career was pretty much scuttled.

I touched his shoulder, then gestured at the tower. "This could be our ticket back into the CEC's good graces." Nothing like a little sabotage—not to mention kidnapping—to redeem oneself. I put the dark thoughts out of my mind and focused on the next step.

When the chatty guard—who hadn't noticed his companion's lack of response—rounded the edge of the butte, Joss and I were hidden again. We waited for him to walk by, still talking up a storm, and we repeated our attack.

The man turned. Caught off guard and still fifteen meters away, I yanked up my stunner and fired. Blue sparks hit his chest and dispersed, harmless. He was out of range.

Joss raised the blaster to his shoulder. As I zipped closer, the guard tapped his wrist device. I fired again. The blue lightning wrapped around him, forming a bright net of sparks. As the man fell, a voice spoke from his device.

"Joss, what did it say?" I dropped beside my victim.

"I think it said, 'report.' He must have contacted headquarters."

The voice spoke again, more urgent this time.

"Tell them everything is fine. That it was a mistake." I lifted the man's limp hand.

Joss raced across the dirt, staring at me. "I told you, I don't speak Gagarian. I don't know what to say!"

"You can say 'sorry,' right? Isn't that one of the first things people learn when they go to a new place?" I waved the guy's arm urgently.

"I've never been to Gagarin." He took the man's wrist and muttered into the device. The voice queried again. Joss uttered a couple of liquid syllables.

I tapped the translation button on my collar. It should be converting this conversation into Standard for me.

"—full report when you get back. Where's your partner?"

Joss gabbled in Gagarian and made a semi-comic, terrified face at me.

My translator told me, "He's watering the flowers."

I bit back a snort of nervous laughter.

"Tell him to call when he's done. Argent out." The signal went dead.

"We now have however long it takes to uh, water the flowers, before they demand another update. I think they thought I—he—was drunk."

I pulled the smaller guard's hat over my head and helped Joss roll the second man out of his jacket. "You did sound a little rough. Let's get our pink slime deployed and get out of here." We piled the weapons near the treeline and left Liam standing guard.

We zipped up the slope and ducked under the lowest supports of the tower. We were in the line of sight of the Gagarian cams as soon as we reached the tower, but hopefully whoever was watching had redeployed them to look for their "drunk" coworkers. Either way, we didn't have much time.

I stood close to the support, my body between my hands and the security cams. I tipped the vial and ran a line of slime along the plastek just above the first joint—the point of greatest stress, if my memories of my engineering class were correct. I capped the vial and flew to Joss, making sure to hand off our treasure where it would be unseen by any watchers.

Joss applied another line of slime, and we bolted for the jungle. A quick stop to grab the weapons delayed us only seconds. Liam leaped to my shoulder, and we launched into the sky. Skimming above the top layer of leaves, we listened for the alarm to go up. Thirty seconds later, the voice called again. This time, my translator caught it.

"Simonson, report."

No response. Luck had been with us, and they hadn't seen our sabotage run.

"Report."

Flying beside me at top speed, Joss yelled. "Should I answer?"

I shook my head. "If that slime is anywhere near as fast acting as it was on Qureshi, that tower should have fallen by now. Besides, Simonson's wrist thingy is back there. They'd know you weren't him." I glanced over my shoulder. "Maybe the slime doesn't work here?"

"You saw it work in the vial."

"But there was Qureshi air in that thing. Maybe some of the toxins in this air—"

"We opened the vial. Saha air got in there. But there are no toxins. Marika said so. That's why I'm so sure the interference is also fake. The Gagarians didn't want to claim this system, but they don't want us on this moon."

We were still a klick away from the ship when a wordless shout rang through my audio implant followed by a curse. "Son of a Colonial politician! The comm lock is offline! Check the alignment."

We turned to look. The tower leaned precariously, as if the two legs had weakened but not broken. As we watched, it sagged farther, then crashed to the ground.

With a smothered whoop, Joss and I dove into the top layer of leaves. We skimmed under the top canopy, our progress slowed by the need to dodge branches and trunks. The Gagarians argued about what could have caused the tower to stop transmitting.

Another voice reported the guards at the site were no longer responding. Yet another drew attention to the loss of surveillance cams.

I grinned as I raised my hand to signal a stop. We were approaching our downed ship. I tapped the wrist device and found the vids from the crash site. Two Gagarian guards hovered over the clearing, both of them watching their wrist devices.

"If we come up from the fissure, we might be able to get inside without them noticing," I whispered.

Joss gave a thumbs up and pointed toward the cliff side. We worked our way through the foliage, then burst out of the jungle and dropped into the gash. On my screen, neither guard noticed our appearance and sudden disappearance half a klick upstream.

We swooped along the canyon, staying in the deepening shadows as theu sun dropped below the horizon. If the guards used low-light tech, the glow from the lava below should help conceal us. I nearly choked on the fumes as a magma bubble burst beneath me. The air of this moon might not be toxic but flying over a bubbling ribbon of molten rock couldn't be healthy.

We reached the crash site and hovered beneath our dead ship. The huge structure of metal and plastek hanging overhead made my inner cave woman howl in fear, but I shoved her into her cave and rolled a mental stone across the entrance. "Do we take them out or try to sneak around?" I whispered.

Joss tapped his wrist device and brought up the cams. One guard hovered over the ship, facing the butte. His gaze moved back and forth between the distant hill and his wrist device. The second guard was not in sight. "I wish I still had access to our drone."

I shrugged and pointed upward. "Let's wing it." I swung the blaster around. It hung by its strap across my body, and I placed my left hand on the trigger. I didn't want to kill anyone, even a Gagarian, but I'd fire if necessary. I gripped the stunner in my right, hoping I'd be close enough to any targets to use it instead.

Joss did the same, then counted us down. On zero, he swooped around the side of the ship, aiming for the emergency airlock in the deck of the cockpit. I looped around the opposite direction.

As I rose, I squinted into the darkness. One of the guards we'd seen on cam floated above the cargo hold, still focused on his wrist device. I eased forward and fired my stunner. Blue lights crawled over him, and he slumped in his grav belt.

Fire seared my back, enveloping me in a haze of pain and static. Then everything went black.

CHAPTER THIRTY-FOUR

"Siti. Wake up." A loud crack, like a hand against a bulkhead, pierced my over-sensitive ears. My head rattled, but I felt no pain, only fog. I tried to open my eyes, but they only flickered. My body rocked, as if someone had shaken it. I sucked in a deep breath and forced my eyelids up.

Light spiked into my eyes, and I slammed them shut. "Too bright."

"Sorry. Is that better?" Joss stared down at me, a small battery powered lamp giving off a soft glow. "You need to shake it off. We've got a mission."

"Wha—what happened?" I forced my eyes open. I was on the cockpit overhead, staring up at the floor.

"Second guard hit you with a stunner." He hefted a large, clumsy-looking weapon. "I rammed her as she fired, so you got hit with the edge of the field. Otherwise, I think you'd be out for the count. This thing is set on max."

"I don't think that's how stunners work." I sat up slowly, holding my fuzzy head. "Where's the guard?"

"I stunned her and left them hanging while I got you inside the ship. Now they're napping on a ledge a few meters below the top of the cliff, without their gear." He pointed at a pile of weapons, grav belts, and wrist devices. "I took down the cams, too. Our friends are all busy trying to fix the tower and didn't notice."

"Nice." I raised my hand for a high-five. "Did you find the goo?"

"I can't do all the work." He scooped the Gagarian gear into a small crate and set it aside. "I was getting ready to look when you started making noise."

Liam jumped to my shoulder and made worried sounds in my ear. I stroked his head. "I wish I could understand you." I grabbed the lamp and cranked it brighter. Then we lifted off the cockpit's overhead and shot through the open hatch into the cargo hold.

"Nice to see you again." Marika sat on an overturned crate, pointing a blaster at us. "I hoped you'd come back. What are you looking for?"

"Crap."

Joss moved, but Marika jerked the blaster. "Drop your weapons. I won't hesitate to shoot you."

I lifted the blaster off my shoulder and held it out by the strap. "You want me to drop this? Won't it go off? I've heard Gagarian weapons are a bit touchy."

"Set it down carefully." She pointed at the overhead near the hatch to the sleeping area. "Then drop the stunner I know you've got in your pocket."

I shifted the lamp to the hand holding the blaster strap and reset my grav belt to zero relative. As the device lowered me to the floor, I maneuvered to land behind a large conduit. It was only half a meter tall, but maybe I could fire from behind it as I set the blaster down. I put the lamp on top of the conduit.

"Joss, stop right there. Siti, put the blaster on this side of that conduit and step away. I'm not as stupid as you think." She held out a hand. "Liam, come here."

The little blue and white glider stood motionless on the conduit, blinking at her. After a second, he leaped into the air, disappearing into the darkness.

Two meters above me and to the right, Joss spoke. "We don't think you're stupid—you're probably the most dangerous adversary on this moon, since you know us."

Marika smiled, a gratified expression. Then her eyes narrowed. "Don't try to use your Earth boy charms on me, Torres. I may know you, but you don't know me at all. I'm nothing like sweet, little Marika LaGrange."

I blinked. "That isn't your name?" It was a stupid question—of course she used an alias.

"You're smarter than that, Siti."

"What should we call you?"

As Joss asked the question, I took a half step back toward the blaster. Marika's head swung around, homing in on me. "You can call me ma'am. And don't try it. Put the stunner down and take off the belt. Then move over there." She jerked the blaster to my right.

I dropped the little weapon on top of the conduit but missed. It fell to the overhead. "Sorry."

"Leave it." Marika jerked the blaster again. "Move out of the way."

I released my belt and set it next to the blaster, shoving the stunner with my toes as I went.

"I said move." Marika glared.

I took a few steps to the right and waited.

"Torres, your turn." She watched while Joss removed his weapons and belt. Then she threw a handful of white strips toward him. The pieces of plastek fell short, dropping to the overhead. "Pick those up. Wrists and ankles."

Joss scooped up the slip ties. I took a reluctant step toward him.

Marika stopped him. "Don't get too close. Arms' length. Siti, hold out your hands."

I held out my hands, and Joss leaned forward to wrap the slip tie loosely around my wrists. I caught his gaze and dropped my eyes to my stunner, half a meter from his left foot. His left eyelid dropped in a half wink.

"Make it tight, Joss. Show me."

He pulled the tie snug, and I held up my bound hands.

"Pull."

I pulled my arms apart, demonstrating he'd bound me tightly. Joss backed away, stopping near the stunner.

"Sit down and put your feet on that vent thing." Marika pointed at a round tube that protruded from the ceiling.

I sat on the conduit. "I don't have to stay here, do I? This conduit is cold."

"Stop whining. That always was your strong suit."

"Hey, that's not nice. And you said we were friends." I banged my feet against the vent as I followed her instructions. The hollow sound rang like a badly built drum. "Remember that vid you sent me at the end. You said—"

"I know what I said. But you've caused me a lot of trouble. Taking you back to camp is going to go a long way toward clearing the cloud over my head. Get busy, Torres. Her feet won't tie themselves."

"Crap." Joss fumbled and dropped the slip tie.

"Nice try." Marika pulled another from her pocket. "Leave it. Take this one." She tossed the plastek, and it fell short. She muttered under her breath and pulled out another. She moved two steps closer and hung the tie on the end of the blaster, pushing it toward Joss.

"You don't expect me to—"

Marika cut him off, using the weapon to fling the slip tie at us. Joss snatched at the tie and missed. He dropped to a crouch, reaching for the dropped strap.

"Don't try anything funny." Marika pointed the blaster directly at me.

I stared at the huge barrel, cold spreading through my body. I started to tremble, fear pushing my bravado aside. I curled in on myself, lost my balance, and fell off the conduit with a thud.

With a flash of blue and white, Liam appeared from the darkness, leaping straight at Marika.

Joss snatched the stunner and fired twice. The blaster went off, singeing the air over me. The ship's bulkhead sizzled, and something exploded. Someone screamed. The light went out.

Cold and shaking, I huddled on my side behind the conduit. "Joss?" My voice shook.

"I'm bleeding." His sounded hoarse. "I think Marika is down."

I squirmed to my back, then sat up slowly. Black pressed against my eyes, with a faint ghost of the explosion leaving a red imprint on the darkness. I rolled to my feet and, staying hunched over, shuffled toward Joss.

My toes hit something—probably one of the many smaller conduits crisscrossing the cargo bay's overhead. "Where are you?"

"Here." His voice came from the floor near my feet. I crouched, patting the air with my bound hands. He grunted when my fingers hit his body. "That's my shoulder."

"Where are you hurt?" I brought my wrists to my face and tapped the Gagarian device against my nose to activate it. A dim light spilled across my friend lying beside the conduit. Blood seeped between the fingers he had clamped to his thigh. "Oh, God, that's not an artery, is it?"

"I don't think so, but I never took anatomy." His face looked pale, but it was hard to tell in the dim light.

"That's a lot of blood." I pulled the Gagarian jacket off and pressed the sleeve against his wound. "Do you think there's a medical kit here?"

"We took it with us—it's in the Gagarian camp." He clamped his hand over the fabric.

"I'm going to check the HLP—you aren't going to pass out and bleed out while I'm gone, are you?"

He bared his teeth at me in a terrifying, pain-filled grin. "You can't get rid of me that easily."

I slapped my wrist device when the light died and flashed it around the hold. Liam sat on the conduit, holding a slip tie in his tiny paws. "Good boy." I took it and linked several together, then slid the length under Joss's leg.

He made a sound like a hurt animal.

"Sorry." I pulled the ties on either side, folded the jacket into a thick pad, and secured it with the ties. Then I propped his leg up on the conduit to keep the wound above the level of his heart. I put one of the stunners under his hand. "Just in case. Stay alive. I'll be right back."

Before leaving, I took a second to remove Marika's weapons and wrist device. I wrapped her grav belt around my waist and dumped the extra devices in a dark corner near the airlock. Even if Marika revived before I returned, she wouldn't have time to find them.

CHAPTER THIRTY-FIVE

THE HLP SAT where we'd left it, in the center of the crash zone. I pulled away the vines that had already started growing over it and activated the control panel. The emergency batteries—designed to hold a charge for months of inactivity—showed ninety percent. I hit the open button and found the first aid kit—right on top where an injured explorer could easily find it.

I grabbed the kit and the extra beacon, then closed the HLP, adding a security code to the latch. They were designed to be used by anyone who survived a crash, so there was no security protocol on first use. But after that initial opening, a lock could be engaged—in case the crash was in hostile country with sentient aliens. Or hostile humans, apparently.

In less time than it takes to explain, I was back in the hold with the ScanNSeal. I found Joss unconscious, so I cut the slip ties and slapped the ScanNSeal on his wound. The device checked his vitals, evaluated the wound, and administered treatment on its own.

While it worked, I used the remaining slip ties to secure Marika. Then I spread an emergency blanket over Joss, picked up the stunner near his hand, and retrieved some meal pacs and a light from the HLP. I considered activating the beacon, but didn't want to lead the Gagarians to us.

As I settled beside Joss and opened a packet of Chewy Nuggets,

Marika whimpered. I flicked the lamp to low and leaned back against the conduit, watching the Gagarian woman.

"Wha—?" She tried to sit up, but with her left wrist secured to a conduit support and her ankles tied together, her mobility was limited.

"That didn't go as well as you'd hoped, did it?" I popped another Chewy Nugget into my mouth and waited for her reply.

She scooted her butt back and carefully levered herself into an upright position. "Where's Joss?"

I glanced at my friend. His color looked a little better, but it was hard to tell in the dim light. I twisted the controls on the lamp to turn up the lumens. "He's here. No thanks to you."

Her eyes settled on him and widened. "Did I hit him?"

"You hit that." I pointed over my shoulder at the blackened bulkhead and the remains of a no doubt vital piece of equipment. "The shrapnel took him down. He's alive. If he wasn't, you wouldn't be either." I patted the blaster across my lap, so she'd know what I meant.

Her face went white. "I didn't mean to kill him. And you wouldn't shoot me. You're not like that."

"Not normally. But if you had killed him..." I left the statement hanging. "You'd better hope the ScanNSeal can patch him up because if I have to get him to a med pod, I'm blasting a hole through your base and taking hostages."

It was an insane bluff, but Marika nodded. "I don't want him to die."

"What do you want? Why are you here?" I held out a nugget to Liam, who took it with chirped thanks.

"I came to recapture you and take you back to camp. To redeem myself."

I shook my head sharply. "No, if that was your plan, you would have brought backup. You came alone, even though you knew there were two of us, and we were armed. You want something from us, and you don't want your superiors to know. What is it?"

She lifted her chin. "I don't need anything from you. I'm a loyal daughter of Gagarin, and I'm here to take two enemy spies into custody."

I choked on my Chewy Nugget. A swig from the water pac got the coughing under control. "Enemy spies? We're stranded explorers. Castaways from a mission legally underway in this system. Under every Inter-Colony Treaty, we should have been provided with medical care and returned to our ship. But your superiors chose to lock us up and threaten us. And you...*what do you want?*" My voice cracked on the last word.

Marika swallowed hard. She looked away for a long moment, staring into the dark corners of the inverted cargo hold. Finally, she whispered, "I want to come home."

"Home? I can't take you to Gagarin."

"I don't want to go to Gagarin. I want to go back to the CEC." Her eyes went glassy with unshed tears, and she took a ragged breath. "I've never felt as much a part of anything—the CEC—I had friends. Not just you. Anivea, Rico, Chasin. I was shocked how much it hurt to betray them. Living with them for almost four years—they felt more like my family than anyone I knew on Gagarin."

"Then why did you do it?"

"I told you—I've always been a loyal daughter of Gagarin. I was raised by the state—with hundreds of other kids. We were trained to love the mother planet and pledged our lives to her. Then I went to Grissom. Basic training was easy—I was ready for everything. I scored high. And my first mission was easy—a phase 3 to Lovell. I worked security at the platinum mine. Big deal. But I stayed focused and was rewarded with the mission to Earth."

"Rewarded? Or assigned by a Gagarian mole in the personnel office?"

"Probably that." She rubbed the tears from her cheeks with the back of her free hand. "That's where I made friends. I started fitting in—"

"Spare me the angsty drama. You're trying to play me again. It won't work. Even if it did, you'll never get back into the CEC. They don't take traitors."

She flinched at the word.

The device on Joss's leg pinged. The screen said his wound had been medicated and sealed. No broken bones or internal injuries. An hour in a med pod and additional fluids were recommended.

"We can do one of those," I muttered.

"What's it say?" Marika demanded.

I gave her a death glare, then relented. "It says he'll be fine if he gets plenty of fluids and rest. No exertion. Which means you should stop trying to take us prisoner."

That surprised a laugh out of her. "Being a prisoner isn't so bad—it's the running and attacking that's hard on a half-healed wound."

"You would know better than I." Or maybe not. I'd been a prisoner too many times already in my short CEC career. I nudged Joss. "You awake?"

He blinked and lifted his head. "Did someone shoot me?"

Marika raised her free hand. "I wasn't aiming for you. If I was, you'd be dead."

"She says she wants to be friends. Now that we've got her trussed up in a derelict ship."

"If you want to be friends, I recommend you prove it by helping us escape." Joss rubbed a hand over his face. "You got anything to drink?"

I handed him a water pac and turned back to Marika. "Can you help us contact Lee?"

"The kid who stole the shuttle? Shouldn't he have brought the cavalry by now?"

"Yeah, what's up with that?" Joss threw aside the now empty water pac and made a gimme motion at me. "Even if he claimed to be the sole survivor, the CEC would have sent a SAR team to check on the ship." He grimaced at Marika. "Can't have it falling into enemy hands."

She smirked. "There's no tech on this ship that we don't already have."

"Hah." Joss pointed at her. "Who would 'we' be? The Gagarians? So much for wanting to come over to our side."

She flushed. "Old habits. But you're right. If your friend—"

"Not my friend!" Joss and I said together.

"Whatever. If this Lee kid made it safely to the *New Dawn*, they would have sent a team."

"You know the name of our ship?" I demanded. "Are you saying someone shot him down?"

"What? No. We don't have any anti-air weapons on this moon. We're not supposed to be here. Low profile. Undercover."

"Maybe building a huge base in the middle of a jungle was a poor choice, then." I pulled a blue packet from the meal pac and tossed it to Joss.

"What, no Chewy Nuggets?"

I held up the empty packet. "Sorry. You get the next one. I heard some of the officers say Lee hadn't gotten out of orbit, but they were speaking Standard, so I figured it was part of a plot to draw me out."

"It may have been. But it also might have been true." Marika chewed on her lip a moment. "Little known fact—Gagarian shuttles require two pilots to leave orbit."

Joss barked out a laugh. "That's the stupidest thing I've ever heard. What if one of the pilots is injured?"

She shrugged. "They don't have to be conscious, just on the ship. It started as a way to keep pilots from defecting." Her lips twisted. "Yeah, it's fairly common on Gagarin."

Joss leaned closer to me. "Shouldn't we get moving? How do we know she didn't call back to camp? There could be a platoon of Gagarian soldiers camped outside this ship."

"There wasn't when I got the ScanNSeal, and I have her wrist thingy."

"It's called a Chet, after its creator. And I told you, I'm here alone."

"That's what you'd say if you called for backup. We've been here too long." Joss pushed himself up, favoring his right leg as he went. "Did you get the goo?"

"Crap! I forgot about it, what with all the shooting." I darted a glare at Marika and stalked past her to the rear of the ship. A flick to my grav belt took me up to the deck of the hold. The crate that had been secured there before we left still hung from its straps. I tapped the control panel on the side and activated the grav lift. The crate hummed and strained against the straps. I tethered it to my own belt and released the restraints. The crate dropped a few centimeters and righted itself.

"Inventory says samples, so I think we're good." I dropped to the overhead and tapped the open sequence.

"We probably need to take this crate with us—I'm sure the boss won't want *that* falling into enemy hands." Joss kept his voice low. He'd replaced his grav belt and now hovered beside me.

I lifted the lid, revealing stacks of trans-lu vials packed in heavy padding. "Looks like they all survived intact. We probably shouldn't use this stuff here—leaving traces of it for the Gagarians to analyze."

"Too late now. Besides, you got a better way to create havoc and mayhem?"

"What are you two whispering about?" Marika asked. "If it's the snail goo, I know all about it."

I swung around and advanced on her. "We've been here way too long. Joss, cover me." I waited until he had the stunner aimed at Marika, then cut her wrist free from the ship. "Hands behind your back." I secured her wrists, put a piece of tape over her mouth, then put one of the spare grav belts around her waist. "I'm tethering this to yours, Joss. Two-meter trail so she can't get close enough to cause any trouble. You'll go ahead of me. We'll put the plan into action."

CHAPTER THIRTY-SIX

Full dark had engulfed the ship by the time we left. I took the crate of samples out through the cockpit exit. It might have fit through the rear cargo hatch, but we needed it at the front end of the ship. As I pulled away from the ship, I peered toward the side of the cliff but couldn't see the Gagarian guards Joss had marooned there. "Are they far enough away from the ship?"

He waved beyond the capsized shuttle. It spanned the narrow gorge, wedged into place between the two sides. "They're down that way. They'll hear the crash, for sure, but they're out of range. They should be able to attract attention when the base sends someone to investigate."

"I'll do this—you watch her." I glared into the darkness where I could barely make out Marika's outline. "Do you believe her?"

He nodded. "Kind of. But it's better not to take the chance."

"You think she wants to defect? She's changed sides so many times I can't keep track anymore."

Beyond Joss, Marika tried to speak through the tape over her mouth.

"Shut it, Marika. Where's Liam?"

The little glider chirped from his perch on Marika's shoulder.

"Traitor. But I guess she's safer than me right now." I slapped Joss's shoulder. "Keep watch while I drip the goo." Without waiting for a reply, I pulled one of the flasks from the crate bobbing along in my wake and lifted over the ship.

In the distance, bright lights shone on the tallest butte. Tiny figures buzzed around the remains of the tower.

"We should activate the beacon," Joss called softly. "Before they get the tower operational."

"Not yet—it will bring them right to us. Let me get the sabotage started, and we'll hide it somewhere."

I pulled the stopper from the top of the trans-lu flask and poured the pink goo onto the inverted ship. Painting it on would be more accurate, but I didn't have a trans-lu brush, so I had to improvise. I trailed a thick line across the top, then ran it at an angle around the sides. When I reached the top of the ship—currently the underside—I stopped. There was no way to get it onto the flat roof without dripping some on myself. Before we left the ship, I had trailed a line across the overhead of the sleeping compartment inside.

Now I went back up and over, angling farther back on the ship. When I was finished, a wedge of ship was outlined in pink goo. It glowed in the darkness, giving my hands a rosy cast. I stoppered the flask and returned it to my crate.

Plastek groaned. Metal grated against metal in places where the goo had melted the plastek away. "It's going a lot faster here." I hit the forward button on my grav belt and sped away from the wreck, the goo crate and the HLP sliding along behind me.

I reached Joss and Marika and waved for them to precede me. "Stay in front. I want to keep her where I can see her."

Joss tossed me a salute. "You got it, boss. Holy crap!"

I spun around. The glow had intensified, as if the goo was pulling energy from the ship. The bright pink line widened. The ship slowly folded in on itself, the wedge I had cut free collapsing under the weight.

With an ear-shattering groan, the cockpit ground against the stone that had been holding it up. The goo-edged section crumpled accordion-style, and the heavy cargo hold tilted forward, folding like a book. The rear ramp tore free from the boulders that had prevented it from opening.

Plastek and metal screeched, and the collapsed ship fell into the lava river below.

As the ship hit the lava, Joss and I raced toward the camp. I looked back, once, to see the craft beginning to melt from the intense heat. My breath caught at the sight. We were committed. Not that the shuttle would ever have flown again but seeing the CEC craft slowly disintegrating made me want to cry.

About halfway between the base and the ship, we stopped to activate the emergency beacon I'd taken from the HLP. Joss tucked it into a sturdy tree and turned on the miniature force shield. That would stop any creatures from messing with it, but it wouldn't prevent the Gagarians from throwing it into the lava after our ship. We had to hope it would take them long enough to detect and find the signal that we'd have a chance at rescue.

In the meantime, we headed for the base. There was more havoc to wreak.

When we reached it, the place looked like a kicked anthill. Soldiers loaded equipment onto grav lifters and disappeared toward the antenna tower. Others packed boxes and crates, stacking them on the landing pad.

"Are they leaving?" Joss asked as we hovered in thick foliage across the chasm from the base.

I looked at Marika and raised my eyebrows. She shrugged and said something behind the tape.

"We got a signal out," I said. "The CEC will come looking. Game over."

"Then we can wait for rescue." Joss sagged in his grav belt.

"Are you feeling okay?" I put a hand against his forehead. "You feel kind of hot."

He shrugged me off. "Probably from flying over hot lava."

"You can barely feel it up here. I think you've got a fever. I'm going to get the ScanNSeal."

"We have a mission to complete first." He gestured at the base.

"If the CEC is coming, we don't need the mayhem, do we?"

Marika made more noises.

I motioned to Joss. "Cover her. I'm going to remove the tape." As he pulled his stunner from his pocket, I approached the redhead. I stayed at arm's length and out of Joss's firing line. The tape peeled away with a loud rip, and Marika winced.

"You may not be home free yet. There are others embedded in the CEC. Why do you think you ended up here?"

I glanced at Joss, then turned to Marika, carefully backing away a few more centimeters. "What are you talking about?"

"Too many coincidences. I can't believe you didn't see it." She ticked things off on her fingers. "You and Joss assigned to the same mission. Your name used for the accounts that attacked the CEC systems—"

"How'd you know about that?" I demanded.

She held up three fingers. "That major expecting you to fix the decon system, then blaming you when it failed."

"Are you saying Bellincioni is a Gagarian spy, too?"

She shook her head. "Not her—at least, not as far as I know."

"But someone else," Joss said. "Jankovic? I couldn't believe he thought Siti was the cause."

She shrugged. "Maybe."

"You seem to know an awful lot for a low-level soldier." My eyes narrowed. "You aren't, are you?"

"A low-level soldier? No. I'd outrank your Major Evy if we were at a diplomatic event. Rank doesn't count so much when you're undercover."

"How old are you?" She'd told me she was twenty-two when we first met almost four years ago.

She laughed, but it sounded a little sad. "I turned thirty-one last week. There was no cake."

"That's terrible." Joss tried to move closer, but with Marika tethered to his grav belt, he ended up pushing her past me. "Oops."

"A major." I turned the idea over in my mind. "Do you outrank the base commander? Wait. *Are* you the base commander?"

"No and no. I'm second highest rank, but I'm not part of the chain of command here. I'm a special liaison, due to my expert knowledge of the CEC."

"Your base *is* here to spy on us." I played with the piece of tape that had been stuck over her mouth.

"And looking for an opportunity to defect." She held out both hands, still bound together. "Please, believe me. Let me help you."

"How'd you get your hands in front?" Joss poked his stunner at her.

She glanced at her hands and shrugged. "That's easy." She pulled up her knees and slid her feet between her bound wrists. "Flexibility is the key to space power." It sounded like a quote, and she chuckled before pulling her hands to the front again. "The important thing is, I can still help you."

"How?"

"We need to get ahold of your frie—" She swung up her hands to ward off our denial. "Your non-friend, Lee. He had to have landed that shuttle somewhere on this moon. We call him and get him to pick us up, and we're out of here."

"I still don't get why you're suddenly interested in defecting. You could have done that at any point during the Earth mission and been welcomed with open arms."

"I told you. It was the Earth mission that convinced me to defect. When I got back to Gagarin, I realized how good you have it in the Colonies."

Joss moved closer, pushing Marika away from me. "What about Evy?"

"We'll have to go on base to call Lee. We can grab Evy at that point. If they're really abandoning the moon, they might let her go." She looked from me to Joss. "I assume he has a holo-ring? I can reach it through the comm system, but not from a Chet."

I pointed at her. "You took his. He has *my* holo-ring. And the comms have been deactivated."

She waved that away. "That was us. You don't think the CEC normally deactivates comms for explorers sent back to the ship, do you? I can fix it."

"You can?" I asked.

"We have no way of knowing if she's telling the truth," Joss said. "Do you trust her?"

"Less than I trust Lee, for sure. But what are our options? We can wait and see if they leave Saha and hope the CEC comes looking for us because of the beacon. Or we can sneak onto the base and try to call the CEC. Or we can rescue Evy and try to escape."

"They were putting that antenna back up. That doesn't look like they're leaving. And here's something—Marika says there are people inside the CEC. What if Lee is one of them?"

"His mom was a CEC officer. And we've known him for years."

"You heard what she said—she went through basic training and spent four years in the CEC. Maybe Admiral Lee was a deep plant. And she indoctrinated her kid to be one, too. That would explain why he didn't come back for us. He could have set up those accounts in your name."

"That's ridiculous. Lee might be a *terkvard*. And he's a suspiciously capable pilot. But he doesn't know anything about programming."

"That's what he wants us to think." Joss pointed at Marika. "We never suspected her until she showed her hand. Why would Lee be any different?"

"Good point, but we still need to get out of here. Which means trusting her." My head spun. "I'm still willing to give Lee the benefit of the doubt. If he was a spy, he wouldn't have been so obviously stupid plebe year. I say we grab Evy, then try to call Lee. And if they capture us, at least we'll all be together."

"Deal." Joss turned toward Marika. "You heard her. We're trusting you—to an extent. If you turn on us, I will stun you and leave you with a note in Gagarian that says you tried to cut a deal with us." He nodded at me. "Ready?"

"Go."

CHAPTER THIRTY-SEVEN

WE SPLIT UP. Joss and Marika headed to the far side of the base, staying as low in the gorge as they could. Liam and I crept to the closer corner. I watched the chrono on the wrist device. Marika had showed us how to connect in a private channel and activate a count down. "Private channels are not really private, of course. But unless they're scanning for suspicious activity and happen on our channel while we're talking, the chances of being overheard are slim. We should stick to code, though."

"What do you think?" I whispered to Liam as we perched on a small outcropping below the lip of the cliff. "Should we trust her? What about Lee?"

Liam made a few pithy but unintelligible comments and rubbed his head against my cheek.

"Helpful." The chrono trickled down to zero.

"Your turn." Marika's voice came through my implant, soft and steady.

"See you soon." Liam squirmed into my pocket, and I lifted off the little rocky shelf, swiping sweat from my forehead. A peek over the edge of the cliff revealed soldiers on patrol, but they were far apart and paying more attention to the activity on base than their jobs.

A shuttle had landed on the pad. This wasn't the Gagarin ship Lee had absconded with, but a sporty private shuttle—the kind the ultra-wealthy use for in-system travel and racing. It had no markings—just a tail number that meant nothing to me. And a flag—a Colonial Commonwealth flag.

"That doesn't mean much to me either," I told Liam. "I've heard rich Gagarians often license their ships in the Commonwealth to avoid taxes. Or 'repatriation' of their belongings if they piss off the wrong officials." I toggled the wrist comm and described the ship. "Any idea who our visitor might be?"

Joss whistled. "That's a MorganTech TX-7. They cost a fortune."

"When did you become a racing shuttle enthusiast?"

"It's a pilot thing. I don't know who it belongs to, but if our ride doesn't show, we should 'liberate' it. I could fly it," Joss said.

Marika hissed at him to be quiet. We signed off.

I waited until both guards in view were distracted, then popped up over the side and took up a position watching over the canyon. Marika was supposed to have inserted loops into the surveillance. Although with all the activity here and on the antenna butte, chances were good the cam feeds were not being monitored.

Marika and I had traded jackets—she could get away with wearing Evy's, while I needed a Gagarian uniform to blend in. It had been hard to part with the coat—what if Marika flipped again and I didn't get it back? Of course, if Marika was a double (triple? quadruple?) agent, we'd be back in custody shortly, and the jacket would be gone.

I turned slowly, my blaster held at the ready. The other guards barely glanced in my direction as I strode purposefully toward the buildings. I hurried down the narrow alley, not pausing to admire the scorch marks my blaster had created the last time I'd been here.

Across the wide walkway, a guard stood outside the module housing the cells. I marched forward, my sweaty hands making the rifle slippery. I slung it over my shoulder and halted in front of the guard. Marika claimed the lower level soldiers didn't know or care who the officers were—that this guy wouldn't be alarmed if he didn't recognize me. The officer's rank on the jacket meant he would barely glance at me, and with her hat pulled low, I should be safe.

My heart pounded. I took a deep breath and repeated the carefully memorized syllables that Marika swore—and Joss confirmed—meant, "I need to retrieve the prisoner for the commander."

The guard stared through me for a few seconds, as if mentally processing a difficult religious text. Then he yawned and stepped aside, scratching his crotch.

I pushed the door open and stepped inside. As it shut behind me, I hurried across to Evy's cell. I flicked the wrist thing to unlock the door and sent a brief message. "Step 1 complete."

The door swung open, and three faces turned my direction. Evy sat up in the open med pod. A man dressed in white, with a green medical star on his sleeve, and a woman in uniform stood before the pod, comparing notes on a tablet.

Crap.

I repeated my order. The man said something. My translator murmured in my audio implant. "She's healthy enough."

The woman muttered to the man, so quiet my translator didn't pick it up. Evy—stared at me in shock. "Where are you taking me?" she asked in Standard.

I repeated my memorized demand.

"I already told you, take her." The translator gave the man a whiny tone.

"Who are you?" the woman asked.

I heaved a sigh and pulled out my stunner. "Your worst nightmare." I zapped the woman and the medic with the blue ray, and they crumpled to the floor. Then I turned to Evy. "Sorry, that wasn't very original. But I wasn't expecting them, and—"

"Let's get out of here." Evy raised her hands. They were attached to the sides of the med pod by thick straps.

I unbuckled her right arm, then went to work on her ankles while she did the left. She slid off the bed and yanked the Gagarian woman's sleeve, rolling her onto her face as she tore the jacket off. "You got any shoes? They took my boots."

I glanced at her bare feet, then at the prone Gagarians. "I'm not sure either of those would fit you. Take the grav belt—no one walks around here."

She stripped off the belt and wrapped it around her waist, pulling it to the shortest length. It fit loosely around her tiny frame, but she nodded. "Give me a weapon."

I handed her the stunner. "Keep it in your pocket—you're supposed to be under guard." I pulled the door open and came face to face with Commander Jankovic.

"Sir," I stammered. "What—"

A lance of blue sizzled past me, hitting Jankovic square in the chest. He collapsed. Evy fired again, taking down the Gagarian standing behind him.

I whirled to stare at Evy. "You just stunned the commander."

"He's with them. Help me move him. He doesn't have a grav belt on."

I leaped out of the way as Evy leaned down to grab the commander's legs. She pulled his ankles, but he barely budged. I grabbed his shoulders and lifted, shoving his heavy frame into the room. "I'll get the other guy."

While I wrestled the guard into the cell, Evy went through Jankovic's pockets. "Get that guy's weapons and give me his hat."

"You need an officer's hat." I pointed at the woman lying beside the med pod. "This one will give you away. And grab their wrist devices, too, or they'll be able to open the door."

She nodded and yanked the hat from the woman's belt. "Good intel. Does Jankovic have one? I didn't think to look."

I slid the commander's sleeves up his arms. "Doesn't look like it. Are you sure he's one of them? Maybe he's here to negotiate our release."

"I doubt he'd walk into a Gagarian camp without a CEC security detail if he wasn't. Besides, she said he was with them." She tapped the woman's leg with her toes, then looked up at me. "What's your plan?"

"We're waiting for a distraction and a ride. Although, maybe we should borrow Jankovic's ship. I assume that's his on the pad."

"Sleek little civilian model? It's his." She gestured at the cell. "Hey, you got a cam? We should record all this."

"I'm not sure I want a recording showing I was complicit in disabling my mission commander on a foreign-occupied moon. On the other hand, he did send me back to the ship on trumped up charges." I tapped the device on my wrist and brought up the cam.

While I found the vid app, Evy leaned over Jankovic again. When I panned the vid to her side of the room, she held up a hand. I focused on her.

"I, Major Sarabelle Evy, am relieving Commander Lishan Jankovic of his holo-ring. Commander Jankovic stands accused of treason—infiltration of the CEC and aiding and abetting the Gagarian government in their attempt to set up a spy base on the moon Saha. We will return Commander Jankovic to the CEC for questioning and trial." She pulled the holo-ring from his hand, then made a cutting motion against her neck.

I flicked off the vid. "Treason? There seems to be a lot of that going around."

She looked up from fastening the soldier's grav belt around Jankovic's waist. "Who?"

"Marika, for one. And possibly Lee."

Outside, an explosion roared. The walls shuddered, rattling the med pod. "There's our distraction." I jumped over the young soldier lying inside the door and hurried across the outer room.

Evy tapped Jankovic's grav belt controls, and the unconscious man rose from the floor, drooping from the belt. As she pushed him through the door, his head banged into the frame. "Oops, sorry, sir." She didn't sound sorry at all.

"Even with the distraction, we can't drag him out like this." I grabbed his arm and rotated him upright. "I'll put his arm across my shoulders—hopefully no one will get close enough to ask what's wrong with him."

Evy nodded. She opened the door and rattled out a command in Gagarian. The soldier on the step stuttered a few words and saluted. Then he ran.

"What did you say?" I guided Jankovic through the door.

Evy grabbed his other arm and turned him toward the landing pad. "I told him the commander needed his help in the command center, and he'd get double rations if he arrived in under thirty seconds."

"Does everyone speak Gagarian except me?"

We increased our grav belt speed and flew along the walkway, zipping past Gagarians heading the other direction. One tried to stop us, but Evy barked out another order. The man fled.

"I learned at the Academy. With a brush-up via hypnopedia after we returned from Earth. It's a long story." She pushed me toward the little shuttle. "Get him inside while I do a preflight." She flicked the holo-ring she now wore—Jankovic's—and the door opened.

"Yes, ma'am." I pulled Jankovic into the craft. Inside, no expense had been spared. Four pairs of huge, Lether seats faced each other over small tables with a wide aisle between. Thick carpet hid the deck, and attractive fabric covered the bulkheads. Large screens were embedded in the bulkheads to imitate windows. I pushed Jankovic into the rear right seat and fastened the restraints. Then I took another look around the shuttle.

The cockpit was hidden behind a door at the front of the ship. There were seats for two pilots and a pair of jump seats in a narrow space behind them. A door at the back led to a small galley and sanitation facility. I pawed through the cupboards and came up with a set of slip ties. People reacted differently to being stunned, and I wanted to make sure he couldn't catch us by surprise if he woke up early.

I strapped the commander's wrists to the arm rests, making sure the ties were too tight to slip out of, but not tight enough to cut off his circulation. I considered doing his legs, too, but that seemed like overkill. Then I stuck my head out of the shuttle door, looking for Evy.

Another explosion rattled the base. Flames shot up from behind the ranks of buildings. Sirens blared and a voice barked from my wrist device, demanding fire suppression.

More orders in Gagarian issued from behind the ship. It sounded like Evy, but it was hard to tell in the foreign language. Two low ranking Gagarian soldiers veered around the nose of the shuttle and streaked away toward the carnage.

CHAPTER THIRTY-EIGHT

ANOTHER EXPLOSION SHOOK THE GROUND, louder and closer than the previous. To my right, a fireball blossomed, heat washing over us. What could they have hit? Had they expected it to be that destructive?

Two Gagarians arrowed across the tarmac, making straight for the shuttle. I reached for my blaster. Crap! I'd left it on a table inside while wrestling Jankovic into a chair. Frantically, I searched through my pockets, but I'd given the stunner to the major. "Evy! We have company!"

I dove back into the shuttle and snagged the blaster. Whirling around, I surged forward, then slammed to a halt. The blaster's strap had snagged on Jankovic's arm rest. I stopped to unloop the length of webbing.

Fingers snapped around my wrist like a vice. Jankovic's eyes burned into mine. "What are you doing, you little *crepiv?*"

"Defending myself." I twisted my hand, putting pressure against his thumb while pulling his wrist away from the chair arm. The slip tie pressed into his flesh, and he released me with an oath.

"You'll regret this, you little *crepiv—*"

"Yeah, I don't know what a *crepiv* is, and my translator isn't working right now." I ripped a strip of tape off the roll I'd shoved into my belt pouch and slapped it across his mouth. Then raced to the door, swinging the blaster to the firing position.

Two Gagarian soldiers lay on the tarmac, a few meters from the door. Marika and Joss hovered over them. "We should move them out of the launch zone," Joss said.

Marika flicked their grav belts, and they rose, slumped over their belts. She got behind one of them, dropped to plant her feet on the pavement, and shoved him, hard. He slid away, moving toward the closest building. Joss pushed the second one after the first.

"Preflight checks done." Evy swung around the end of the ship and made shooing motions. "Get inside, children. Time to go." She lifted over the steps and pushed past me. "Joss, you're with me. Siti, close the door. Marika—" She stopped to stare at the other woman. "Stay out of the way."

Marika threw a CEC salute at Evy and sauntered up the steps. Joss followed her. I let them pass, then pressed a button marked "steps." The small platform retracted into the side of the ship.

Across the plasphalt, the first Gagarian bumped into the building and bounced away. The second smacked into the first, sending them drifting in opposite directions like huge, misshapen billiard balls.

I swung the hatch into place and spun the wheel, locking the mechanism by hand. A green light flared on over the door, and a soft ping sounded through the ship.

"Get strapped in. We launch now."

I ran forward, flinging myself into the first seat on the left as the craft lifted smoothly off the ground. Marika sat across the table, staring at Jankovic, muttering under her breath.

"What?" I pulled the straps around me and fastened them.

"We should have left him there. Failure on this scale would net him what he deserves. Commonwealth prisons are too good for him."

"Do you know him?"

Her lips curled. "I know of him. Believe me, he deserves to rot in Friangler."

A chill ran down my spine. I'd heard of the notorious Gagarian "retraining" camp—who hadn't? I wouldn't wish it on my worst enemy—well, maybe LeBlanc deserved to go there. But from what I'd heard, he would probably end up running the place. It was right up his alley.

Which reminded me. I unfastened my seatbelt and staggered toward the cockpit door. "Major Evy? What about Lee?"

Evy leaned back in her chair to look at me. "We've found him. He landed on the far side. We're headed there now. You should strap in. We don't know what defenses they have."

"Marika said there aren't any." I clutched the edge of the cockpit door frame.

Evy slanted a look my way. "I'm not sure she's a credible source." She flicked a switch, activated the internal comm system. "Marika, if you move from that chair, you'll regret it. Joss, keep an eye on her."

I dropped into the jump seat behind Joss. Now that we'd escaped, adrenaline had deserted me. I slumped into the chair and pulled the five-point harness over my shoulders. I rearranged my jacket so Liam wouldn't be squished and clicked the buckles home. Then I closed my eyes and went to sleep.

A CHANGE in the engine noises roused me. I peered through the windows. This section of the moon looked different. Instead of thick jungle, wild grass waved in the breeze, sending ripples across the vast plains. A herd of creatures—so far away they looked like insects—stampeded over a rolling hill. Sunlight glinted on a trickle of water.

"Where are we?" I leaned around Joss's seat to get a better look. "Is this the same moon?"

"It's a big moon—lots of different ecosystems here." Evy turned the hovering shuttle in a slow circle. More rolling grass stretched for kilometers.

"Where's he hiding?" Joss yawned and stretched. His face was red, and a sheen of sweat gave him a greasy appearance.

"Are you okay?"

Evy glanced at Joss. "He's running a fever. I ran a ScanNSeal on him after we got away from the base—he's being treated for infection right now."

"I'm fine." Joss blinked sleepily.

"Maybe you should lie down. Those seats in back fold flat."

"You got any stick time?" Evy asked.

"Me? I've done some time in a simulator, but I wasn't planning on being a pilot, so I never got any real flight practice."

She nodded. "You should remedy that. Never hurts to have flying experience. If we don't find Lee, you can take the right seat."

"Marika probably flies," I suggested hesitantly.

"If you ask me, she should be tied to her seat like Jankovic. But you didn't ask me."

"I'm—"

She cut me off. "It's not a problem. You were running this operation—you made the call, and I can stand by it. I'm just saying I might not have made the same one in your position. And I'm keeping an eye on her." She waved at the array of holo-screens across the front of the ship. Three of them showed the passenger area from different angles. Marika and Jankovic were visible in all three. "I've also turned on the scrambler. Even if they have compatible communications tech, they shouldn't be able to talk to each other without us hearing."

I sat upright with a jolt. It hadn't occurred to me Marika and Jankovic could be working together.

Evy set the craft down on the flattest section of meadow she could find, but we were still canted at a fairly steep angle. We moved Joss to the rear of the craft, laying him on one of the reclining seats.

Evy checked the ScanNSeal, still wrapped around his arm. "It says he's good…"

"Why don't you stay with him, and Marika and I will look for Lee." I turned to the redhead. "You said something about Gagarian tech blocking my comm system. Were you able to get ahold of Lee?"

"Gimme Jankovic's ring." Marika jumped out of her seat and took the device from Evy. She slid the ring onto Jankovic's little finger and grabbed his face, turning it forward. "Tilt his seat back a bit, will you?"

"Why is he so still?" I reached down and hit the seat controls, tipping the seat to a more horizontal position.

"He was making so much noise, muttering behind that tape." Marika waved a pen-shaped item at me. "So, I hit him with this."

"This" was a single-shot sedative from the ship's first aid kit. Usually, the ScanNSeal could be relied upon to take care of emergencies, but each CEC shuttle also carried a fully manual kit. You never knew when you'd need to patch up a teammate up without power.

"You drugged him?" I asked. "Isn't that dangerous?"

"Those sedatives are formulated to be safe to use in almost every circumstance. It shouldn't cause any lasting damage."

Evy nodded. "That's why I let her do it. We've got a mission to complete, and he'd get in the way."

"Okay, I'm in." While we'd been talking, Marika had activated Jankovic's ring. The heavy, signet-style device now hung loosely from her thumb, projecting a holo-screen. Marika flicked through files and made some changes.

"Rings are supposed to be tuned to the user—how'd you get it to work for you?" I watched, fascinated, as she worked.

"How'd you get the Chet to work?"

I explained my process.

"Yeah, it was nothing like that. Rings have more sophisticated security. That's why the higher-ranking officers use them whenever possible." She flicked one last thing and grinned. "Lee, are you there?"

Static replied.

"Hang on, let me..." She flicked a few more things and tried again. "Lee?"

"Who is this?" Derek Lee's voice growled. "How'd you make this comm work?"

I leaned closer. "Lee, this is Siti. We're looking for you."

"I tracked your holo-ring to this location, and managed to fix the comms," Marika said. "We're in a big rolling field—the same field you were in about two hours ago."

"Who is this?" Lee repeated.

"Lee, that was Marika. She's helping us. We are not under duress. You can come out of hiding. Commander Jankovic's shuttle is here to take us back to the *New Dawn*." I made a face at Marika and Evy. It was true, as far as it went.

"I hid the Gagarian shuttle in a cave a half a klick from the edge of that meadow. I'll be there in a few minutes."

"Got him." Marika flicked up another holo showing a grid with two locations mapped. A couple of swipes overlaid an image of the terrain, and we could see Lee's indicator emerging from a rocky cliff.

"I'll move us that way." Evy sprinted to the front of the ship, and we lifted off, traveling a few meters above the ground.

We set down as Lee emerged from the trees at the edge of the vast meadow. He ran across the grass and jumped into the ship before I could get the steps down. He barreled into me, slamming both of us against the shuttle's bulkhead.

"Siti!" He squeezed me in a lightning fast hug and planted a loud kiss on my cheek, then stepped back. "Who else is here?"

I turned. Evy and Marika stared at us from their positions beside Joss's chair. "Everyone."

A stunner appeared in Lee's hand. He jerked the weapon at Marika. "Who's she? And what's happened to the commander?"

CHAPTER THIRTY-NINE

I LET Evy explain what had happened while she and Lee flew the ship to the *New Dawn*. Marika and I sat in the back, mostly ignoring each other but occasionally reminiscing about things that had happened on Earth. I still wasn't completely convinced she'd switched sides, but luckily, that wasn't my call to make

When we arrived on the *New Dawn*, things got complicated. Major Evy presented her evidence to the security officer, and Commander Jankovic, still groggy from his sedative, was turned over to them. Security also took Marika. I offered to make a statement in her defense, but the junior officer waved me off. "We have protocols for defections."

A med team took Joss away on a stretcher pod, presumably for a stint in a med pod, and I returned to our team compartment alone. The rest of the team was still on Qureshi, of course, but that hadn't felt real until I saw the deserted room. I requested a new uniform from the printer, grabbed a set of one-size-fits-none lounge gear, and headed to the showers.

Clean and dressed in baggy pants and shirt, with tight sock-like slippers on my feet, I rolled into the bunk I'd originally been assigned and fell asleep.

A HAND SHOOK MY SHOULDER. "Siti, wake up."

I opened my eyes. A blurry blob resolved into Joss. "Did you finally get fixed up?"

"They said I'm lucky to be alive." He looked normal, with clean hair, a tailored uniform, and the faintest of stress lines around his eyes.

"That wasn't luck, it was a friend with fast reflexes and excellent training." I poked my thumb at my chest and sat up. "You seen Liam?"

"He's over there." He pointed across the room. Liam looked up from the Chewy Nugget clutched in his front paws, cheeped at me, then returned to his meal.

"Thanks for feeding him." I scooted off the bunk, landing lightly on bare feet. I must have removed the tight socks in my sleep.

"I didn't give him that. I think he's learned to use the meal pac dispenser." Joss held out a pile of fabric. "Here's the uniform you printed."

I took the clothing. "I know he's smart, but—" I stared at Liam as I pondered. "No, I bet you're right. He probably knows how to work everything on this ship."

"I don't think we're ready for glider pilots." Joss flung himself on the couch. "Or glider medics."

"You never know—they might be better than humans. Back in a few."

Once I'd washed and put on my new, well-tailored uniform, I felt a little more human. "What are we going to do today?" I asked as I returned to the ready room.

"Try to take over the world," Joss replied. "Or sit on our butts and wait for them to decide what to do with us. I'm not sure which would be more fun."

I tried contacting Evy through the ship's comm system, but calls out of our section were blocked. The door leading to the rest of the ship was locked.

"No one told me we were confined to quarters when I left medical." Joss waved his hand at the sensor inside the door. "But they didn't give me a holo-ring, either."

We dug up a deck of cards and played a few hands of a children's game

Joss remembered. The rules seemed to change with each round, and he won every time. Suspicious, I reached for my holo-ring to look up the game. "Crap. I'm going to try calling Evy again."

I crossed the room to the access panel and pulled up the comm system. Red lights glowed on each of the channels but the one labeled Captain. "Come look at this."

Joss threw his cards on the table and joined me. His eyes popped when he saw the panel. "Are we supposed to call the captain? Maybe they did that in case of emergency. No cadet is going to contact the ship's captain for anything less."

"Try me." I tapped the button.

"Siti, what are you doing?"

"They gave us no other options. What are they going to do, ruin our careers? I think we're past that." I looked him over while we waited for the connection. "You're usually the risk-taker. What's going on?"

"Too many senior CEC officers are crooked." Joss turned and stomped across the deck, his hands waving as he spoke. "Admiral Zimas, Lee, Myers. Now Jankovic. We don't know anything about the captain of this boat."

A voice issued from the speaker. "Admiral Hydrao's office. This is Major Wronglen."

I closed my eyes. Of course it was Wronglen. But her system would tell her who was calling, so disconnecting would only make matters worse. "Hi, Major Wronglen. This is Cadet Kassis. I hate to bother you, but this comm channel is the only one available to us."

Petra Wronglen had been a Lieutenant when we met on the mission to Earth. She didn't like me—I still wasn't sure why. She seemed jealous of my father's fame, and I had overheard her using a less than respectful nickname in conversation with an enlisted member. After that, things really went downhill. "Cadet Kassis, I was told you might call."

Joss hurried across the room. "Hey, Major, this is Joss Torres, from Earth. How are you? Congratulations on the promotion."

Wronglen's face appeared on the screen, and her voice seemed to warm. "Hello, Cadet Torres. I'm sorry to see you in these circumstances."

Her eyes darted to me, and her lips pressed together, as if I'd led a beloved child astray.

I stepped away from the camera and made an exaggerated face at Joss. When did he and Wronglen become friends? Her nephew had been our squadron commander during our plebe year, but Joss had never mentioned any connection to the major. I held up both hands, palms out, to let him know I'd leave the talking to him.

"Yeah, that's why we're calling. If I'd known you were the exec on this ship, I'd have tried earlier. Siti and I just want to know our status. No one has told us anything."

"I'm not sure I can help you with that, Cadet Torres. Accusations have been made and an investigation is under way. Until that's complete and charges are filed—if warranted—we're not allowed to share any information with you." Wronglen glanced over her shoulder, then leaned forward. "If it weren't for Major Evy, you'd be in the brig with the others."

"Others?" The question popped out before I could stop myself.

"Can we talk to Major Evy?" Joss asked. "And what happened to Cadet Lee?"

"Major Evy and Cadet Lee have been debriefed and assigned shipboard duties for the duration." She sat back. "I can't tell you anything else."

"But can we talk to them?" Joss persisted.

Wronglen shook her head. "I'm sorry, you're to be kept incommunicado for the duration."

"Can you at least get us access to the gym?" Joss asked. "This weak Qureshi gravity is bad for our physiology. We need regular exercise to combat it."

Wronglen actually chuckled. "Nice try, but your quarters are set at standard gravity. Don't tell me you didn't notice the difference when you arrived. You weren't in a med pod that long. Do some pushups. I have to go. I'm sorry I can't do anything else for you. Please reserve this comm line for emergencies only."

"Isn't being locked up without communications or legal counsel considered an emergency?" I asked, but she'd already signed off. I sighed and turned away. "My guess is Jankovic is denying everything, and it's going to come down to whether Evy can convince them we're telling the truth."

"Doesn't the fact that he was on Saha incriminate him?" Joss threw himself onto the couch again. "We should have looked for vid of him talking to the Gagarian commander."

"We didn't exactly have a lot of time for that kind of thing. You two really went over the top with the explosions."

"That wasn't all us." Joss ran his hands through his hair. "We did the first one, but Marika said the rest were part of the scuttle plan."

At my raised eyebrows, he went on. "Since they weren't supposed to be there at all, they had a plan for discovery. It included wiping out the base and destroying all records. That big explosion was the command center. Marika says our explosion, after we'd already destroyed their comm interrupter, probably convinced them to pull the plug on the operation."

"If we knew why Jankovic was there, that might give us something to work with." I picked up an open meal pac and dumped the contents onto the table. Only the Chewy Nuggets were missing. "Who ate the nuggets?"

Joss pointed at Liam, now snoozing in my rack. "I told you, he learned to use the dispenser."

"Maybe he can learn to break us out of here," I muttered.

"He probably can, but I'm not sure that's our best option." Joss snagged the blue envelope and squeezed fruit sauce into his mouth.

I shuddered. "How can you eat that stuff? It's one thing if that's all there is—"

"Look around you." Joss waved the empty blue packet. "This *is* all there is. We're stuck here for however long their investigation takes. No one in or out. We'll be living on meal pacs for the duration."

CHAPTER FORTY

A WEEK LATER, I was ready to scream. Joss and I had played every card game we knew more times than we could count. I owed him four hundred thousand fake credits, which he graciously declined to hold over me. We'd set up a workout routine using the furniture in the compartment and our body weight. We'd watched the seventeen approved vids that were available through the restricted library. I'd found a pair of scissors and cut a blanket into thin strips, which Joss taught me to knot into a long scarf using a technique he called "crochet."

"It's a lot easier to do if you have a hook," he said for the umpteenth time. "If I had a knife, I could make one—"

"From that piece of plastek. I know." I threw the length of fabric onto a bunk and dropped to the deck to do a few pushups.

The door swooshed open. I jumped to my feet as Joss came out of his chair.

Dad stood in the doorway. "Siti."

I checked my urge to lunge at him and saluted instead. "Admiral Kassis."

"At ease, both of you." He strolled into the room and held out a gold-colored circle to each of us.

I took the ring and slid it onto my finger. It lit up and accepted my credentials, then presented a standard menu. "Does this mean we've been cleared?"

"No, it means I'm here to ensure proper procedures are being followed." He took the chair Joss had vacated and gestured for us to sit. Then he pulled a small, gray cube from his pocket and set it on the table. He pressed the button on top, and it glowed softly. "That's a confidentiality cube. They're usually used when lawyers speak with their clients. I'm leaving that with you. Your attorneys will meet with you when we're finished."

"Attorneys?" Joss perched on the edge of his chair. "I don't know about Siti, but I don't have an attorney."

"You do now. I've called a friend of mine. His firm specializes in Corps conduct investigations. He's partnering with another lawyer who works on politically sensitive cases. They're both CEC veterans, so they know the system and how our missions work. You need to be one hundred percent truthful with them. Tell them exactly what happened from day one of this mission—they may even ask you to go back before that. Everything you say to them will be kept strictly confidential. I can personally guarantee none of it will come back to hurt you later."

Dad leaned back in his uncomfortable chair. "I think you're aware the CEC has changed in the last twenty-four years—since Siti and I left Grissom to go to Earth. Some of the senior officers are not—let's just say I'm not sure the best candidates were promoted. Young officers I thought would make rank left the service, moving to civilian jobs. As a result, situations—like the one you encountered on Sarvo Six—have occurred. Situations where sworn officers have chosen personal gain over the good of the Corps."

He cleared his throat. "I've been working with a carefully vetted cross-section of officers and politicians to root out the problems, but you cadets have been lightning rods for this stuff." He shook his head. "I had no idea convincing you to join the Academy would land you in so much trouble, Siti." He turned to Joss. "And I'm sorry your experience in the wider galaxy has been less than optimal."

Joss nodded gravely. "I appreciate that, sir. And I know my father will, too. Has he been informed?"

Dad's lips twisted in a grimace. "I called him as soon as I heard about the problems. I have another call scheduled later today. In fact, I'd like you to join me for that, so you can speak to him yourself. He says he trusts me to do what's best for you—I hope I am worthy of that trust."

"I'm sure you will be, sir. And I'd like to talk to him."

Dad stood.

I grabbed his hand. "Before you go—can you tell us about everyone else? Where are Evy and Lee? What happened to Marika and Jankovic? And what about the rest of our flight—Peter, Aneh, Chymm, and the others. Are they all right?"

"Squadron advisors are checking in with all the other cadets on Senior Tour." Dad sank back into his chair. "They'll let me know if there are any other irregularities. Evy and Lee are here on the ship. They're still working—doing drops to Qureshi, but they aren't allowed to speak with anyone on the surface. Marika is in the brig, as you must have expected. She'll be tried for treason when we return to Grissom."

"No!" I leaned forward. "If it weren't for her, we'd still be on Saha."

Dad patted my hand. "All of your statements will be taken into consideration. But first you need to be cleared or else your support will mean less than nothing to Marika. In fact, it might damage her case."

I put my hand over my face. "How has this happened? I was trying to be a model cadet."

"It's not your fault. We have cleared you of the sabotage charges. Based on the timestamps and both Major Bellincioni's and Senior Explorer Unida's sworn testimony, there's no way you could have created any of those accounts that were used to damage the mission. Marika has made it clear Gagarin set all of that up. She's been a wealth of information, but it all has to be corroborated, of course. She could have her own reasons for clearing you."

"What about Commander Jankovic?" Joss asked.

"He has returned to his duties on Qureshi."

"What?" Joss and I both jumped to our feet.

"But he was on Saha!" I added.

Dad made calming motions. "Yes, he was on Saha. And his reasons for being there are being investigated. As are his accusations against you two and Evy. And his private shuttle has been impounded—I can't believe Hydrao allowed him to bring it on her ship. But his accusations are why you're here, and Evy and Lee are under a gag order."

"But Lee got off scot-free." The thought left a bitter taste in my mouth.

Joss's lip curled. "He wasn't sent back to the ship. By Jankovic."

Dad nodded. "That's all being investigated by the IG. And your attorneys will do their own reviews once they have your statements."

"The IG? Can we trust them?" Our flight mate Yvonne had told us years ago that the Academy Internal Affairs office wasn't really impartial —would the CEC Inspector General be any better?

"Commander Origani is working there. Obviously, he can't be involved in this case—conflict of interest since he's known you since you were born—but he's finding out who's loyal to what. Or whom." He pushed out of his chair. "It's time I let your attorneys in. As I said, be completely up front with them. They can't help you if you conceal anything."

Joss and I came to attention and saluted. Dad returned the salute, then stepped forward to hug me. His arms closed around me, reminding me of all the times he'd bailed me out of trouble—even when I didn't really deserve it. My dad had never let me down. I hoped I wouldn't disappoint him this time. I choked back a sob and clutched him tight.

After a time, he released me. The door opened, and Dad had a low-voiced conversation in the hall. Then two younger people wearing civilian clothing stepped into the room. Dad strode away as the door slid closed.

I don't have much interest in fashion and had barely been out of uniform in three years, but even I could tell the woman's clothing was unusual. She wore a narrow skirt and a tightly fitted jacket that came down to her hips. The sharp V of the jacket revealed a scoop-necked shirt, and the notched collar lay flat against her chest. It looked very old-Earth retro.

The man, on the other hand, wore a beige coverall with red piping down the sides and stripes across the sleeves. Wide legs were tucked into his boots at mid-calf. It looked like a flamboyant copy of a CEC ship's mechanic's uniform. He carried a large case of what appeared to be tooled, purple Lether.

"Great, we got the fashionistas," Joss muttered. "I hope their lawyering is better than their taste in clothing."

I smothered a snicker and stepped forward to bump fists with the new arrivals. "I'm Cadet Serenity Kassis. You can call me Siti. This is Joss Torres."

Joss knocked his knuckles against theirs.

"Anders Neverti." The man bowed as he said it, then gestured regally to the woman. "This is Briva Arenti. You can call us Anders and Briva."

Briva's lips twitched as she took the case from Anders and placed it on the table. She opened it with a snap, revealing four tiny drones. "We record everything—I hope that's all right? These drones have no networking capability, so the interviews won't be transmitted anywhere. We'll hand carry the data back to our staterooms and only review them on non-net holo devices."

Joss pointed at the gray box Dad had left with us. "We have a confidentiality cube—that won't interfere with the drones, will it?"

"Not a problem," Anders said. "The tech is built to work together. If someone else got a drone inside, they would be able to record but not transmit. And we have a solution for that, too. Briva?"

Briva pulled out a small box and another cube, slightly larger than the gray one Dad had given us. "Holo-rings inside, please. You'll get them back in a moment." She and Anders pulled theirs off and dropped them inside the small box.

With a shrug, I followed suit, and after a slight hesitation, Joss added his to the collection. Briva closed the box and placed it inside the drone case, which she then closed with a snap. She raised the cube to eye-level and squeezed.

Nothing happened.

"If there had been any drones in here, they were just fried." She opened the case and returned our rings.

"What about other electronics?" Joss asked as he slipped his new holo-ring back onto his finger. "The meal pac dispenser. Heck, even the bathroom has electronics."

Briva pulled out the drones. "The fryer is built specifically for drones. I'm not sure how they make it work, but I've seen demonstrations that prove it does. In fact, I accidentally fried a holo-ring during a deposition a couple of weeks ago." She laughed as she took Joss's arm. "Let's get started."

We split up, with Briva interviewing Joss in one corner while Anders walked me through events in another. Then we switched and went through it all again.

After a quick lunch of real food brought to our compartment by the galley staff, Anders and Briva sat us down together to go through the story again. This time they asked more detailed questions. Taking us through some incidents several times.

Finally, Anders called a halt. "You've had enough for today. Briva and I will go through all of this, then we'll interview the others—including a trip to the planet." His nose wrinkled as if he could already smell the stench of Qureshi. "We'll get a chance to review the data from the wrist devices you brought back with you. Then we'll be back to go through all of the testimony and evidence with you."

"In the meantime, your holo-rings should give you access to other parts of the ship. You can get meals from the mess but should return here to eat them. You can use the recreational areas, but we highly recommend you keep interactions with others to a minimum." He packed up the drones as he spoke. "The crew knows you're here, and they've been instructed to avoid you, so that won't be a problem."

"Great." I stood and stretched. "Nothing better than being a pariah."

"What about the officers?" Joss asked. "Major Wronglen became friends with my dad when she was on Earth, and we met Admiral Hydrao then, too."

Briva glanced at Anders before answering. "If the admiral feels it's appropriate, of course you're allowed to speak with them. But don't discuss the case."

"Roger." Joss bumped knuckles with the two lawyers. "Thanks."

"Our pleasure," Briva replied. "It's more than time for the CEC to clean house."

CHAPTER FORTY-ONE

TWO WEEKS LATER, the *New Dawn* returned us to Grissom. The rest of the cadets went with us, but we weren't allowed to speak to them. In fact, Joss and I were sentenced to a stateroom in officers' country before they returned to the ship. The plusher accommodations were not a fair trade-off.

Liam didn't seem to mind. In fact, he managed to disappear completely for hours at a time, then reappear just as suddenly, with no indication of where he'd been. But he didn't eat any of our rations, so I had to assume he'd found a way to reach the galley. Or a sympathetic glider lover. I hoped he wouldn't abandon me. I'd originally found him wandering loose on the ship to Earth—maybe he'd gotten tired of me and was looking for a new partner?

Hours after the ship arrived in orbit, we were finally escorted to a small personnel shuttle. Liam appeared as the hatch opened, flying to his favorite perch on my shoulder. I rubbed my cheek against his soft body, grateful he'd returned. The explorer waiting at the door eyed Liam but didn't say anything.

Lieutenant Nabiyev—the officer who'd flown with Evy when she arrived to pick us up on Qureshi—met us at the shuttle. "Major Evy says you're on the pilot track, Torres. You wanna sit up front?"

"Hell, yes." Joss leaped over the two steps and into the shuttle's airlock.

Nabiyev grinned as he stepped aside to allow Joss to pass. Then he raised an eyebrow at me. "How about you?"

"Thanks, but I'm not—"

He cut me off. "Sit up front with us. You don't want to be back here. This is *not* one of the nicer shuttles."

"Thanks." I followed him into the craft and strapped my bag to the pallet. Someone had packed up our gear on Qureshi and sent it to the ship, so at least I had a few familiar items. Liam leaped up into the conduits overhead, soaring from perch to perch, following Nabiyev to the front of the ship.

"Who's flying co-pilot?" Joss hovered in the space behind the pilots' seats where the jump seats folded down.

Nabiyev's lips twitched. "I'm pretty sure letting you fly in the left chair would be dereliction of duty, so it's not me."

A smile spread across Joss's face. "Really? You'll let me co-pilot? Even with all this?" He made a stirring motion, indicating me, the ship, and everything.

"I trust Major Evy's judgement." Nabiyev slid into the seat on the left side. "If she says you're a good pilot, that's good enough for me. And I don't care about the rest of that stuff. She made it pretty clear you're both innocent—without actually saying that, of course, since she's under a gag order." He flicked his holo-ring and pulled up a checklist. "Pick a seat and strap in, Kassis."

I pulled down the jump seat behind Nabiyev and did as I was told. Liam jumped from the hatch to my shoulder, then scrambled into my pocket.

Nabiyev spared a glance over his shoulder. "Did you whistle or give a hand command?"

"Me?" I asked. "No."

"How'd your glider know it was time to get into your pocket?"

I shrugged. "He knows. We're on a shuttle, and the pilots are starting it up."

His eyes narrowed. "That's way smarter than any glider I've ever seen."

WE LANDED on the shuttle pad at CEC headquarters. Several other shuttles, most of them in much better condition than ours, sat on the tarmac, each in its own tidy white square. Jankovic's fancy private shuttle sat near the end of the space, next to a large shiny white craft with blue racing stripes and the words Colonial Explorer Corps emblazoned across the side in red.

Nabiyev glanced at the shuttle, then did a double take. "The Chief is here."

"The Chief of the Explorer Corps?" I followed the men out of our shuttle and into the hot sunshine. "Isn't her office here?"

"Yeah, but my wife is her pilot. She was at some high-level summit on Armstrong with the prime minister and the other chiefs. I wasn't expecting her home until next week." He led us along a white walkway between lush green lawns. "Must have finished early. Lucky for me!"

Liam jumped down from my shoulder and scampered away before we stepped into the building next to the flight line. As the wide doors slid shut behind us, Nabiyev looked back. "Aren't you worried about him getting lost? Has he been here before?"

"No and no." I grinned at his look of consternation. "You've seen how smart he is. Our plebe year, he hitched a ride with Dad from Earth so he could get to me at the Academy. It's almost as if he has a homing beacon on me. He can find me anywhere."

We stepped through a second set of trans-lu doors into a wide lobby. Shiny white tiles covered the floor. A pair of modern-looking couches stood on either side. The CEC crest dominated the far wall where an attractive young explorer junior grade in formal uniform sat behind a tall desk. He stood as we approached and saluted Nabiyev.

"I'm delivering Cadets Kassis and Torres for their hearing."

The explorer gawked at us over the tablet he scrolled through. He mumbled under his breath—probably talking to someone via comm—and presented the tablet to the lieutenant.

Nabiyev read the tablet and pressed his thumb against the face of it. "Good luck, guys. Give me a call when you're free—we can take another flight. I suspect you missed out on a few check rides over the last two weeks." He returned the tablet to the young explorer and strode through the wide doorway beside the crest, nodding to two more explorers who entered as he left.

"I need your thumb prints." The explorer shoved the tablet at me. "You're agreeing to follow the regulations for class 4 defendants. You should already have had an opportunity to review those regulations, so press your thumb here." He reached across awkwardly to scroll upside down to the end of the document.

I pulled the tablet away from him. "I've read the regulations, but I always read everything before I sign it." I swiped through the clauses, making sure they still said what I read earlier. The two women chatted quietly, waiting for us, I supposed. The front desk guy fidgeted with his stylus, but I ignored them all. "Looks good." I pressed my thumb to the face of the device and handed it to Joss.

Joss followed my lead, taking his time to read through the entire thing. When the explorer presented another screen, because as a citizen of Earth, Joss's status was different, he read through all of that, too. Finally, he signed.

The explorer sighed with relief. "Stiles and DuBoff will take you to the defendant's quarters."

The two women turned smartly, and one of them preceded us through the wide doorway. The second one waved us past. "Please follow Explorer DuBoff."

The wide doorway led to a long corridor. At the far end, people moved purposefully through another lobby. The corridor between was empty, lined with closed doors. Thick carpet muffled our footsteps. About halfway to the end, DuBoff placed her hand on an access panel, and a door opened.

She led us along another hallway, then we took a float tube to the fourth floor. Three more hallways, each accessed through a locked door, brought us to another tall desk. DuBoff murmured to the uniformed guard on duty, then she and Stiles disappeared the way we'd come.

"Good afternoon." The guard flicked a code slip to each of us. My holo-ring buzzed as it landed, and a screen popped up. She reeled off a spiel as if it had been memorized. "Welcome to the defendants' barracks. Inside, you'll find a gym, mess hall, AR fitted rec center, and chapel. You've each been assigned a room. You're free to move about the barracks as you wish, but you will stay inside this section of the hall until your judiciary action is complete. All areas of the barracks are under vid supervision. Your holo-rings will not have access to anything outside this facility. If legal counsel visits, you may use the assigned meeting room for that visit. Any other guests must be approved by the judge." Here, she paused to look us up and down. "I don't recommend you request any guests."

"I hope we won't be here long enough to want guests." I took the tablet she handed me and scanned the information, then pressed my thumb against the screen. Joss did the same.

The door beside the desk popped ajar, and the guard waved us through. "Follow the code slip to your room. Enjoy your stay." The last bit was added with a sarcastic edge.

We entered a small, empty room with one door on the far wall. The door through which we entered snapped shut, and a blue light passed over us—a scan, probably for weapons. Thirty seconds later, the far door opened.

This dumped us into a short hall with beige walls and brown plastek floors. Three closed doors stood on either side. My holo-ring pulled me toward the last door on the right, so I pushed it open. Inside, I found a bed, a dresser, and a tiny bathroom. No windows, no entertainment center. I threw my bag onto the bed and turned.

Joss stood in the doorway across the hall, staring back at me. "Wanna hit the gym?"

"I'll take a look at it, but we've already worked out today." I tapped my holo-ring and brought up the information the guard had given us and tapped the gym. The door on my left popped open, revealing a room the same size as mine with a single multi-function aerobotron, a weightlifting system, and a padded mat down the middle.

"That's underwhelming," Joss said over my shoulder. "Let's try the mess hall."

The door across from the "gym" opened to reveal a small table with two chairs and a meal pac dispenser. Behind the remaining two doors, we found a table with four chairs—the meeting room—and, across the hall, a tiny Sanctuary with two chairs facing a screen. A panel by the door allowed the occupant to choose which religious symbol appeared on the screen and offered a selection of music.

"Where's the rec center?" I asked.

"It's the hallway." Joss tapped a panel at the end of the hall. It opened to reveal a rack of augmented reality equipment. He fingered a pair of AR glasses then returned them to the rack. "No expense spared."

"I guess we know where we stand in the CEC scheme of things." When Joss raised an eyebrow, I held a hand by my thigh to designate levels. "Bottom of the barrel. Well below new recruit. Basic training has better facilities than this."

"I guess if you consider these cells were built to house people accused of crimes, it makes sense." He closed the cupboard. "I mean, innocent until proven guilty isn't a thing in the CEC, is it?"

"Theoretically it is, but by the time you get sent here, there's probably a huge pile of evidence."

"Like what we're fighting?"

"I think—I hope—there's usually more than that." I wandered into my room and dropped beside my bag. "Maybe I'll take a nap."

"Briva and Anders should be here soon." Joss crossed the hall and threw himself down on his own narrow bunk. "I hope they have good news for us."

CHAPTER FORTY-TWO

"I'm not sure it's 'good' news." Anders's face was pale, and a sheen of sweat covered his upper lip and forehead. "The trial has been moved up to tomorrow."

Briva tried to look unconcerned. "We're ready. There's no point in drawing this out."

We sat in the small meeting room. Briva had smuggled in real food in her briefcase which Joss and I fell on like animals. The barracks' official information claimed the meeting rooms were protected by client-attorney privilege and that vids were suspended during legal team meetings, but Anders had deployed a privacy cube just the same.

"Is Jankovic here?" I asked. "I saw his ship—are they letting him fly it?"

Anders sat down on one of the uncomfortable chairs, which squeaked alarmingly. "No, he arrives tomorrow. The ship has been impounded. But I've heard they might be getting ready to return it to him."

"When is *his* trial?" Joss tapped his fingers on the table. I reached across and gripped his hand, stopping the noise.

Briva looked away. Anders ducked his head.

"What?" I demanded. "Don't tell me there isn't a trial! What about Marika's evidence?"

"Marika's evidence isn't admissible—she's a known enemy agent."

Briva twisted her fingers together in an uncharacteristic display of nerves. "Gagarin would love to get a decorated officer disgraced. Don't look at me like that—I'm just telling you what the prosecutor told me."

"What would it take to get him to trial?"

"The prosecutor has to have enough evidence to convict, or they won't even attempt it. That would mean incontrovertible proof he had worked with the Gagarians." Briva flipped files onto the tabletop projector and flicked through the images. They all showed Jankovic in locations around the base on Saha, speaking with Gagarian officers, but none had audio. "There was no vid, just these stills. Everything we gave them could be explained away—he was on Saha in an effort to negotiate with the Gagarians."

"But the Gagarians aren't supposed to be on Saha. How was he supposed to know they were there?" I asked.

"He said he noticed the base when he flew to the *New Dawn*." Briva sorted through virtual files, never stopping to look at any of them. "We asked why he was returning to the ship—why he didn't go with you in the VIP shuttle. We were told that wasn't relevant to the case. I have someone trying to get more information, but so far, nothing."

Anders cleared his throat. "Let's go over our case one more time."

FOUR HOURS LATER, Anders called a halt. "You've got your responses down. We'll meet you here at oh-seven-thirty and escort you to the hearing."

"Thanks for your help." I bumped fists with each of them.

Joss followed my lead. "Yeah, thanks."

As the door closed behind them, Joss turned to me. "I don't feel very good about this. I mean, they've been amazing, and in a fair world, we'd win, but if Jankovic is going free…"

"I know what you mean." I dropped into my chair and cradled my head in my arms. "At least it will be over soon."

"What are you doing here?"

I lifted my head. Joss was crouched on the floor in the doorway, petting a blue and white sair glider.

"Liam!"

The little glider explained in his usual unintelligible fashion and dropped something in Joss's palm. Then he leaped over the young man and landed on my shoulder.

"I knew you'd find me, but I didn't think it would take this long." I rubbed my cheek against his warm body. He chittered and curled around my neck.

"Siti, look what he brought." Joss held up a small drawstring bag. He tipped it over, and a silver ring dropped into his other palm. "Where do you think he got it?"

"I dunno but put it on and see what happens."

He started to slide the ring onto his finger, then paused. "These things can't hurt you, can they?"

I laughed. "You've had one for three years. Aside from that time you jammed your finger in rev ball and had to have the ring cut off, has it ever hurt you?"

"No, but you hear stories. Or at least on Earth there were stories of found artifacts causing physical damage."

"You mean that ancient vid you used to watch with the warehouse, and the agents dumped possessed gizmos into purple goo? That's pure fiction. Give it to me if you don't want to try it yourself."

"No. Liam gave it to me. Besides it's probably too big for your fingers." He slid the ring on and flicked it.

A vid popped up, and Dish Elsinore's face grinned at us. "Hi, guys. This is a vid, obviously, but as soon as you finish watching it, give me a call. Your friend Nibs contacted me and said you need help. He claimed your little squirrel friend would get this ring to you—we'll see if he was correct."

I stared at Dish's face. "Who's Nibs?"

Joss shrugged and gestured at the vid.

"We're doing a little reconnaissance for you." The vid disappeared. "Call him."

Joss flicked the ring again. "The call is going through. How's he doing that? This facility is supposed to be a blackout zone."

Elsinore's face appeared again. "Good afternoon, Siti Kassis."

I leaned closer to Joss so he could see us both. "Dish! Hi! This is my friend Joss."

Joss waved.

"How are you doing this?" I gestured to Joss and the ring. "The Justice Center is supposed to be secure, and we have a confidentiality cube running."

"I have a tri-vector interpolator parsing over a multi-net block-neural transcode inhibitor with three—" My eyes glazed over as he explained. "It's quite effective in infiltrating CEC communications. All communications, really."

"Jeez, do the CEC know about it? What if the Gagarians get it?" Joss asked.

"I'm a member of the CEC communications security master panel. They know this is possible but have dismissed it as unlikely. I created this script in part to prove it can be done. I'll be demonstrating it next week. Apparently, they don't understand the urgency of the matter."

"I guess not—" I started, but Dish continued as if I hadn't spoken.

"We have initiated a covert operation to clear you. Nibs—"

"Who is Nibs?" Joss interrupted this time.

Dish blinked and stared at us. "That's the only name I know. I shall have to check his credentials."

"You're undertaking a covert and possibly illegal operation with a guy you know only by his call sign?" Joss asked.

"Oh, it's a call sign." I laughed. "That makes sense, but it isn't one I've heard before. Do you know this guy?"

"Nope, never heard of him." Joss jerked his head at me and grabbed the cube on the table. "These chairs suck. Let's go sit on one of the bunks."

We moved into Joss's room while Dish muttered to himself about credentials and call signs.

Once we'd settled on the infinitely more comfortable mattress, Joss waved to get Dish's attention. "You can check his credentials later. Tell us about this mission."

Dish's face brightened as he refocused on us. "Nibs is going to have a talk with Commander—" He glanced around the room and leaned closer to the cam. "With the treasonous miscreant. We believe with the correct social pressure, he can be convinced to elucidate his position."

A headache started throbbing behind my right eye. "I didn't understand any of that."

Joss scowled. "I think he means they're going to get Jankovic to brag about his treasonous activities, like a cartoon villain."

Dish's expressive face fell. "We aren't going to ask him outright. Our plan is more subtle than that. Make sure you're watching tonight at ten. In the meantime, is there anything you need from the outside?"

"Ice cream," Joss said.

I smacked Joss's arm. "We're good—you can focus on your scheme. We'll check in at ten."

After Dish signed off, Joss pulled the ring from his finger. "Probably best if I'm not wearing this. In case anyone else wanders in."

I waved at the ceiling. "Vids. They might already know."

Joss picked up the little gray box. "This thing fogs the vid. They can tell we're sitting here, but they can't see details."

I stood and stretched. "How do you know so much about confidentiality boxes?"

"I'm smart that way." He pressed the button, turning it off. "Plus, I looked at the specs."

CHAPTER FORTY-THREE

AT A QUARTER TILL TEN, I wandered into Joss's room with the confidentiality box. He sprawled across his bunk, reading on his holo-ring. When he saw me, he closed the file and sat up. "Sup?"

"I ate hours ago." I pressed the button on the gray box and dropped beside him.

"You're so funny." He knocked his shoulder against mine. "Where's Liam?"

"I dunno. He disappeared after dinner." I always felt deserted when he took off, but I knew he'd be back. As I'd told Nabiyev, he always found me.

"Probably roaming the base looking for girl gliders."

"Don't let the xenobiologists hear that. They only approved him because their testing showed he was nonreproductive. By the way, I looked up 'nibs' on the net. All I got was 'a person of authority or someone who is full of themselves,' and something about chocolate. Oh, and it was the name of one of the 'Lost Boys' from an ancient book named *Peter Pan*."

Joss chuckled. "Any one of those could be a good source for a call sign. Probably got lost on a check ride and was a nob about it when he got back."

Promptly at ten, the holo-ring activated. A live vid popped up, showing a dark expanse, illuminated at regular intervals by small blue lights. Along the side, spotlights shone on various shuttles, each sitting in a white square painted on the dark plasphalt. The flight pad—or at least a flight pad. In the darkness, it was impossible to see landmarks that would indicate the location.

The view swooped and turned—obviously an airborne drone—focusing on a small, expensive personal shuttle. It looked like Jankovic's. A figure stood in the shadows, watching it. The wind swooshed, then muted.

A second window opened showing Dish's face. "Sorry about the wind noise. I've recalibrated to eliminate that."

"What are we seeing?" I asked.

"That's Nibs. He has a meeting scheduled with the target. We're following by drone."

We waited. The vid changed angles several times, but nothing happened. The figure in the shadows shifted. We waited some more.

"When's this meeting supposed to happen?" Joss asked.

"He must be running late." Dish played with something out of sight of his camera, and the drone view shifted again, moving higher and farther away. It rose above the buildings, then focused on a tiny figure in the distance. "There he is."

The figure sauntered along a pathway, pausing in a circle of lamplight to activate a va-pipe. He puffed on the mouthpiece a couple of times, then continued toward the flight line.

"I wonder if he knows he's being watched?" I asked. "That could have been an acting exercise named, 'man who is unconcerned taking a walk.'"

Joss snickered. "He's probably trying to make Nibs nervous—get the upper hand."

"I wish we knew who this Nibs is."

The drone dropped to eye level again. The figure in the shadows stirred, peeling away from the wall he'd been leaning against as if someone had spoken to him.

"We're go for the mission," Dish intoned.

Jankovic appeared around a corner, heading toward his ship. Nibs followed him at a distance, the drone hovering over his shoulder. As he stepped into the light, we got a shot of the back of Nibs's head, but his hat didn't allow us to see anything useful.

Jankovic opened the rear cargo hatch and stepped inside, leaving it open behind him. A few minutes later, we followed him inside. The sound of a hatch clanging behind the drone accompanied a sudden blackout. The airlock was unlit. We continued toward the dim outline of an internal hatch and moved into the tiny cargo hold.

Jankovic turned and held up a small cube. "I hope you followed my instructions and didn't wear a holo-ring."

"Crap! He's got a comm fryer." I waved at Dish's vid. "Dish, we're going to lose—"

The larger vid went black.

"Don't worry." Dish swiped through a few screens. "We have that covered."

Seconds later, another vid opened. This one hovered at ground level for a moment, then rose and turned slowly, revealing the dark airlock we'd just come through. A small box sat on the floor, similar to the one Briva had used to protect our holo-rings. Next to the box was Liam.

Joss and I stared at the screen. I'm sure our expressions were hysterical.

I snapped my jaw shut. "How did you—"

Dish laughed. "That glider of yours is really smart. Using him to open the box was Nibs's idea."

"Who is this guy?" I whispered.

Joss shrugged.

The vid shifted as the drone rose, then moved into the cargo bay. Nibs stood with his back to us. Jankovic faced him, a stunner in his hand. "—one reason I shouldn't just turn you over to CEC internal security."

"I have connections to people you might want to meet." Nibs stood with his hands raised over his head. The voice sounded familiar, but I couldn't quite place it.

"Lee?!" Joss jolted so hard, the vid shook. "Nibs is Derek Lee?"

"Yes, your friend Cadet Lee." On the small vid, Dish nodded. "I couldn't remember his name, but that's it."

"He's—" I started to say he wasn't our friend but stopped. I'd been insisting that for weeks, but was it true? Everything he'd done since we landed on the *New Dawn* together had been the actions of an ally. Sure, he'd made scathing remarks, but we'd been equally rude to him. And some people thought that's how friends talked to each other. In fact, since his first companions at the Academy had been Felicity and LeBlanc, it was no wonder he was caustic toward those he considered friends.

"He's going to sell us out," Joss muttered.

"Is he? He's come through more than once on this mission."

Jankovic said something, and Joss shushed me.

Lee was speaking. "—might be in prison, but she still has connections to people with vast sums of money."

"And you're trying to convince me this consortium of wealthy individuals is willing to use an Academy cadet as their mouthpiece?"

Lee lifted both hands. "After that disaster three years ago on Sarvo Six, the consortium, as you call it, has had to improvise. Keeping me in the Academy took significant effort, with the intention that I would carry on their work. My patrons, if you will, believe you must have an income that doesn't get processed through the CEC finance office. No one can afford a MorganTech on a commander's salary."

Jankovic laughed. "If you think I'm getting paid under the table, why would you think you can bribe me?"

Lee shrugged. "There's always a higher bidder. It depends on what you're selling."

The blaster lowered as Jankovic turned away. "If, for a moment, we assume I'm willing to sell information—" He swung around and pointed at Lee. "I'm not saying I do that. But if I were, what kind of bids are we talking about? How many zeros?"

Lee shifted. "I'm not authorized to discuss specific amounts. I can tell you that if you work with us, you'll have enough credits to buy the new MorganTech that just came out. The one with the heated seats."

"Heated seats? Is that the slang you kids are using now?" Jankovic slung the blaster over his shoulder, so it was no longer actively threatening Lee. "What kind of proof can you offer that you represent who you say you represent?"

Lee pulled a small item out of his pocket and handed it to Jankovic. The drone rose but couldn't go high enough inside the cargo hold to see what was passed. Jankovic examined it, and his face flushed. "Is this for real?"

"Test it yourself, sir."

Joss leaned closer to the vid. "What are they looking at?"

"It's a piece of senidium," Dish said. "It is more valuable than the ship they're standing in."

"How's he going to test it?" I asked.

"Microspectrometer."

Jankovic took the stone and disappeared into the passenger area of the ship. The drone zipped forward, but the door shut before it could enter. It turned, catching a direct shot of Lee's face for the first time. He appeared calm except for the thumb of his right hand, rubbing against the middle finger. He paced across the small hold, his steps easy and measured, then turned to lounge against the bulkhead.

After a few moments, Jankovic returned. "That was a valuable little trinket."

Lee pushed himself away from the wall. "Was? I'll need that back, sir."

"No, you don't. Go tell your handlers I've accepted their gesture of goodwill and look forward to the opportunity to do business with them in the future."

"I can't go away empty-handed, Commander. LeBlanc—" He broke off as if he'd said something unwise.

A crafty expression crossed Jankovic's face. "LeBlanc. I suspected he was involved in this. You were friends with his son before the big blowup, weren't you?"

Lee didn't say anything. Jankovic nodded to himself, as if this confirmed his suspicions. "Ser LeBlanc has his fingers in every pie. I might have information that would benefit him. What is he looking for? Military secrets?"

The younger man swallowed uncomfortably. "We can get military information, for the most part. We still have enough connections there. He—we need details on new discoveries—for example, the scientific research on that plastek-eating snail. I have shared what I know from the mission, but you have access to the test data."

Jankovic nodded. "What else?"

"Certain members of our consortium are interested in the possibility of doing business in other parts of the galaxy. Gaining access to high-level officers in the Gagarian or Leweian governments would be worth much more than mere scientific data."

Jankovic stroked his chin. "Seems reasonable."

"May I have the stone back?" Lee held out a hand.

"Don't be ridiculous. I'm taking that to the CEC IG and filing charges of attempted bribery against you, boy."

"What?" Lee gaped at the man.

"Crap," Joss muttered. "He didn't take the bait. We've lost."

Jankovic laughed. "You should see your face, kid. You like to think you can tangle with the big boys, but you don't have the stones to see it through. Never let on that you've been beaten." He smacked Lee's shoulder, rocking the younger man on his feet. "Tell your friends we can do business. I'll leave a drop at this location." He handed a slip of paper to Lee. "Tomorrow morning at oh-six-thirty. If they're happy with the information, we can do business."

Lee took the paper, his hand shaking. "Thank you, sir."

Jankovic put his arm around Lee and led him into the airlock. "Let me give you a piece of advice, boy. Don't call your adversary 'sir'. It makes you sound weak. If you're going to run with the big boys, you gotta be tough."

"Thank you, s—thanks." Lee stepped away from the man's arm as the outer hatch popped and hurried into the darkness.

CHAPTER FORTY-FOUR

"Was that enough?" Dish asked as the drone followed Lee out of the ship. "Did we get enough to clear you?"

"Are you asking us?" Joss shoved his hand into his hair. "How would we know? Can you get a copy of this vid to our lawyers?"

"They're watching live." Dish swiped, and Briva and Anders popped up in the feed.

"I think this will do," Briva replied. "Nice work."

Anders nodded in agreement. "He'll probably try to convince the judge he was running a sting but combined with his visit to Saha—and the fact that he kept that piece of senidium—we'll at least bring his testimony into question. If he actually leaves sensitive information at that drop location tomorrow morning—that will seal the deal."

"We're cutting it awfully close, though," Briva said. "The trial starts at eight. I hope he isn't late."

"Get some sleep, guys." Anders leaned forward to grin into his cam. "We'll see you in the morning."

The two lawyers disappeared, leaving Dish and the drone still transmitting from the flight pad.

"Thanks for the help, Dish. Did Lee really set this up?" I asked.

Dish nodded enthusiastically. "He contacted me from the *New Dawn*.

He said you told him about me and that you needed help. Then we figured out the rest and contacted your lawyers. He wanted to go to CEC security, but the lawyers convinced him to— What's happening?"

Lee had stopped moving, and the drone stopped with him. It dropped lower to peer over his shoulder. Three large men wearing black clothing and dark face paint stood across the walkway. One of them slapped a thick metal rod into his hand. A second one cracked his knuckles. The third stood like a statue, his eyes glittering in the dim lamplight.

"What are you doing out here alone, little boy?" the middle one asked.

Lee looked around quickly, then squared his shoulders. "I am returning to my quarters. Are you doing an exercise? I'm not involved."

"An exercise." The knuckle cracker cackled. "Sure, let's call it that. We're going to get some exercise teaching you to stay out of our business."

Lee took a couple of slow steps backwards. "What business would that be? I'm just out for a walk. And this is a CEC base. You know there are cams everywhere."

"I know the cams don't always work when we're around." Knuckles raised his hand and waved his holo-ring at Lee.

"They're going to kill him," I whispered. "Dish, call base security."

"I'm on it." Dish's vid disappeared.

The three thugs advanced on Lee. "Who are you?" His voice shook, and he cleared his throat to try again. "What do you want? What business am I supposedly interfering with?"

"You need to stay away from Jankovic. We have business with him, too, and we don't need you getting in the middle." The taller guy slapped his rod into his palm again with a meaty splat.

Lee held up both hands. "Message received. I'll get out of your way."

"Yes, you will. After we're finished with you."

"What's that?" Lee pointed over the men's heads. The silent man jerked around, but the other two didn't even flinch.

"Nice try, kid." The heavy rod swiped through the air, whistling.

Lee jumped back. The rod missed him by centimeters. Something blue and white exploded out of the dark, landing in the taller man's face. He stumbled back, flinging up his hands to protect himself. Liam roared—a noise almost identical to the felines on Saha—and sprang away. The man swung his rod blindly, catching Knuckles in the shoulder.

Liam landed on the silent guy, scratching at his eyes. The glider's tiny claws left surprisingly large gouges on the third man's face and bald head.

Lee waded into the fray, slamming his palm against Knuckles' nose. Blood gushed and Knuckles roared.

Sirens blared. Security officers converged from three directions. They deployed a gas canister, leaving all four men on the ground, gasping.

There was no sign of Liam.

THE GLIDER WAS WAITING in my room when I went to bed. I checked him for injuries but found nothing. He ate the packet of Chewy Nuggets I provided, then curled up beside me in bed and went to sleep.

I laid in bed, my brain spinning with all the information I'd received in the last day. I tossed and turned for hours, finally falling into a fitful sleep around two. My dreams were haunted by scenes of black-clothed thugs, a smug Jankovic, and a giant sair-glider with a sword.

At five thirty, I sat up and rubbed my eyes. I took a quick shower and donned my dress uniform. At six, I met Joss in the tiny mess. He bolted down his meal pac while I picked at mine. Finally, at six twenty-five, he activated the new holo-ring.

Dish's drone was up again. It hovered above a pond in a park on the far side of the base, the cam focused on a bench. People streamed by in both directions, most of them running. A small troop of explorers rumbled past, jogging in step and chanting as they ran. Birds tweeted in the background, and a large web-footed one landed in the water, paddling out of the frame.

At six-thirty, Jankovic jogged up the path. His thick body and muscular shoulders were unmistakable. He nodded to a couple going the opposite direction, then stopped, putting one foot on the bench as if to adjust his shoe. He leaned close, peering at his foot, and his hand causally dropped to the bench seat.

Jankovic jogged away, nodding to a man and woman coming the opposite direction. They exchanged greetings, and Jankovic disappeared over the hill. The couple checked over their shoulders, then inspected the bench. The man took a flat package from the underside, unwrapped it and scanned the contents with his holo-ring. He raised it as if toasting the drone cam.

"Can we follow Jankovic?" Joss swiped at the feed, as if trying to locate the controls. "When will they arrest him?"

"They have to review the evidence first," Dish said. "Then, present it to the proper authorities."

I glanced at the clock over the door. "I hope they get it done in time."

AT EIGHT, Joss and I took our places beside Anders and Briva at a table in the front of an austere courtroom. A panel of nine officers sat in a box on the right, and a scattering of people watched from the gallery. My dad sat directly behind me. We hadn't had a chance to speak to each other, but he gripped my shoulder before I sat.

The judge, a CEC admiral, entered, and we all stood to attention.

"Be seated." Admiral Ponste hit a wooden gavel on the table and took her seat. "The conduct review of Cadets Serenity Kassis and Joshua Torres begins now."

She turned to the panel of officers. "The court would like to thank you for your service, but you are dismissed."

The officers in the box exchanged confused looks. The senior ranking, a major, stood. "Sir, is the review not going to happen?"

"There will be a review, but due to classified information that has come to light, your services are no longer required. You are dismissed."

The major stood, and the others rose, too. They straggled out of the box, many of them peering over their shoulders as they left the room.

When they'd finally left, the admiral turned to face us. "All spectators must go, too. This matter is now classified. The gallery is to be cleared at once."

As the few observers stood to leave, my dad stepped forward. "I am here as the Academy Commandant, since the defendants are cadets. Also,

I have been asked by the Earth government to stand as their representative, since one of the defendants is an Earth citizen. As such, I request permission to stay."

"Admiral Kassis, your status is noted. Understand that the details of these proceedings are classified top secret and must not be shared with anyone without sufficient clearance and a need to know as determined by the chief of the Explorer Corps." She peered down from her high table. "This includes any members of the Earth government, of course. You can reassure them as to the impartiality of the court and the technical aspects, but details of any witness statements must not leave this room."

"I understand, your honor."

She waved her hand, and holo-rings of those remaining vibrated. An officer of the court handed tablets to me and Joss. "Everyone must read and authorize the classification documents. Take your time."

We all read through the legal agreement.

"This is completely normal for hearings involving classified information." Anders tapped the edge of the tablet. "As your counsel, I recommend you agree."

"Since the hearing can't go forward without it, and that would leave the cadets in custody indefinitely, I'd agree," the admiral said dryly.

Dad waved his hand through his document, agreeing to the terms, and nodded at me. Then he returned to his seat.

When everyone had signed, the judge turned to me. "Cadets Kassis and Torres, serious charges have been levied against you by Commander Jankovic."

I opened my mouth, but she held up a hand. "After a thorough review of the evidence, I have decided to throw the commander's charges out. You were clearly not involved in the software attack on Qureshi, and you didn't interfere with the CEC mission. In fact, your participation in the discovery of the plastek-eating snail, Cadet Kassis, has been recommended for commendation by Dr Li Abdul-James. Unfortunately, the snail's ability to demolish most man-made materials is hugely disruptive, so all information pertaining to it is classified."

She looked at Joss. "Cadet Torres, while your statements and implied threats against Commander Jankovic when he accused Cadet Kassis were most impolitic, I am dropping the charge of insubordination due to extenuating circumstances. And frankly, to prevent an interstellar incident between the Colonial Commonwealth and Earth."

I suppressed the urge to whoop. Joss leaned around Anders and Briva and grinned at me.

She peered down at us. "In addition, we have received very clear evidence this morning that throws Commander Jankovic's testimony into question. I believe you are all familiar with that evidence?"

We nodded.

"I'd like to caution you, cadets—and all of you—" She glared at Anders and Briva. "Attempting a 'sting' is dangerous. That could have gone badly wrong, and all of you could have been implicated. Were the evidence against Jankovic not completely overwhelming, all of you—including Cadet Lee and whoever helped with the technical aspects—would be facing much more serious charges. As it is, well done." Her face pursed, as if the words tasted sour.

"As to your actions on Saha, Major Sarabelle Evy has spoken on your behalf. I must say, I was impressed with your ingenuity. However, knowledge of the Gagarian incursion is currently classified top secret, as is Commander Jankovic's involvement. Therefore, nothing that occurred on that moon can be entered into your records."

She knocked the gavel on the desk again. "All charges are officially dropped. You are released from custody and will return to the Academy. In the absence of your mission commander, Admiral Hydrao will sign off on your Senior Tour. Case dismissed."

The admiral stood, and we snapped to attention. "At ease." She stepped down from the platform behind the desk to speak with us. "Siti, Joss, thank you for your service. You've both performed admirably. I wish we could publicly celebrate your contributions to the mission—and I deeply regret that a shadow has been cast over you. Due to the classification, you won't be able to tell anyone what happened, so there are likely to be rumors that you cannot—must not—counter. The fact that you will graduate and be commissioned tomorrow should be enough to clear any doubts, but please be prepared for detractors to call your loyalty into question.

"This next bit is off the record," she continued. "I suspect you've both heard from Admiral Kassis that the Corps has changed in the last twenty years. Your father, Siti, is in a unique position to see that firsthand as are the officers who went to Earth with you. We believe the officers caught up in the Sarvo Six incident, as well as Commander Jankovic, are a symptom of that decay. We hope we will be able to continue cleaning house and bring the Corps back to its former glory. We may call on you to assist in that as you begin your CEC careers."

She turned to Dad. "I leave it to you to give the Earth government—and Cadet Torres's family—a satisfactory yet fully redacted explanation. I expect we'll both hear calls of favoritism—that's natural since Siti is your daughter. But we also know reforming the Corps is going to take time and sacrifice."

"Yes, sir." Dad hesitated, then spoke. "What about Marika LaGrange?"

"She will be held and tried for treason." The judge looked from Dad to me, then to Joss and back to Dad. "I know you worked with her on Earth. I'm sure you have ambivalent feelings about her—I do, and I don't even know the woman. If I had to guess, I'd say she's likely to get off with an easy sentence and may even be allowed to defect. But she'll never rejoin the CEC, which was what she claimed she wanted to do. She's too big a risk."

"Excuse me, sir." I stepped closer to the two admirals. "What about Major Evy and Cadet Lee?"

"Major Evy is receiving a commendation for landing the shuttle without loss of life. The crash has been investigated, and pilot error was ruled out. The cause appears to be negligence, which will be thoroughly investigated."

"You said 'appears' like you don't believe it," Joss said. "Do you think it might be sabotage? Who would gain by crashing a shuttle into an uninhabited moon? They couldn't have been trying to kill us—that's a crazy big risk for two cadets."

"We believe it was Jankovic's way of getting the snail data—and samples—into Gagarian hands. Getting rid of you two was a bonus."

"But why do they care about us?" I asked. "Like Joss said, we're just a couple of cadets."

"You're not just random cadets." Dad put a hand on my shoulder. "Like it or not, you're my daughter, and I'm seen as a threat to that echelon of corrupt officers. And Joss is the son of one of the leaders of Earth. You'll both be targets for the foreseeable future."

"Are you sure you want us in the CEC, then? We're lightning rods. Is having us around worth it?"

The judge smiled. "That's a risk worth taking."

CHAPTER FORTY-FIVE

THE NEXT MORNING dawned clear and bright. As we left the shadows of the building, the chatter of hundreds of people reached us. We crossed the wide quad, our white shoes swishing in time against the succulent leaves underfoot. I marched in the middle of the block, trying to keep the grin off my face.

A martial brass fanfare played, and we waited as the white-uniformed staff marched past us in into the arena. Horns blared again, and we followed them through the shaded tunnel. A stage had been erected on the lawn, leaving a green strip between the stands and the stage. We took our places among the rows of white chairs, standing at attention.

My eyes strayed to the sides of the arena, where a straggly group of kids in civilian clothing watched. These were the new plebes. It was hard to believe we had stood there only three years before—it felt like a lifetime.

On the stage, my father stepped forward. A huge hologram of his head and shoulders appeared behind him. He welcomed the families of the graduates, drawing attention to Joss and Peter's families in the front row, as the first representatives from Earth to attend a commissioning ceremony.

He talked about duty and honor and all those things senior officers always blather on about at ceremonies. Or so I assumed. I tried to listen, but I was too excited to hear a word.

The grav belt team took to the skies. Even though Aneh and I had been members of the team during our time here, the synchronized loops, spins, and proximity maneuvers still made my stomach drop. Behind us, the audience gasped and cheered.

The team flew across the arena, low over the heads of the spectators, dropping a trail of streamers in all the flight colors. Thunderous applause erupted as the fliers zoomed away.

Dad rose again. "And now, cadets of class fourteen-nine, it's time to take your oath." He looked up at the observers in the stands. "Here in the Explorer Corps, we don't commission individuals. One of our prime values is teamwork. Explorers don't survive when they go solo. And so, even at commissioning, we do things as a team." This was our cue to file out of the seats and form up into squadrons.

Dad looked at the cadets. "Alpha squadron, step forward!" The two halves of Alpha—Red and Green flight—took two steps forward and stopped. A rank of officers—teachers and their squadron advisor—marched to the front of the stage, facing the cadets.

As one, they raised their right hands and repeated the words of the Explorer Corps oath. "I pledge to explore the galaxy, protecting and defending my Explorer team, and finding new worlds for humanity. I owe my allegiance to the colonial government and the officers appointed over me. I will strive to bring no harm to the planets we explore." Bravo Purple and Yellow went next. Then it was our turn.

I stepped forward with the rest of Charlie Blue. Aneh, Yvonne, Terrine, and Marise stood in front of me. Chymm, Franklin, and I filled out the second row, with Joss, Peter, and Rendi in the back. Our squadron advisor and two of our instructors led us through the oath. My chest tightened with pride as I proclaimed the pledge with my flight mates—my family.

When Delta White and Black finished their oath, we returned to our seats. Dad stepped forward again. "Congratulations, class fourteen-nine. You are now ensigns in the Colonial Explorer Corps. Go forth and find!" A wild cheer burst out of my throat, echoing my classmates.

The admiral's party marched off the stage. A voice echoed through the speakers: "Families, you may come down and pin your new ensigns." The music returned, louder and brassier.

And then Dad was beside me, pinning his old ensign's bars on my collar. Nearby, Joss's parents and his twin sister Zina cried and hugged him. Peter's mom and his brother Jake pinned on his rank and congratulated him.

"Come with me," Dad said in a low voice. We wound through the celebrating throngs, accepting and giving congratulations as we went. When we finally got away, he led me through the Academy to a quiet corner where a monument stood to the early explorers from Earth who founded the five colonies. "This is why we're here. To find new planets for humanity. No matter what happens, despite the politics and greed, always remember that's our mission. To go forth and find."

Later we would meet with the rest of my flight for a celebratory dinner. But for now, I stood beside my dad and stared up at the memorial. I leaned my head against his shoulder for a second, then stood at attention. I took a deep breath and yelled, "Anyone want to chicken out?"

Dad flung his arm around me with a laugh. "Hell, no!"

I HOPE you've enjoyed Siti's story. There will be more books in this series, but while you wait, check out *Recycled World*, where you'll meet Peter and Joss. If you've already read that series, there's a full list of my other books at the end of this one.

AUTHOR'S NOTE

August 2021

Hi Reader,

Thanks for reading! If you liked *The Saha Declination*—and if you're still reading, I'm guessing you did—please consider leaving a review on your retailer, Bookbub, or Goodreads. Reviews help other readers find stories they'll like. They also tell me what you like, so I can write more.

This story completes the first CEC trilogy, but I have future plans for Siti, Joss, Peter, Lee, and the gang. If you sign up here, I'll let you know when that is ready. You can also download free prequels—including one featuring Joss's dad, Zane Torres, as a teen—and find out about sales. I promise not to SPAM you.

Also, if you haven't read the series leading into this one, Recycled World is available on your favorite ebook retailer, including direct from my website. That's primarily Peter's story, but Joss and his family feature in it, too.

I've had a couple of readers asking me about "Declination" and why I chose that title. I liked the fact that it has an astronomical meaning, but I picked it because the Gagarians *declined* to claim Saha out right—thus setting us up for a secret base. Plus, it sounded good with the other two titles.

AUTHOR'S NOTE

It's late summer here in the northern hemisphere, and fortunately, we've seen a lot less wildfire than last year. The temps have been crazy high, strangely low, and everything in between. We've gotten out and about a bit—a huge change over last year's lockdown. I was able to attend a writing retreat in Lake Tahoe—where I finished the first draft of this book—as well as an author's lunch in Portland, and my brother's wedding up near Canada.

I'm currently working on a romantic comedy series that I will publish under a new pen name. The name won't be secret—it's mainly to keep my science fiction separate from the hearts and flowers. If you like romantic comedy, then you might enjoy these stories, too. I'll post the news in my newsletter, social media, and website when it's ready to publish.

After that, I'll be back to my *Former Space Janitor* series to finish off that trilogy.

As always, I need to thank a few people. Thanks to my sprint team: A.M. "Google-fu" Scott, Paula "Marathon" Lester, Kate "The Potato" Pickford, Hillary "The Tomato" Avis, Tony James "The Decapitator" Slater, and Marcus Alexander "Piano Man" Hart. They keep me working when I really don't want to. (Can you tell we were procrastinating on our writing when we came up with all those callsigns?)

My appreciation goes to my faithful readers who helped me with tech names—most notably thanks to BJ Jones, who came up with the name "Chet" for the wrist communicator. Named after Chester "Chet" Gould, the creator of Dick Tracy, who owned the first wrist communications device. And thanks to my Patreon supporter Rosheen for being the first to jump aboard!

Paula at Polaris Editing polished my manuscript to perfection, for which I thank her profusely. Any mistakes you find, I undoubtedly added after she was done! My deepest appreciation goes to my alpha reader and sister, Anne Marie, and my beta readers: Anne Kavcic, Barb Collishaw, and Jenny Avery.

Thanks to my husband, David, who manages my business, and to Jenny at JL Wilson Designs for the beautiful cover.

And of course, thanks to the Big Guy for making all things possible.

AUTHOR'S NOTE

Use this QR code to stay up-to-date on all my publishing:

BOOKS BY JULIA HUNI

Colonial Explorer Corps Series:
The Earth Concurrence
The Grissom Contention
The Saha Declination

Recycled World Series:
Recycled World
Reduced World

Space Janitor Series:
The Vacuum of Space
The Dust of Kaku
The Trouble with Tinsel
Orbital Operations
Glitter in the Stars
Sweeping S'Ride
Triana Moore, Space Janitor (the complete series)

Tales of a Former Space Janitor
The Rings of Grissom

Planetary Spin Cycle

Krimson Empire (with Craig Martelle):
Krimson Run
Krimson Spark
Krimson Surge
Krimson Flare

If you enjoy this story, sign up for my newsletter, at juliahuni.com and you'll get free prequels and short stories, plus get notifications when the next book is ready.

Printed in Great Britain
by Amazon